ONLY THE DEAD
(Know the End of War)

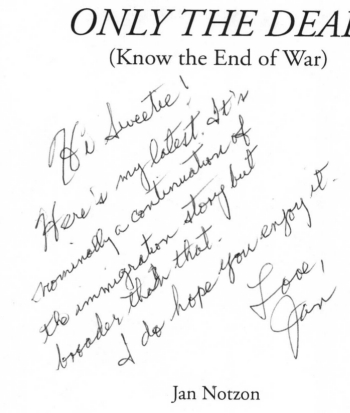

Hi Sweetie!
Here's my latest. It's
nominally a continuation of
the immigration story but
broader than that.
I do hope you enjoy it.
Love,
Jan

Jan Notzon

Chapter I

I live, but I shall not live forever.
Mysterious Moon, only you remain,
Powerful Sun, you alone remain,
Wonderful Earth, only you live forever.

--Death song of the Texas Kiowa

We only came to sleep.
We only came to dream.
It is not true, it is not true that we came to live on the earth!

--Aztec poem

"Hold them up, *hijo*," Miss Luz commanded from her station on the buckboard next to me. "But don't put on the brake."

A week and some out of Saint Hedwig and she'd finally let me take over driving the mule team. The way ahead didn't seem particularly complicated, so I wondered about the heightened awareness I was sensing in her. I guessed that it was because the foothills to our left and the waterless draw on our right narrowed the road so (if you could call it a road). But I wondered.

I started to hand the reins to her.

"No, you'll do it. Just stop first, so I can talk you through it."

I was glad she had the confidence in me to negotiate the maneuver, but wondered why, if she considered me capable, she seemed so intensely focused, so sharply at attention. I'd felt the same hyper-vigilance from Mister G.P. Macalister, the man who'd just taken my mother to wife, ahead of us on horseback. Could there be some danger besides the narrowness of our passage?

My question was answered in a flash just as I pulled the mule team to a halt. The first arrow passed centimeters in front of my chest, grazed Miss Luz's right leg and impaled itself murderously deep into the side of the buckboard. If I hadn't stopped, that missile would have buried itself ever-so-much deeper into my side.

In one motion, Miss Luz snatched the reins away from me, pulled the team to the right inches short of the side of the draw, set the brake and pulled me down underneath the cart.

As I was going down, I caught a glimpse of Mister Macalister jumping from his horse, with his rifle in hand, onto the wagon that carried my mother and the little girl I had been informed was an orphan the family had adopted. He pushed them both down in the bottom of the cart against some sacks of grain mushed against its side and laid down on top of them, rifle firing.

By the time I hit the ground, many more arrows whizzed by or turned the cart into a giant pincushion. Accompanying the arrows, the murderous whizz of bullets instantaneously followed the crack of rifles.

Mister Macalister had already killed one Indian with a rifle shot and wounded one other. It was the first time I had ever seen a person shot. Even if it was an Indian, it is a truly horrific sight: the sickening swat as bullet meets flesh and tears so mercilessly through it, the accompanying cry of agony, the sight of blood gushing from the wound, the knowledge that that being, yes, that *human* being will never again eat, sleep or breathe air, will never cuddle his children or embrace his wife.

Miss Luz, meanwhile, had pulled two more rifles from the wagon, thrust one into my hands and started firing herself from just above the side of the wagon. As she shot, she said, in a tone so measured it had the air of casual conversation, "Do you know how to use a rifle, *hijo?*"

"Uh…Mister Macalister let me fire his a few times." I wondered just for a second why, if I was trying to match her moderate delivery, I was yelling to beat the band.

"Well," she continued, as she caught an Indian on his way down the hillside, "just point and *squeeze*—don't jerk—the trigger. And above all, control your emotions. Aim and shoot with the coldness of the north wind." As she said it, she caught another Indian coming out from behind a large bolder with arrow cocked on his bow. She hit him square in the chest just as he released the deadly projectile.

With the dire hollering of the Indians and rifle shots from all directions, I barely heard the grunt from Mister Macalister in the cart above. My heart pounding like a stampeding bull, I wondered how on earth I could maintain the piercing but apparently stone-cold concentration of Miss Luz and Mister Macalister.

The latter had just caught an Indian who'd managed to sneak up among the rocks and mount the mule cart with a knife in his teeth. I just caught a glimpse as he fell to the ground on the other side of the wagon, one eye missing where the bullet had entered his skull.

From the time Mister Macalister had showed me how to fire his rifle, I was pretty dead-on with my aim. But actually shooting at moving targets—and, more than anything, at human beings, however savage—sucked all substance from me and left me a hollowed-out human silo.

I'd come close a few times, and at least succeeded in making the heathens duck for cover, but never actually hit the mark. I was having quite a time trying to keep myself from shaking as each one came into view. Later, I wondered if my misses were totally accidental.

Suddenly, I heard the blood-curdling, interrupted scream of one of the ranch hands who'd stationed himself by the side of the chuck-wagon to our left. One sneaky Indian had somehow managed to make his way along the draw behind us and come upon him from the back. I just saw the cowhand named Mauricio fall as a fountain of blood gushed out of his throat like a geyser.

The Indian then made his murderous way toward the back of our cart, just a few feet from us. Without a thought, I slung the rifle from its perch on the wagon to where the Indian was approaching and fired point-blank just as the renegade was about to climb up over the back of the cart. It was a good thing I'd had no time to think, to realize that I was killing a man, for this time my aim was true.

As he fell, I was stunned. I stood frozen, staring at the being I'd deprived of life. It had happened so suddenly that I wondered if it had really been I who'd done the deed. I felt all life drain out of me. I was an empty shell, a hollow air-filled cipher, barely able to stand, totally unaware of the arrows and bullets that whizzed by me.

It was a good thing I was so insubstantial, as Mister Macalister, who'd shifted toward me as the Indian I'd shot fell backward, easily pushed me back down behind the wagon. He was back in his position on top of my mother and Amelia just as I hit the ground.

Thank God that by that time the remaining Indians were retreating, for I was now trembling too frightfully to be able to do anything, much less fire the rifle.

After a few moments of relative quiet, Miss Luz turned to me. "Are you all right, John Michael?"

I wasn't sure I could even talk. "I, uh…I th-think so. Y-yes, ma'am," I barely voiced before the contents of my stomach, meager as they were, exploded out of me in a terrible torrent.

"*Hermano?*" she asked, ignoring my epiphany, as she stood and looked in on the cart's occupants to assess their condition. "Ah," was all she said as she (and I) saw the arrow impaled in Mister Macalister's right leg. "Let me see, Gerardo," she continued as he struggled over to let her inspect the wound. I marveled at how matter-off-act they were as they considered the action to be taken.

As she took her knife and split Mister Macalister's pantleg up above the arrow, his only reaction was a clenching of his jaw. "Lucky it's in the side. It won't do too much damage to push it through. The point is even poking out a bit."

"Was that Mauricio that blasted Injun got?" I couldn't believe his chief concern was his hired hand and not his injury.

"Yes."

"Da…uh, darn," he muttered under his breath as he glanced at my mother. "Rosalie, Amelia? You alright?" he asked of my mother and the child. He then repeated the question in what sounded like German for my mother, although it was the sorriest German I'd ever heard. Though like me with sparse language skills, my mother knew enough German to answer that she was okay. She was already inspecting her new husband's wound. She looked at Miss Luz and asked in her broken German what was to be done about it.

Miss Luz answered her in kind, "Push it through and clip off the barb," she answered with sign language to aid my mother's understanding. My mother just nodded, unemotional and prone to practicality in a crisis as she is.

I wondered how many languages my new family spoke.

As Mister Macalister got down from the wagon aided by my mother, his only reaction was again a clenching of the jaw as his right foot gingerly touched the ground. "Jacob," he called to his son as the latter was just about to remount his horse from the other side of the chuck wagon. "Come on, boy. You got to push it through."

Jacob came forward, leading his horse behind him. He dropped the reins, not looking particularly happy about the task Mister Macalister had called on him to perform. "Come on, boy. Get behind me and push the arrow through when I tell you."

I usually get a feeling about someone new I meet, good or bad. But this son of Mister Macalister's I couldn't get a sense of one way or the other. He hadn't said a word to me either before or in the week and a half we'd been on the road. I figured it must be an adjustment for him, having a new stepmother and brother to get used to.

He was already a man, at least by years, but… I don't know, I felt like there was something unformed about him. I did notice that he furtively took a drink from time to time out of a flask he kept on his person.

He hesitantly positioned himself behind his father. I couldn't get a fix on what was going through his mind. He obviously didn't want to be tasked with the job Mister Macalister was calling on him to do. But there was a coolness about his resistance, a… what's that word my brother Alexander used: *nonshallance*, or something like that? It was a weird combination.

With my mother under Mister Macalister's left arm supporting his body and Miss Luz in front holding his right leg steady, a barely audible grunt oozed out of him as he tried to put as little of the weight as he could on that leg. "Now, boy. Push."

I felt kind of bad for Jacob; it was obvious he hated having to be the one put to such a disagreeable job. The strange thing was, though, that it seemed like he was more annoyed than revolted. He put his hand at the back of the arrow, his other hand holding the arrow just at the point where it entered Mister Macalister's leg. I supposed that was to try to steady it so it would go through as cleanly as possible. I could see that despite his outward calm his hands were trembling.

"Steady those hands and push, boy!" Mister Macalister commanded. He then began to mumble something that sounded like a recitation—or an incantation. I could just barely make out the words: "*I live, but I shall not live forever.*" I was amazed that, as Jacob started to push, Mister Macalister continued reciting, squeezing it out in obvious agony, "*Mysterious Moon, you only remaiiiii-n!*"

But I could tell that Jacob was losing heart. "*Push! Damn it boy, push!*"

"I ca… I can't, G.P." I was astounded that he called his father by his name, or the name that all the hands called him by. The way he said it also sat kind of strange with me. It wasn't like a plea, like he was sorry but just didn't have the heart to do it. It was more like a casual observation. Almost like he couldn't be bothered.

"Yes, you can. Now, *do it,* boy*! Do it!*"

More like resentful than squeamish, Jacob started to push again as Mister Macalister groaned out, "*Powerful Su-uuun, you alone re...mainnnn!*"

I could see a tiny bit more of the arrow's barb begin to push through the front of Mister Macalister's leg. Blood quickly formed around it and flowed down his knee and shin. As it did, Mister Macalister's grunting became ever-so-much more direful as he recited that poem or prayer or whatever it was. "*Wonderfulllll Earth...nn-nnn!*" he groaned in agony.

As he did, Jacob finally lost his nerve—or maybe just lost interest. He stood, grabbed his horse's reins, mounted and rode off. "Jacob! Damn it, boy!"

My mother said in her broken German, "Lie down, GP. Muscle soft. Push through, better."

"But who's gonna push the dang thing through? It takes a lot of strength."

"I will," I said, and helped him down onto the ground and got behind the arrow to push it through. My mother held him steady, and Miss Luz kept his leg in place as I began to push the barb through. But boy, Mister Macalister was right. It took practically all my strength to get that arrow to budge. As I could feel it finally moving forward, Mister Macalister grunted out in agony, "*Wonderful Earrr-rth, only you live forever-rrrnnnn!*"

"That's far enough, *hijo*," Miss Luz told me, and I was ever so grateful the torture was over. She quickly lopped off the barb with a pair of wire-cutters. "Now, pull it back and out," she directed as she placed her hands on the opposite side of Mister Macalister's leg. As I pulled the arrow back and out of his leg, Mister Macalister just groaned and again clenched his jaw, "Uhnnnnn." It took a hearty, and steady, tug to pull it out.

My mother asked in here pigeon-scratch German, "What have to clean? Eh…" She looked to me and said in Polish, "Disinfect?"

Somehow Miss Luz understood and called out to their Negro cook, "Cookie, bring me a bottle of whiskey and some strips to use as bandages." She turned to my new stepfather. "We will do the best we can, Gerardo, until we reach Fort Concho."

My mother asked me what they were saying. Miss Luz seemed to understand, so she addressed her in German. "There's a doctor—of sorts—at the fort on the way to the ranch. Two-three days out. Meanwhile, we try to disinfect the wound as best we can with what we have."

My mother wiped the sweat from her new husband's face with the hem of her dress. "Thank you, Rosalie. Daynkuh" he responded, his breathing becoming a little steadier now that the painfullest part of the process was over, and he could rest a little easier. I supposed that what he'd said was his best effort at *danke*. My mother smiled patiently.

When Camp Cookie came with the supplies, he stayed, apparently knowing what to do as he held Mister Macalister's leg steady. "John Michael, you help Cookie keep his leg steady while I pour in the whiskey," Miss Luz directed. "Then we turn him over and do the same on the other side."

She proceeded with the treatment and Mister Macalister hardly reacted, except for stiffening his leg that Camp Cookie and I struggled to keep in place. He was one powerful man, even at his age, rock-hard and sinewy.

Once the process was over, Miss Luz went around the wagon with the whisky and a bandage, I assume for modesty's sake, and attended to her own wound.

"How bad?" Mister Macalister asked her when she returned.

"A scratch. It will heal before we get to Fort Concho."

He started to rise but my mother quickly put a stop to that. "You rest," she rather ordered. "We stay night. Tomorrow better." Mister Macalister looked at Miss Luz. She gave a firm nod, so the four of us lifted him into the cart, rolled him over on a blanket and put another on top of him. The wind out of the northwest cut like a straight razor and seemed to whine in muted anguish.

After a hearty stew and biscuits Camp Cookie made with my mother's assistance, Mister Macalister fell into a restless sleep, quietly moaning as he frequently woke. I noticed that Miss Luz, while she attended to the tasks involved in making camp, at the same time kept a watchful eye on her *brother*, as she called him.

I lay down myself in the cart with my back against the cab, a blanket wrapped tightly around me as the temperature had been dropping since the sun went down, and that constant and contrary wind never ceased its murderous onslaught. I looked out at the last vestiges of the painted western horizon as the sun from beneath it pasted its artwork on the few clouds there, trying to take stock of what we'd just been through.

What sort of people would brave this kind of danger to carve out a life for themselves in this seeming wasteland? What was the difference between them and the others who stayed behind in relative safety? Was it the cruelty of the life out here on the frontier that made them so hard, or was it that steel-spined people are attracted to a life of danger, to the challenge of conquering an untamed frontier? Was it maybe a little of both? That would be a question for my brother, Alexander.

I thought about the question he'd asked when our father first told us about the plan to emigrate: "Are there savage Indians?" Oh yes, Alex, there are. There sure are.

The dark had fallen as quickly as a hammer blow revealing a cloudless night sky emblazoned with a banquet of starlit wonder. A platinum moon rose over the flatland to the east, shedding a pearl-light grace so that the outline of cart, wagon, cattle, horse and rider could be faintly discerned through the inky blackness.

The air was as crisp as a starched collar, and the awesome silence of the desert was only interrupted by a bird Miss Luz told me was called a poorwill in English, because its song sounded like it was saying, "Poor Will's Widow." Its call seemed to match the awesome vastness of the desert. Then the high-pitched wail of what she had earlier told me was called a coyote echoed plaintively across the prairie. "Like a wolf," she'd said, "only smaller and more wily."

Next to the chuckwagon, I could just make out Jacob as he took out his flask and took a furtive sip of whatever was in it, then lay down to go to sleep. I wondered what it was that made that ole boy tick.

In the mule cart, somewhat protected from the icy northwest wind by its walls, I lay down myself, thinking about my new adoptive family. I wondered how Jacob would react to the fact I'd done what he couldn't bring himself to do. And I wondered why he couldn't—and why I was able to. What was the difference between us? Where did it come from? And how would it affect our relationship—that is, and this thought burrowed in the folds of my innards, if we ever come to have one?

It made me think of my own family: how we'd made our way with the rest of our group of immigrants from the coast inland to found Panna Maria, Texas. How we'd suffered such want, such stumbling, groping our way in this new land, operating first as the collective my brother Alexander had always touted as the ideal.

Was it when we came close to starving that first year that he began to have second thoughts? No, I think it was earlier than that, and that turn of events merely confirmed the lesson for him.

Boy there was a lot of bellyaching. Understandable, I guess, when people ain't got enough to eat. A lot of our colony wanted to go back to Poland. Then some people struck out on their own, still keeping a relationship with our colony but pursuing their own and their own family's welfare outside the colony.

I think it was Alex that first noticed how much better they were doing than any in our group; how they were trading with each other and even with people outside our company. He must have mentioned it to Father Moczygemba, because it was when

12

Father let us start working for ourselves and our own families that we began to do better.

Alex pointed out to me that when Father did that, all of a sudden people began to work harder. Wives came out of the house to help with the plowing, planting and harvesting. The children pitched in more.

Alex also explained to me that it was then that people started finding more efficient ways of doing the same tasks they'd always done—mostly the people who had struck out on their own. They even started experimenting with improvements to the tools we used. He noted that some were starting to specialize and what he called *barter*. I guess that's a fancy word for trade.

The Mazurs were the first to look into selling some of their crop. That allowed them to save up to buy a cow and at first bartering the milk she produced, then actually selling some to people outside our party of Poles. They invested a lot of what they made and bought more cows until they had a thriving business.

That allowed Krystian Zielinski to start marketing Pan Mazur's milk and crops to cheesemakers and bakers and resume his life as the merchant he was in Poland. He started mostly with German farmers and businesspeople until he learned enough English to start doing business with local folks.

Konstantyn Michnik found he had the strength and energy to do the heaviest work on his own farm and then hire himself out to others while his wife and children completed the less stressful tasks on their own farm. That allowed his family to at first trade for and then even buy the wonderful bread that Pani Zizik made.

And since Pan Michnik sometimes worked for people outside our group, he had the opportunity to introduce Pani Zizik's bread to a wider market. I heard that now the Ziziks dedicate themselves almost exclusively to their bakery, with Pan Zielinski marketing it to a wider and wider clientele. Funny how one person's success helps others to succeed.

I mentioned all of this to my brother, Alexander, marveling at how it had all worked out. He said it had to do with something some philosopher he mentioned and his... "invisible hand of business", or something like that.

I am so proud of him, getting a full scholarship to Baylor University in Independence. I had to laugh at my mother, afraid he would be converted to Protestantism there, it being, as I understand, a Baptist institution. I told her with a laugh that it would probably be an improvement for him to have any kind of religion at all.

As I think about it, though, during that first year he seemed to begin to truly participate in our church, in the Mass; and to read the Bible, even. Funny, he seemed particularly fascinated with the Book of Exodus, like our father. Oh, how I wish Papa could be here to see how we're flourishing here in Texas! I do so wish he could be part of it.

Our family was helped during those first couple of years—saved, actually—by the kind ministrations of Josef Kotula and a few other Poles who'd come to Texas years before, Pan—or, I should say, *Mister*—Kotula from a different part of the United States. It was providential that he took an interest in our family in particular, hiring my mother and sister, Mariana, as domestics, and giving me work as a farmhand.

Adam Mazur and my sister Ursula had married and moved to San Antonio by then, Adam finding plentiful work as a carpenter there once he learned the English system of measurements.

It was so good of Mister Macalister to let us stop there to visit on our way from Saint Hedwig. Ursula seemed so happy, already in the family way with their first child. Despite my mother's ever-present hardihood, I know it was agony for her to leave knowing that soon she'd have her first grandchild.

Mariana stayed with the Kotulas, as I could see that their eldest boy, named Joseph after his father, had his eye on her—and the feeling was obviously mutual. I know my mother hated to leave that potential joy as well.

But as grateful as she was for the employment Mister Kotula provided—and especially hiring my sister and me as well when he probably didn't need that much help—I know being wife and mother is not only what she prefers, but what she lives for.

So, when Mister G.P. Macalister came to the Kotula ranch seeking to buy some of the English Herefords Pan Kotula had imported, his and my mother's needs seemed fulfilled in each other. They married scarcely a week later, my mother insisting, of course, on it being in the Catholic Church with Father Moczygemba officiating. It was interesting hearing him try to accommodate all parties by conducting the ceremony alternately in Polish, German and his English that was scarcely better than mine.

Mister Macalister was a widower, I'd found out from Miss Luz. I took to her right off the bat. I could feel a strength from her like I did from him, although she didn't seem so distant—didn't seem distant at all, really. I felt right at home with her the first conversation we had. There's something just...I don't know, *genuine*, about her.

Mister Macalister looked like he was well past middle age, but I could just feel a strength from him, a power over most younger men. Miss Luz said she thought he'd taken to my mother so quickly because the one thing lacking in the Lazy Eight lacked was that woman's touch that makes a house a home. She said she'd heard a Chinese saying, that "it takes a hundred men to build a fort but one woman to make a home".

I lay back and drank in the sequined canopy of twinkling majesty above, happy that my mother seemed so content to be Mister Macalister's wife—and at the way he treated her with such respect and concern. I'd wondered how I would feel if their union in marriage were to take place. Now I knew. I had a real good feeling about my new stepfather. I just wish I could say the same about his son.

This Texas sky is so huge! And it is so awash with the delicate wonder of starlight spread out from horizon to horizon. It makes me think of the ocean—an ocean of stars in infinite space, it is. It makes me think of my brother and sisters I left behind. I wonder why it is Alexander I think of more than the others when I was always closest to Mariana.

I wonder what life will be like on Mister Macalister's ranch. I hope I can reach some sort of understanding with my new stepbrother. Then there are the two daughters Miss Luz mentioned who stayed home while she and the others made the trip. Will they be anything like my own two sisters? I wonder what my place will be there. I hope I'll have one.

The sky just seems to stretch out forever ... forever.

Chapter II

*The Conquest was the means through which
the civilization and religion of this country
were established, and Don Hernán Cortés
was the extraordinary man sent by Providence
to achieve this purpose.*

--Lucas Alamán, historian

*Cortés was that great outlaw who has been raised
to "hero" by his own good fortune, because his
life was no more than a web of vile actions and
betrayals.*

--Pérez Verdía, historian

*The most miserable European, without education,
without intellectual cultivation, thinks himself
superior to whites born in the new continent.*

--Alexander von Humbolt

José Nicolás de Cos de la Portilla sat on his horse outside the Indian hut waiting for his father to finish his "business" with the peasant woman who lived there. Despite the beauty that surrounded him, a kind of spiritual nausea crept about his soul's innards.

He gazed across the landscape trying to distract himself, devouring the verdant hills and valleys that had always filled him with a rapturous sense of peace. The Lerma River flowed languidly in the fertile swale below, its riparian beauty the lifeblood of the *Bajío*'s (as this part of New Spain was called) gracious tranquility.

Aromas of river-sodden earth wafted up on a tentative spring breeze, and mirthful birdsong lilted tenderly through the inviting air. At an impossible height in the sky above, a stately golden eagle imperiously glided on updrafts, scouring the area below for a fish or fowl or rodent to take home as sustenance for his hungering chicks. In the distance lay the town of San Miguel el Grande, creeping lazily up one hillside from the floor of a separate valley a quarter-league or so away.

Ensconced like a statue upon his steed atop the grass-carpeted hill that overlooked the waterway, José Nicolás tried to ignore a tremor of disgust that chafed like a burr under the mattress of peace this tender scene always inspired.

Was it that this was the home of Papaplotl, his wet nurse and nanny for so many years? The thought of his father taking his pleasure with her sent a potent wave of revulsion through him. He tried not to think of his mother, Anastasia de la Portilla de Cos, but those efforts proved futile.

He shifted nervously in the saddle. His father, José Maximiliano de Cos de Asunción, routinely took him on these junkets touring their vast estate, an *encomienda* granted to his great-grandfather by King Carlos the Fourth more than a century before. These excursions always ended as this one had, with his father taking his leisure with one Indian girl or another.

José Maximiliano de Cos de Asunción had that natural air of superiority that all pure Spanish *encomenderos* possessed, that sense that the world was his playground. It served as an impenetrable bulwark against any imagined alternative theory of social organization. He was, like all of them, a *criollo* after all, born in New Spain but of pure, unadulterated Spanish blood.

And he was rich! Proof that God had favored him. He owned all the land from the edge of San Miguel el Grande down to the Lerma River and continuing for leagues in all directions. His fertile lands produced corn and wheat and barley in abundance which his Indian peasants farmed for a percentage of the bounty. In his own mind he treated those, his tenant farmers, with great magnanimity, and he was certain he had their abundant love and gratitude.

But the great bulk of his wealth came from his silver mines. He was proud of the fact that through it, he gave other peasants meaningful jobs as miners. The complaints he got about the working conditions from the priest in Dolores he chalked up to Father Hidalgo's ignorance of how a business is administered and the great need of the Spanish Crown for the resource.

It all worked as God intended, he mused, and mirrored the divine order of Heaven. As the Council of the Indies had so articulately explained, "hierarchies and classes are of the greatest importance to the monarchical state, since a graduated system of dependence and subordination sustains and insures the obedience and respect of the last vassal to the authority of the sovereign."

As God rules in Heaven and all beings there are ranked in order of sanctity, so the King rules on earth and shepherds each of his subjects according to their station. He thanked God for his own exalted place in the hierarchy of New Spain and anticipated with relish passing it on to his sons, José Antonio and José Nicolás.

Now that younger son, José Nicolás, sat astride his beloved mare, Dulcinea, looking down at the graceful valley below and wondered why these stops at different women's huts bothered him so. After all, as his father said, "This royal bequest to our family included everything on it, the land, the minerals, the game, the Indians...the fertile soil and gentle rains that produce such bounty. It is all ours to enjoy and enjoy it I will. As your brother does and as one day you shall."

This is what the lord of the estate does—what all men of means do—including, of course, his adored older brother José Antonio. He never sensed any of these misgivings in the big brother he idolized so. Why couldn't he be more like Antonio, confident, afraid of no one and nothing, brazen in his appetites for good food, aged wine and beautiful women? What was wrong with him?

Besides, according to his peers from the other *latifundios* of the area, their fathers take similar advantage. Except for one, it seemed: the sons of José de Arreola y Riaño never seemed to participate in the usual tall tales of their father's self-pleasuring prowess. José Nicolás was quite intrigued by that and felt a confraternity with them.

There was something different about Don José Sebastián de Arreola. Whenever the fathers gathered in their exclusive groups at parties enjoying brandy and cigars, he always seemed to distance himself or seemed ill-at-ease when the conversation elicited a kind of conspiratorial laughter among them. José Nicolás had an inkling of what might have been the subject of those discussions, as the tenor immediately changed when a wife or child or even a female servant came within hearing distance.

José Nicolás had a vague sense that the uneasiness Señor Arreola y Riaño sometimes—or even to a degree, generally—seemed to feel with the other *encomenderos* was reciprocated in kind by them. He'd wondered about that and tried to catch some of the conversations engaged in by the other fathers when Don José de Arreola was absent.

He'd only caught snippets, vague references to "spoiling his peasant tenant farmers", or "conspiring with Father Hidalgo to overpay the miners", or "institute safety measures that would sorely cut into profits". José Nicolás even heard disparaging references to Arreola's young sons and their lack of experience—in what, José Nicolás imagined he knew.

Most of the older boys had followed in their fathers' footsteps. Or so they bragged. The exceptions were Fernando de Arreola y Riaño and his younger brother, Felipe. Though José Nicolás felt a kind of undefined admiration for Fernando and Felipe, he was aching to join the club of the experienced, to do what real *men* do, to pass this milestone into adulthood, to the favored, the experienced, the knowledgeable.

Astride his horse, overlooking the bucolic rapture of the valley below, he thought to himself, *I'm on this very day thirteen years old, after all, and must start thinking and acting like a man.*

So why did he have this feeling of unease, at least as far as his father and this particular peasant woman were concerned? And would his first experience be with an Indian woman, like his peers? Like his father? Was his father's first an Indian peasant woman? He thought it likely. A shiver of misgiving like an autumn chill rifled through him.

Finally, Don José Maximiliano emerged from the hut. He stopped and stretched, taking a deep breath and exhaling with a sigh of satisfaction. Then he ambled indolently up to where his young son was. He took the reins of his own horse from José Nicolás and addressed the boy with a slightly impish air. "All right, Nicos—José Nicolás! You are thirteen years old today and a man. It is time you do what real men do. She's waiting inside and expecting you."

José Nicolás felt a noxious wave of queasiness trundle through him. It raised the hairs on the back of his neck and turned his skin to gooseflesh. "But Papá...it's—it's Papaplotl."

"Precisely why I brought you here, for your first time to be with a girl you know, one you might feel comfortable with."

A bare treacle of perspiration beaded on José Nicolás' temples. He started to dismount, then hesitated. To refuse this opportunity would be consummately shameful. He could not bear to live with the stigma. But with the woman who'd cared for him so lovingly, who'd cossetted and played with him as a child, who had been more his mother than his own? The thought was...sickening.

Don José Maximiliano was somewhat bemused and perhaps a bit concerned by his son's hesitation. "Go on, Nicos. She's waiting."

He weakly answered, "But..."

"No buts, *hijo*. It is time. Now, go on."

José Nicolás slowly dismounted. He tried to think of some excuse to avoid this pending challenge that twisted his guts in knots of repugnance. But could he deal with the shame of failure at this most manly of pursuits?

He walked the short distance to the typical dilapidated Indian mud hut that housed his nurturer who was now to also serve as his prey. He hesitated at the blanket that served as a door. He knew that his father's eyes were on him, however, and could not falter lest shame pursue him all the rest of his days.

All avenues of escape dissolved into ether in his mind; they'd all be known for what they were, flimsy pretexts that no one, least of all himself, would believe. No, even if by some miracle others were convinced, he would know. *He* would know.

As he pulled aside the blanket, the full battery of odors there contained washed over him like an ocean wave. There were some rather pleasant ones like the sumptuous smell of corn tortillas and the lard that goes into them, although the fresher scents were rather overpowered by the stale ones used over and over. Most sickening of all was the day-old, week-old, months-old and maybe years-old odor of sweat that cloyed the air like a thin film of pond scum.

He stepped in and at first was blinded by the darkness, the tiny mud hut having only one small frameless window allowing a bare suggestion of light. Finally, his eyes adjusted, and he made out the silhouette of his one-time nanny sitting up on her crude corn-shuck mattress on the bare dirt floor, the threadbare blanket pulled up to cover her naked body. He could barely make out parts of her ample breasts through the holes the covering bore. The sight momentarily overcame his revulsion and triggered a tiny flame of desire in him.

As his pupils continued to widen, letting in more of the paucity of light in the room, he could finally make out the world-weary features of his nanny's face. He reflexively tried to read any feelings about this situation that face might betray. But she was a study in impassiveness.

Maybe deep inside those windows of the soul there might have been a fading sense of the irony at this turn of events, but it was buried so profoundly beneath a fatalism acquired over a life of simply being an object of use that it was too occulted for him to discern.

"Hello, *mihijo*. You've grown," she simply said, and lifted up one side of the blanket for him to lie next to her. She spoke to him in her native tongue, Náhuatl, which he had learned from her as a child. Although Papaplotl had learned some Castilian, spoken language was unnecessary with the boy's father.

He hesitated. The idea of this kind of intimacy with one who'd actually been his surrogate mother made his head spin. Yes, he'd had the stirrings of desire. He'd fantasized about some of his neighbors' daughters, seeing their nubile young bodies at dances and parties at the homes of different *latifundistas* in different parts of the *Bajío*, including at his own.

He'd even had to quickly distract himself when anatomical changes as a result of those fantasies threatened to embarrass him. Then all his thoughts during the times he pleasured himself were on fully developed female figures.

Why did this…this situation so repulse him? As best he could decipher, it was a typical milestone on the path to adulthood. At least according to the stories of those older sons of fellow *encomenderos*. And to those of his brother, Tony, it was an honored ritual. Again, what was the matter with him?

The fear that there *was* something wrong with him propelled José Nicolás to the edge of the mattress. It crackled most annoyingly as he sat down on it. He began to tremble. *Why am I afraid?*

he despairingly wondered. *What is wrong with me?* And the more he worried, the more he quaked, and the farther he was from the required anatomical changes that might enable the consummation of the affair.

Papaplotl, from somewhere in the past experience of care the two had shared, seemed to have a sense of what the boy was going through. Perhaps she had entertained other boys who'd had the same difficulty. The impulse on her part was light years from being articulated into coherent thought. It was rather pure instinct that induced her to pull Nicolás down on top of her and hold him as he shook like an earthly tremor.

Thoughts buzzed through his mind like a swarm of agitated fire ants. Contradictions swirled: how wrong it felt to be held against his nanny's naked body—and at the same time, how warm and safe. How can it possibly be both? He was at the same time grateful for the tenderness and furious that it calmed him. He shouldn't need this calming!

Gradually however, the gesture began to work its magic. His shaking ameliorated to an occasional quake. As it did, he even began to feel the distant stirrings of desire. The necessary change a male must go through for intimacy to occur slowly started to make itself felt. As it did, his trembling ceased altogether.

The warmth of her body now felt good. He could now return the physical gestures of affection, the squeezing of her ample breasts and caresses of her curvaceous thighs, both of which she herself initiated. She seductively slipped off his shirt, allowing him to feel the softness of those ample breasts against his tingling flesh.

Then, just as he was about to consummate the affair she so generously directed, a baby's cry split the dark. José Nicolás pulled himself up and looked around, astonished. "It's all right, Nicosito," Papaplotl said, using the appellation of affection she had given him as a child. "She's just hungry. She can wait."

But the crying was insistent, demanding. It was so distracting that José Nicolás' body recoiled into itself, and the moment was lost. This caused Papaplotl considerable concern; satisfying the boy, after all, was as much her responsibility as pleasing his father. She hesitated, unsure of what to do.

"Uh...y-you'd better...I can't, with that..." Nicolás stammered in Papaplotl's native language and pulled himself all the way off her.

"All right. Just give me a few moments," and she went to the dirt floor at the foot of the mattress. There José Nicolás could see the baby on a fluffed-up blanket. He or she had obviously been asleep and woke up hungry. Papaplotl immediately put the child to her breast and she hungrily latched on and suckled.

Such a jumble of emotions this caused José Nicolás! At first, he was embarrassed, feeling that he was intruding on such a private moment. But then, as Papaplotl seemed perfectly at ease, he began to find the gesture rather erotic. He would wait, perhaps availing himself of what was left after the baby had had its fill. The thought aroused him like nothing before and he impatiently waited for the process to be over with.

But then out of nowhere, a most unsettling thought struck him: what if this baby was his half-brother or sister? Or could it be a nephew or niece, Tony's child? A wave of utter repugnance banished those erotic sensations and pulsed through him so that he shuddered in disgust. He quickly grabbed his shirt and threw it on, not even noticing that he had it on backwards.

Now Papaplotl was truly unnerved. What if the boy reports to his father that she had failed him? What would the consequences be? "Wait, Nicosito. The baby is almost finished. We can still…" But José Nicolás was already heading for the doorway. "Please, *hijito*! We can do it. The baby is done. She'll go to sleep now." She put down the baby on the blanket and in two steps was with him at the door.

"Please, Nicosito," she pleaded as she wrapped her arms around him and crushed her naked body against his, taking his hand and placing it on her breast. His whole body, save that one part necessary for consummation of the act, stiffened. She started trying to take off his shirt, certain that the feel of her naked flesh against his would rekindle the flame of passion.

There had been too many interruptions, however, too many unarticulated thoughts—or vague sensations, rather—of this Indian woman as a mother and a person, with ideas and feelings of her own, hopes and dreams and worries all her own. José Nicolás was simply incapable of considering his childhood companion, the woman who had actually been to him more his real mother than the woman who birthed him, as merely an object to be used for his pleasure.

And perhaps because of those vagrant notions, José Nicolás had an inkling of the source of his erstwhile nanny's fear. He tried to reassure her. "I'll…I'll tell my father that we did it. That, uh… that it was good…very good."

Papaplotl wondered if he truly meant it. She was, in fact, truly astonished that a member of the ruling class, even if he was her surrogate child, would actually consider taking an Indian's safety into account. "Are—are you sure, *hijito*?" she asked as she turned his shirt around and fitted it properly on him.

The feeling of gratitude and relief he sensed from her stirred in him a twinge of satisfaction. Was it the power he felt at her dependence on his willingness to protect her this way? Or was it simply the pleasure of caring for the woman who was more mother to him than his own? Or was it some combination of the two?

Whatever the case, that tiny and fleeting kernel of comfort lay entombed beneath a mountain of piercing shame at his failure. He could never honestly claim to be a part of the "experienced"—a *Man*—and the terror of being separate, apart, not welcome in the community, this very *Spanish* community, crushed his sense of self-worth to a pitiable powder liable to be taken on the wind and dispersed to non-existence.

Belonging, having an inviolable place in New Spanish—in Mexican—society was the sine qua non of all New Spaniards, as it was in the mother country. Even in the civilizations that Spain had conquered—the Aztecs, the Zapotecs, the Maya, the Incas—it was the collective, and one's place in it, that gave each member a sense of surety, of grounding—of their very identity.

Even those who suffered horrible privations under it would not trade membership for personal success if it meant being on one's own, forsaking the community, the collective. For all the New World territory that the Spanish claimed, there were New Spanish—Mexicans—only in the tiniest portion of that vast expanse.

And try as they might to colonize those outer territories with cross and sword, Spanish sensibility cleaved to its own, to itself—like bees to membership in the hive.

So, José Nicolás de Cos de la Portilla exited his surrogate-mother's hovel in a harrowing state of conflict. His feeling of belonging, of being among the favored, the worthy, on which depended almost in its entirety his fledgling sense of self-esteem, was crushed in the grist mill of failure.

At the same time, to save his beloved childhood companion, his guardian and nurturer, he had to give off the air of the conqueror, of one who had risen mightily to this determinative feat of manhood.

As he started out ambling diffidently to where his father awaited him, a broad smile emblazoned on his progenitor's face, José Nicolás quickly changed his pace to an affected stride brimming with confidence. He effected a smile of complicity of his own and swung his arms in a swagger, as he had seen from those of his fellows who must have passed this rite of passage of maleness with flying colors.

He threw his shoulders back in a heroic gesture and almost stumbled with the length he had increased his stride to. As he approached his beaming father, he grabbed the reins of his horse with such show of force that he made the sensitive animal shy. His anxious mare almost reared at the way he flew into his saddle, the poor equine so unused to such behavior from her quondam rider.

For a moment after he mounted himself, his father just glowed with pride as he looked upon this, his youngest son, who was now a man. José Nicolás, doing his best to simulate the air of braggadocio he repeatedly saw come from his brother and his brother's compatriots, gave a tenuous kick to his horse before his father grabbed the reins to keep her and him in place.

With a smile from ear to ear, his father addressed him with a giant sigh of satisfaction. "Well? Tell me boy, how was it? How do you feel now that you've had your first woman, now that you are a boy no longer but a man among men?" He gave his son a hearty slap on the back and hugged his shoulder, rocking him back and forth on his horse. "Tell me all about it, Nicos!"

José Nicolás felt no compunction about lying to his father, only a deep and abiding shame at having decidedly not measured up to this rite of passage. But he also knew how to put on the mannerisms and gestures he had so carefully studied that his brother and his brother's experienced and confident contemporaries displayed.

He again threw his shoulders back and pushed his chest forward with a fairly convincing air of bravado. "It was fantastic, Pap—" he interrupted himself and in consonance with his bodily affectations of pride, finished the sentence with "Father. Truly fantastic."

The explosion of laughter that exited his father filled the valley and echoed against the surrounding hills. He now grabbed his son by the back of his neck shaking him again and letting out a victorious howl of delight as he kicked his horse to a sudden gallop.

José Nicolás' horse, following the other's lead, galloped after him, a doubt planted in both rider and horse.

Chapter III

Hierarchies and classes are of the greatest
importance to the existence and stability of a
monarchical state, since a graduated system
of dependence and subordination sustains and
insures the obedience and respect of the last
vassal to the authority of the sovereign.

--Council of The Indies, 1806

What we have to undertake is to systematize
the foundations of the house...until finally...
the scaffolding will be taken away and there
will be a family in a great building...where
men can live as a single community, co-operative
as in a perfected coordinated beehive.

--Woodrow Wilson, 1912

Title being in nature neither hereditary nor
transmissible to children...or relation, the
idea of a man born a magistrate, lawgiver, or
judge is absurd and unnatural.

--Massachusetts Constitution of 1780

José Necahuatl de Arreola was not surprised or embittered when he was sold by his mother into an *obraje*, a woolen mill, there in the town of San Miguel el Grande. He understood that, like many of his Indian and fellow *mestizo* (mixed-blood) peers, it was the only way for his mother to pay off the family debt that all Indians and *mestizos* in New Spain were essentially born into.

He could feel his mother's anxiety building as visits from his creole father, José Sebastián de Arreola y Riaño, became more and more infrequent. As they did, his material support began to fade with it.

Young José was disappointed himself at that turn of events, mostly because he enjoyed those visits so much. Señor Arreola y Riaño had always brought with him such delights: a good portion of beef or a leg of lamb or even a whole cabrito. They were the only times the boy had the chance to savor meat. Then there were the sweets his pure Spanish father brought for him and his little brother and sisters.

But the greatest treat of all was Don José Sebastián's simple presence. He seemed happy while he was there, and sad when he had to leave and go back to his other, legitimate, family. He was always kind and loving. He had instructed the peasants who lived on his lands to stop calling him *Amo* (Master) and rather address him as *Jefe* (Boss).

Little José so looked forward to practicing his Castilian with him. His father even brought books written in the mother-tongue and gave José some elementary lessons in reading. He peppered his father with questions about life among those of pure Spanish blood, meetings with the other *hacendados* of this part of Guanajuato province and his part in its governance. The love and respect his father gave him stirred in him his first misgivings about this rigid system of hierarchy in New Spain.

Don José Sebastián recognized a powerful intellect in this his eldest "natural" son and was impressed at how he taught himself during the periods of the patriarch's absence. The boy had always read the books his father had brought on his previous visits several times over and anticipated new ones with even more relish than the culinary delights the patriarch provided.

Don Sebastián was most astonished at the boy's interest in the world around him, always peppering his father with questions not only about his father's other life and family, but about New Spain in general.

What did the difference between his own family and his father's other family consist of? Why were there those like his own and other *mestizo* families that lived in relative poverty while others, like his father, luxuriated in stately palaces, traveled in elegant buggies and wore such fine clothing?

Much of Don José Sebastián's wonder lay in the fact that he had only relatively recently considered these issues himself and marveled at those same inquiries in one so young. The child seemed to have a ravenous appetite for knowledge and learning and was, for the most part, self-taught. It prompted this gentleman of two families to bring more books and he was astounded that the boy had read them all more than once upon his return.

So, he expanded José Necahuatl's education with basic math, the history of New Spain and the mother country, elementary lessons on the governing structure of the country and other subjects.

Again, he was astonished at the ease with which the boy absorbed the lessons, answered all the problems Don José Sebastián had left with him to solve, and even made up some of his own even more complex ones. The sophistication of the questions his son asked him about the material he had provided only added to José Sebastián's awe.

Something had begun to change of late, however. During his father's most recent visits, José had gotten from him a feeling of some trouble brewing, something unsettled or unsettling among the people of New Spain, of Mexico. He had a vague impression that it was this tension that impeded his father's visits and made him less at ease when he was there. José Necahuatl ached to question him about it.

The boy's infrequent forays into town with his mother seemed to confirm the feeling. He couldn't say what it was, as vague a sensation as it continued to be. There just seemed to be something in the air, especially among the *criollos*, those of pure Spanish blood but born here in New Spain and not in the Mother Country.

He asked his mother about it, his uncles, other fellow *mestizos*, but no one else seemed to be particularly aware of it. He began to think that it might be just some peculiar phantasm of his own and wondered what it could be, where it might have come from.

Of course, when he was finally confined to the *obraje*, all contact with the outside world was summarily cut off. His life was one of constant weaving and spinning with all-too-short breaks to eat and sleep. The only workers who ever saw the light of day were those with families, and that was only for a brief period on Sundays.

That was the hardest part for José de Arreola. One thing he truly loved was being out in the sun, working in his mother's garden or attending the livestock, or cleaning and stocking the store of

Don Pedro Allende, a local and, he thought, prosperous merchant and prominent citizen of San Miguel.

That perception lasted until Don Pedro died, leaving his family mired in debt and practically destitute. José de Arreola wondered how people of pure Spanish blood could have such a reversal of fortunes. Where did all their money go?

As time in the mill dragged on, a previously inert seed of doubt about the society of which he was a part began to flourish and articulate itself into coherent thought in him. He recognized that that seed was planted by comments from his father and the resulting discussions they engendered. It was the overarching question as to why those born in Spain, seemingly regardless of ability or industriousness, held all the positions of power and wealth.

Why was it that even the creoles with pure Spanish blood but born here in Mexico were excluded from those positions? And why all second-tier positions seemed to be reserved for those very creoles—again, however talented or incompetent they might be?

It struck José that the vast majority of New Spaniards just accepted this rigid system as natural—perhaps as ordained by God. What else did they know, after all? But then why was it that *he* was aware of it, and they never seemed to give it a second thought—or even a first, for that matter?

He wondered if it was truly so ordained by the Creator, and if it was, why God had made it so. Above all, he ached to know if there might be others like himself who questioned it, who wondered if there might be another way—if perhaps room could be made for those low-born but of talent and intelligence to put those abilities to work.

Life, if one could call it that, in the *obraje* was so horrific that many of his fellow indentured servants and slaves faked injuries or illness, or even provoked their master-supervisors to beat them to where they couldn't work, just to have a moment's respite from the constant, soul-crushing monotony.

Some others simply went insane, standing, running to-and-fro, spouting madness of demons pursuing them or mouthing unintelligible blather in their particular Indian dialect. They were all bone-crushingly beaten; some—many even—ground to death.

To save himself from such an ignoble fate, José taught himself to do the mind-numbing work by rote, so that his imagination could be free to ponder these questions. He also tried to occupy his mind making up simple math lessons of quantities of wool leading to bolts of cloth produced. He listened carefully when the mill's managers and even owners came in speaking Castilian so he could improve his own.

But to what end? The pervasive sensibility in the mill was that there was no escaping this purgatory. Still, he clung to hope, however fruitless it might be. He realized that hope was all he had and that without it, he was doomed to follow those who succumbed to madness.

Another way he distracted himself was to imagine biographies of his fellow workers: Negro slaves, convicts, vagabonds and debt peons like himself. He even let his mind fantasize about the lives of the brutal supervisors with their canes and whips constantly urging faster work.

He managed to avoid those stinging slaps and cracks for the most part by mastering the art and maintaining a greater speed than his fellow slaves. Even beyond that, he soon invented a more efficient manner of weaving, so that his production now greatly outpaced that of his fellow workers. As a result, he noticed that for their one meal a day he had a few more beans than normal in the gruel, courtesy of those slaves who'd been in the *obraje* longer and had graduated to being cooks and servers.

He'd learned an important life lesson from the experience, as well. His greater speed and efficiency had made his fellow weavers and spinners look bad by comparison, incurring their supervisors' wrath. Plus, having more beans in his soup meant the others got less. Most troublesome of all was the fact that those who were slower were subject to the cane and whip, notwithstanding the fact that their productivity hadn't slowed, it just seemed so by comparison.

That lesson came cruelly home during one rest period when his fellow workers caught him just as he was dozing off and beat him mercilessly. Such was the price of individual accomplishment in this inflexible system, he thought to himself.

For a while, José simply slowed himself down to avoid outshining his fellow bondservants. That, however, incurred the displeasure of the masters. Then, an alternative idea occurred to him: one-by-one, he began teaching his fellow vassals his improved method.

Of course, there were some who balked at having to learn anything new and others who simply had not the capacity. But there were enough who mastered the technique that José Necahuatl was saved from further mistreatment—at least by his fellow workers.

As production increased across the board, one of the more compassionate—or better said, less cruel—supervisors noticed and brought it to the attention of one of the owners. For a while it resulted in slightly better food for the whole assembly. He even noted a tiny savor of salt that made it a bit more palatable.

It didn't last long, however, as the managers and owners quickly became accustomed to the higher output.

Then one day, opportunity struck: work was agreeably stopped to demonstrate a whole new system imported from England. It consisted of a device called the flying shuttle and the mechanized loom it enabled. José Necahuatl watched closely as the textile worker imported with the devices showed the assemblage of workers, supervisors and managers how the system functioned.

As a result of his careful attention, José was the first to master the art. He remembered his earlier lesson of the resentment of the less gifted, however, and this time immediately tried to teach his fellow workers the skill. He was astonished and dismayed when the majority would only learn the procedure grudgingly. Had their curiosity, their very sense of industry been beaten or bred out of them?

José Necahuatl de Arreola even took to the study of the device's construction, so that when one of the shuttles broke, he suggested a way of manufacturing a replacement, saving the company the expense of importing more.

But despite having to teach the supervisors and even the manager how to use the flying shuttle and the mechanized loom, he remained in the caste of indentured servants. He had to be careful not to openly question the system, as it was his work in the *obraje* that was paying off his family's debt—or at least, he hoped, keeping it from growing.

He was granted one reward for his diligence, however. He was notified that he would be allowed to join the familied workers on their brief Sunday periods of liberation.

It was unimaginable: that he might once again know, if only for an all-too-brief interval, life outside this hell on earth! The prospect made him giddy with excitement. What would he do? How many activities could he crowd into those few hours?

Would he be able to see his family? The possibility brought tears of joy to his eyes. The night before the first blessed event, even though exhausted from work and teaching, he could only attain a fitful sleep, burdened as it was with outlandish dreams.

When he walked out that front door, for a good while he just stood, mesmerized by the sheer exhilaration of finally seeing a choice bit of the world outside those prison walls. The light, even the early morning light, was rather painful after all those months (years, had it been?) in that sultry, lightless dungeon. But still, he was grateful for the pain as it was a reminder of his wondrous, if temporary, emancipation.

After his eyes adjusted somewhat, he wandered, swallowing like a starving man his first taste of food the luscious rolling plains of green grass, those majestic, misted hills that surrounded them, so wondrously tall and stately. He'd forgotten how pleasing it was to drink in the sight of the town structures, some quaint and some ostentatious, of wood, of stone and some of plain dried mud. There was birdsong and laughter.

And the people, oh the people! An old *campesino* driving a don-key cart full of hay, children chatting playfully on a street corner on this day of rest, men and women idly strolling, and many others flocking to the market or to Saint Cecilia Church. How he ached to converse with them all!

He would finally be able to attend a Mass! Of course, he must thank the Almighty for this blessed delivery from his prison walls, this oh-so-welcome reprieve from the torment. He recognized that it was his God-given talents that had won him this treasure of liberation, and so bountiful thanks were in order.

The fact that he wouldn't have time to visit his family, a half-league or so from the town, was a pea under the mattress of his temporary deliverance. Perhaps he might see them in church!

It so happened that a visiting priest from the town of Dolores, a Father Miguel Hidalgo y Costilla, was saying the Mass that particular Sunday. José Necahuatl was disappointed at seeing no signs of his family, but he was delighted that as the priest gave his sermon, he translated bits of it into Náhuatl, his mother's, and of course his own, first language.

José smiled to himself that he had to conceal the fact that, despite Castilian being his second language, he spoke it better than the supervisors and even most of the managers and owners.

Father Hidalgo's sermon intrigued him. The priest spoke of his ceramic workshop in Dolores, some day or two's journey from San Miguel, using the process of fashioning the pottery ware as a metaphor for the crafting of one's soul. He even brought some pieces, including some poorly made, to illustrate. He presented other pieces that appeared, as he said, perfect, then pointed out that there were tiny flaws in some and almost invisible cracks in others that made them prone to breakage and loss.

Significantly, he said the best and most enduring and valuable pieces were made by common Indians. He even seemed to imply that, like their pottery pieces made with greater attention and care, their souls might be the purest of all.

José de Arreola was truly astonished. Indians could be better craftsmen, because no Spaniard or creole would ever stoop to practicing a craft. But to imply that Indians are purer of spirit was as close to heresy as he could imagine. He'd heard of a priest who'd been investigated by the Inquisition for questionable remarks and wondered if this were he. At any rate, he knew he had to become acquainted with this man of the cloth.

But how? Though he was quite encouraged by Father Hidalgo's apparently egalitarian tendencies, he knew that when the priest greeted parishioners outside the church, he would be surrounded first by peninsular Spaniards—those born in the mother country—then, outside them would be an outer ring of creoles. *Mestizos* and Indians would not have any chance of getting near him, nor would any even try.

Though José de Arreola looked more creole than Indian, his threadbare clothes and sweat-stained countenance besmirched with endless toil reeked of a lowly station in life. He could be severely punished for effrontery if he tried to push his way forward, perhaps even being shunned from the mill. Then where would his family be?

When he made his way outside from the back row of the church and Father Hidalgo finally emerged, he found his expectations woefully fulfilled: the prelate was surrounded by a thick circle of aristocracy. So how was he going to get close enough to speak to this extraordinary man?

He noticed a block of stone left over from the church's original construction among the crowd. It was one of two placed on either side of the entrance as adornments with potted plants atop. Trying his best to slip unnoticed amid the throng, he succeeded in making his way to one block without causing any notable disruption. He climbed atop it so that he could see just above the assemblage that blocked the priest from view.

Concentrating all his attention on Father Hidalgo as the prelate stood in profile to him, he aimed for some sort of silent communication: a gesture, an ephemeral meeting of eyes or the like.

After a relatively short period of time, Father Hidalgo suddenly stopped speaking and turned to the boy. Their eyes met in mutual curiosity, and because the priest was intrigued, the attention of all the gaggle of the well-healed were drawn to José de Arreola.

José immediately hopped down and made his way away, since interrupting the gentry's contact with a new spiritual leader could have dire consequences. He waited some distance apart, secreting himself behind a tree, hoping that his brief wordless contact with Father Hidalgo might entice the priest to an audience.

As the aristocrats melted away one-by-one, José had the impression that their real interest was more in outward demonstrations of piety—in being seen to pay respects—than genuine concern with church affairs or the status of their own souls. Again, he wondered if he was alone in recognition of the phenomenon. He remembered the parable of the beggar and the Pharisee.

He tentatively stepped out from behind the tree, hoping to once again catch Father Hidalgo's attention. He began to lose heart when the priest turned back toward the open doors of the church.

What was he to do? To actually speak out could end in truly horrific consequences—for him and therefore for his family. But to lose this opportunity was simply unthinkable. In desperation, he blurted out in Náhuatl, "Bless me Father for I have sinned. My pottery is flawed!"

The whole remaining entourage turned to José, all but the priest with a condemnatory scowl. Who could this impudent rustic be, and how had he the effrontery to address the reverend at all, much less in his crude native tongue?

José Necahuatl stood paralyzed with all substance sucked from him like a bitten quarter-lime after a shot of mezcal. A wave of nausea turned him the color of sheet-metal and almost made him flee the scene. He had breached so many unspoken rules that he was sure his condemnation was inevitable. What had he done to his family? To himself? He waited, trembling.

Somehow fortune was with him. Though Father Hidalgo had made the feint toward retiring into the church, (perhaps to draw the boy out?), his silent communication with José de Arreola had more than fascinated him. He turned and looked directly at the young waif and addressed him in kind. "Come here, boy, and speak with me."

The few gentry still in Father Hidalgo's entourage were astonished, wondering what he had said, and what this uncivilized lout that stopped him had expressed—and, above all, how he had dared to! They were fairly scandalized that the priest addressed this lowly street urchin at all, much less in his native language. They and the deacon took a threatening step toward the boy before Father Hidalgo stopped them with a gentle, but firm, gesture.

There was something in the boy's manner, his very bearing, that spoke, for all his disheveled appearance, of intelligence—even of something akin to nobility. He waved José to come to him and continued speaking to him in the Indian dialect. "Come closer, my son, and tell me who you are and where you come from."

Those in the gathering were scandalized. They slowly moved away, looking at each other in bewilderment. They knew that it was a part of a cleric's obligation to minister to the commonplace, to instruct the crude in the superior Catholic culture—to save their souls. But to do it when their betters were in attendance was the height of impropriety.

It was the kind of egregious offense that only Father Hidalgo could get away with—that only he would commit. They quickly peeled away with significant looks at each other that this insult would be addressed at some later time. Even the deacon kept his distance from this upstart.

As he approached the priest, something told José Necahuatl to switch to Castilian. It was perhaps to show the retiring swells that his command of the mother-tongue was formidable, and hopefully to placate them somewhat by demonstrating that he recognized the superior nature of Spanish culture.

"I am José…" he started to say his second name but thought better of it "…de Arreola, the son of…" and he knew somehow that this priest would appreciate absolute candor "…the illegitimate son of Don José Sebastián de Arreola y Riaño."

At this public disclosure of illegitimacy, the scandalized deacon, Manuel Urbáñez, could take no more and moved to chase this slovenly peasant away. "Look here, boy. You are addressing the

44

pastor of Dolores, Guanajuato, graduate of San Nicolás Obispo College and its onetime rector. This kind of impudence—"

But he was cut off by Father Hidalgo: "Please, Manuel, as the scripture says, 'Suffer the little children...'" The deacon was quite discomfited by the priest's interest in this young heathen but knew he must defer to his authority.

Father Hidalgo turned back to the boy, again causing the deacon to withdraw in consternation. "And what do you do here in San Miguel, José de Arreola?"

"I am paying off—trying to pay off—my family's debt working in the local *obraje*, Father. Although the longer I wor..." José stopped himself, realizing that what he was about to say would not be taken kindly by the deacon and the few of his cohorts who remained.

Father Hidalgo seemed to recognize the boy's quandary and came to his rescue. "Have you family at your age? How comes it that they let you out to attend Mass?"

José breathed a sigh of relief and resolved to be more careful in how he talked about his "employment". "It is a reward for being the first to learn how to operate a new device called the flying shuttle and eventually more than doubling the production of cloth per day."

"More than twice the normal amount? How did you learn to use this new technology so quickly?"

"I—I'm not sure, Father. I just watched the Englishman they brought with the device to demonstrate its use."

Now the prelate was doubly impressed. "You learned just by watching? Was it difficult?"

José was a bit hesitant to answer. The last thing he could afford to be witnessed doing, especially with the deacon and a few of the upper class within earshot, was bragging. "Well Father, I… Uh…no, not really. It just takes a bit of concentration." He knew he needed to mollify those aristocrats, so he added, "Most of the workers are Indians and Negro slaves."

"Humph. I see," Father Hidalgo responded thoughtfully, having a suspicion of the reason for the boy's qualification. "And how is it working in the *obraje*? I've heard that the conditions are rather harsh." This was a reference to the scathing report on the *obrajes* by the *Corregidor* of the province to the governing council in Mexico City, the *Audiencia*, calling it essential slavery.

Now José felt a noose of indecision tighten around his neck. If he honestly said what life was like in the mill in front of all these witnesses, it would without a shred of doubt doom him with the dispatch of the Almighty. On the other hand, Father Hidalgo was obviously quite cognizant of the mill's true conditions.

So, hoping against hope that this Reverend Father would be discreet, he said in Náhuatl in as casual a manner as he could, "It is Hell on earth, Father," and smiled to dissimulate the actual message.

The deacon, who happened to be part owner of the mill, together with the other elite still present, looked to Father Hidalgo for a translation of what the boy had said. "What did he say, Father?"

José braced himself. Would this priest betray him to his remaining entourage? Why had he stepped out on such a dangerous ledge, trusting in this complete stranger, however much a man of the cloth? What horrors might he have subjected his family to if that trust were misplaced?

Father Hidalgo adopted the same neutral outward appearance that José had as he answered his deacon. He knew that if he made the boy's depiction a song of praise, this aristocratic assembly, and particularly the deacon, would automatically be suspicious.

So, with a gentle smile of his own, he responded, ameliorating the representation with his tone of voice, "He said it was... not quite Heaven on earth," and let the deacon and others wonder for a bit at that characterization. Seeing their disapproving reaction, however, he added, "but that he's learning from the experience."

The deacon was not quite mollified, but couldn't condemn the boy's description, either.

Father Hidalgo turned back to the boy. "Well, José de...?"

"Arreola, Father."

The deacon was concerned about the direction this conversation between the cleric and this vagabond was taking. He tried to urge the priest away. "Father, we uh...we must prepare for this afternoon's Mass. It—"

"Oh," Father Hidalgo cut him off, "we have plenty of time for that, Manuel. I want to get out of these vestments for a little while, anyway. It's rather uncomfortably warm today." He turned to José. "Come with me, José de Arreola. I could use someone with your capacity for learning in my pottery mill."

The deacon was aghast. "But Father, you...he..."

"Don't worry, Manuel. I'll pay you handsomely for stealing him away from you." With a wink at José, Father Hidalgo escorted the boy through the doors of the church and back to the parish rectory.

The deacon and the rest of the aristocracy, audience to this most distressing marvel of condescension, looked to each other with astonishment and consternation as the pair made their way into the church.

Chapter IV

*Calvin, through Knox, destroyed the old Christian
concept of a station in life and built a new cosmos
in which men and women should have not place but
functions. The act of being was meaningless and the
worth of any man could only by judged by what he did.*

                       --"Lone Star", T.R. Fehrenbach

God helps those who help themselves.

                       --Old Scots-Irish Expression

*They fear God so much, they have no fear left over for
anything else.*

                       --Said of Scots-Irish Presbyterians

"You're right, *hijo*. He is a hard man."

I was startled to hear Miss Luz answer the question rummaging about my brain that I hadn't had the forwardness to voice. It was the day after the attack by the renegade Apache, and we'd only been on the road a short while. I was surprised to have awakened and seen Mister Macalister and Miss Luz already up and starting to harness the mule team. I immediately rose and joined them.

There's something about this work I really like. Well shoot, I just like being busy working with my hands. I wonder if I'll get any chance to use my carpentry skills on Mister Macalister's ranch. Well anyway, I know I'll be working outside and working up a sweat like I like to do, using my hands and body and maybe learning some new skills. I'd already learned a lot working on Mister Kotula's ranch.

I'd watched Mister Macalister limp around in such obvious pain that when he mounted his horse with barely a grimace, I was really surprised. Referring to my club foot as he hobbled about, he'd quietly flung off, "Guess we got something in common now, huh boy?"

The sun had finally completed its ascent above the eastern horizon and quickly burned off the few clouds that had so gloriously reflected the burnt orange glow of its coming. There was quite a chill in the air and as we continued in a northwesterly direction a sabertoothed wind did its best to try to check our progress.

I was fairly trembling with the cold till Miss Luz reached back in the cart and wrapped a blanket around me. Neither Mister Macalister nor Miss Luz even seemed to be aware of the chill.

It's a real different kind of cold here in Texas than in Silesia. There the unrelenting dampness penetrates so deep into your joints that they want to go on strike. Here that constant juiceless wind seems to slice through and suck every ounce of moisture out of you. The strange thing is that it warms up so quickly that you're stripping down layer by layer through the day. That bone-bleaching wind never seems to let up, though.

I hoped that that first thing Miss Luz had said to me was just a prelude to giving me a feel for Mister Macalister, as short-spoken a man as he is. Actually, I'd already got a feel for him. I mean I could tell he was a man of honor, a man of courage and discipline. I guess making a life out here in the wilderness, as hard and scarce as it is and with so many dangers, you'd pretty much just have to be just to survive.

Even with such pain as he must have been in, he rode square-shouldered and tall in the saddle. I noticed when he hitches up the rigging on the wagon or bridles and saddles his horse that his right arm just didn't seem to move past a certain point. It was obvious that shoulder didn't quite work right.

And yet I never saw any expression of pain or discomfort when he performed those tasks beyond a clenching of his jaw. I'd never heard him complain about anything—except maybe about losing his hand Mauricio to the Apache raiders. Never a peep about his own injury.

I just wanted to get to know everything I could about such a man, so different from my own father. And yet so much like him in some ways. Papa, after all, had not just braved a new and uncultivated stretch of land but a whole new country—with five children in tow!

I was real curious about Miss Luz as well. I noticed both she and Mister Macalister had considerable scars on their wrists. Of course, with Miss Luz those scars paled in comparison with the scars on her face and neck. I wondered what on earth could have caused the tip of her nose to look like it had been cut off. That was something I knew was far from my place to ask about.

There just seemed to be an understanding in the Macalister family, just like ours, that you just didn't ask about personal things at all. And that suits me just fine. I would just have to be content with whatever Miss Luz felt all right talking about.

My discretion paid off. Besides, it's almost like this lady can read my mind. After a bit of time as we lumbered on, she continued right where she'd left off. "To survive in this God-forsaken country, it is the only way."

As the terrain flattened out and seemed to stretch out to infinity, she took a moment to drink in its vastness. "And beyond that, to actually build something, something fruitful and lasting… Well, it sucks the life out of most who brave it. This land is littered with the graves of those it conquered.

"The Lazy Eight, our dominion, is that something—that creation that gives us purpose…that gives us place."

I felt like Miss Luz was talking about more than her brother, Mister G.P. Macalister. That led me to another mystery that this time I would express: "Miss Luz, I've heard you address Mister Macalister as '*hermano*'. That means 'brother', don't it?"

A barely visible closed-lipped smile broke easily across her face. "Yes, *hijo*. It does."

When she didn't continue for a few minutes, I knew not to pursue it. "Oh," I just said, and left it up to her to decide if she would explain or just drop the subject cold.

"You wonder how we can be brother and sister when I'm Mexican and he's Anglo."

"Well…yes, ma'am, kinda'; but I—I don't mean to pry."

"It's quite all right. There's nothing personal about it. It is a story of survival, of the savage brutality of the Texas frontier and the primitive peoples that inhabited it and some that still do. It's a tale of the greatness of human decency that daunting challenges seem to foster in us."

She took a moment in which she seemed to look out at the vast expanse of all human history. "I'll start at the beginning—at least, from *my* beginning. Hand me the reins so that you can listen carefully and at your ease."

She took the reins and then a deep breath which she exhaled with a sigh that seemed to contain all the grief and joy of a lifetime. "When I was six or seven years old—it's kind of hard to remember now—my father, who was a captain in the army of New Spain—Mexico, now—was sent on a mission to establish a colony in what was then the Spanish province of Texas. With him went ten other soldiers and their families together with two Franciscan priests and various Indian servants.

"The project was intended to reaffirm Spanish sovereignty over the province now that Anglo settlers, though they'd sworn their allegiance and accepted Spanish citizenship, outnumbered our own. To that end, our cadre made its way from Veracruz to the mouth of the Brazos River and moved north, searching for an old post established in the past by the French called Fort Saint Louis.

"We found what was left of it and immediately began working on repairs, although as my father said, it was in such poor condition that it might have been no more difficult starting from scratch.

"Since I was so young and a girl, my contribution could only be minimal, so I was often free to explore the area. My father said that there had once been a fierce Indian tribe called the Karankawa in the area that had killed all the French settlers in the original fort, but that yellow fever and malaria had wiped them out.

"I started sampling some of the nuts and berries in the area. Made myself very ill once and learned to be more careful. There was one nut with a hard shell called a *nogal* that was very tasty. My uncle Enrique, who was one of the other soldiers, taught me and my cousin, Rafael, how to set traps and fish in the river. He took us on forays to find edible roots and plants as well.

"One day, maybe two years or so after we'd come to the area, I was upriver fishing when I heard a commotion from the fort, yelling and horrible screams. I ran back to it and saw from a distance…"

Miss Luz hesitated to describe whatever it was she'd witnessed. "Miss Luz, you don't have to…" I could tell that it was horrible, maybe too horrible to give a picture of.

After a moment's silence, however, she continued with the story. "Yes. Yes I do. You need to know, *hijo*."

She paused a moment like she was trying to gird herself to be able to tell the story. I could tell it wasn't going to be a pleasant one. "Well, it was evident that not all of the Karankawa had been wiped out. I beheld such acts of savagery that…are perhaps best left to your imagination.

"But the true horror was still to come. Those who weren't immediately slaughtered were taken prisoner. I followed at a safe distance as they were dragged, bound hand and foot, back to the Indian camp. I had taught myself to move through the forest without making a sound."

I felt the air take on a heaviness and a warmth flowed through me as Miss Luz paused before continuing with the story. She seemed almost buried in so dark a place that I started to ask her to leave off recounting the hard parts. But I didn't get a chance to.

"When I got to the Indians' camp late that afternoon, I saw the true depravity that human beings, if they could be called that, are capable of. A ritual I later found out was called the *mitote* I watched until I couldn't watch anymore—and that happened very quickly. The Indians..." She hesitated, her face hardening into granite.

"...Please, Miss Luz, don't—"

"No. I must," she said with the conviction of tempered steel. "You need to know the kind of barbarity that those who settle in this land have faced and still face." She took another deep breath and silently exhaled. "The *mitote* is a ceremony in which flesh is carved from captives' bodies while they are still alive. The prisoners are then forced to watch as those parts of them are roasted and eaten before their eyes. Sometimes those parts are...unmentionable. The screams...

"I'd never seen or even imagined that such evil could occur, could exist, but I suppose it prepared me for what was to come."

She took an extended moment to collect herself, and I was grateful as it gave me a little time to gain control over my inclination to purge my breakfast. What she described seemed...I don't know what. I wondered if she sensed what she'd described had done to me.

She was silent for a long time, and I respected her need for a respite from recounting her and Mister Macalister's story. I needed the time anyway to try to process what she'd related already. I wondered what she meant about this horrific episode preparing her for what was to come. It sent a shiver like the cold north wind through me that there could possibly be anything more hideous than what she'd already described.

In the ensuing silence that bellowed louder than the west Texas wind, I watched her carefully observing her *hermano*, Mister Macalister. Every time he shifted in his saddle and let go a furtive grimace, I could tell she noticed. It was obvious from the time I'd been introduced to them how much Mister Macalister meant to her.

She'd of course tried to get him to ride in the cart. He didn't even bother to argue; he'd just saddled his horse and mounted without a word. He'd taken a good long moment to let the pain subside before he once again moved out in front of our train. And now he wasn't looking quite so steady in the saddle.

So, we talked for a while about this and that while she carefully watched her "*hermano*". She was curious about my family's history and what it was like to come to such a culture so different from our own. I did my best to describe my feelings about it and why we'd made the trip in the first place. Sensing she needed a break from the horror of what was done to her family, I asked her about life on the Macalister ranch.

At about noon the chill of the morning had tempered quite a bit, and I chucked off the blanket and was perfectly comfortable in a shirt and jeans and jacket. As we continued on, that afternoon sun began to beat down to where I was starting to get a mite uncomfortable and had to throw off my coat. Boy, this weather out here in the desert sure is changeable.

I hoped by then that enough time had passed, and Miss Luz had hopefully gotten past the hideous part of her story. So, I ventured a word about what came next to my buckboard companion. "Gosh Miss Luz, were you left without anyone? All by yourself and miles from anyone besides those Indians?"

"Yes," she answered matter-of-factly, "I was completely alone."

"I can't imagine what that must've been like. What did you do? How did you survive?"

"Because I had to," she answered like it was as simple and obvious as two plus two. "The will to live is indomitable. Even in those for whom life is an unendurable burden, that instinct usually stays the hand of their own self-destruction.

"Survival, at least physical survival, was not the problem. We'd been at the fort quite a while by the time of the Indian attack. I had learned the necessary skills from my uncle, and my cousin and I had ample opportunity to practice them. Besides that, I was frequently on my own as my cousin was older and often involved in affairs of the fort."

"Weren't you scared?"

She exhaled a breath that had a kind of ironic laugh in it. "I'm certain *scared* isn't the word for it. I cried and cried even as I tried to take stock of my situation—to think logically about what I was going to do. I had to will myself to calm my mind enough to think clearly.

"Fortunately, through the fear, the panic, I was finally able to. I knew I had to get away from those barbaric Indians. In the time we were in the fort, I'd heard the grownups speak of a tribe further north that was peaceful—or relatively so. They'd talked of moving there, away from that mosquito-ridden coastal establishment. However, the order from the *Audiencia*, the government, was to establish a colony at Fort San Luis. So, we followed orders. We always followed orders.

"In the time I've had as a Macalister, I've come to the conclusion that there is an inherent difference in the—the *character* of the Spanish and Anglo peoples. The Spanish had to force or bribe people to colonize Texas, to populate all the lands in America they claimed, even the northern parts of Mexico. Our colony was an example.

"From what I've seen, my people—the people I was born into, I mean—came to conquer and exploit. But they, as well as the people they conquered, are social people; they need company, society. To pioneer unsettled land as individuals, even families or small groups, is contrary to their nature.

"And I wonder if it comes from the rigid hierarchical system that characterized not only Spanish society, but that of the civilizations they conquered as well. My parents' family were *criollos*, born in New Spain but of pure Spanish blood. I'd even begun to question our exalted position before we were sent to colonize this then Mexican province of Texas."

"Why was that, Miss Luz?"

"I'd just had the feeling that there were some Indians and *mestizos*—you know what that is, of mixed Spanish and Indian ancestry?"

"Well, I do now," I said with a smile.

"Yes. Well, there were some of those, those considered inferior, who seemed to know more about farming and even business than my father knew, even though he was a capable man. It actually bothered me a bit that one of those *mestizos*, a Guadalupe Surem González, would caution my father about some decision he'd made and convince him that there was a better way, and when the change resulted in greater success, my father would take credit for the idea.

"Of course, I was still a child. I hadn't really articulated it in my mind. It just seemed funny to me then and only came clear to me years later. What seemed strange to me was that no one else seemed to question or even think anything of it.

"By contrast, my adoptive Scots-Irish father and mother came with a wave of colonists that their government had nothing to do with—gave no incentive or even encouragement. The settlers even agreed to renounce their United States citizenship and become citizens of Mexico—or New Spain as it was then called. They came like a wave. The United States government, in fact, only followed the people."

I thought about that, and she gave me time to consider it. "Well, I know my family came here to hopefully find—create—a better life. I only wish my father could have been a part of it."

"I'm sure you do, *hijo*. The only solace I can offer is that now you have as fine a man as God ever made in your stepfather."

That was the first time I'd heard Mister Macalister referred to as my stepfather. It felt like it kind of tickled my mind and sent that tickle out to my skin in a touch of gooseflesh. It was a funny feeling, but not a bad one.

Mister Macalister struck me as an admirable man. He had a really commanding way about him—but not domineering; all his orders were given quietly and considerately. There was no question they'd be followed, though. I could just feel that all the workers, including Miss Luz, relied on his judgment and leadership. I truly felt privileged when he showed me how to shoot a rifle and care for the horses and mules and stuff.

I couldn't figure out what the heck was going on with his son, though.

I'd leave that for later, however, because I was too interested in Miss Luz's story. "But Miss Luz, what did you do, all on your own then? How did you...even survive?"

"*Por los pelos.* 'By the skin of my teeth', as you say in English. It was touch and go, at least at first. I was fortunate that my uncle had taught me so many survival skills. I followed the river north, so I'd always have fresh water and fish to eat and still put distance between myself and the Karankawa. I found more trees that produced *nogales*. They're called 'pecans' in English. I set traps, caught beaver, muskrats, raccoons and...*nutreas—este*...'otters'.

"One thing I needed that my uncle hadn't taught me was how to build a shelter. I'd learned a little from the colony's efforts to rebuild the fort, but I hadn't paid much attention. I grew to really regret that."

As she recounted her travails during her time alone, I noticed that for the most part she kept her eyes on Mister Macalister. Now she abruptly stopped, and a frown of concern rippled across her face. "*Hermano?*" she called out to him. I looked up and saw my stepfather pull himself upright onto his saddle from a considerable lean. I wondered if his wound was bothering him more than he let on. Had he almost fainted?

"I'm all right, Luz," he answered rather curtly.

"We should stop, Gerardo. It's already late in the afternoon and the breakfast we had was hours ago. Everyone must be hungry, including yourself."

"We still got a measure of light left. Let's get a little farther on our way."

I was surprised to hear Miss Luz give what almost sounded like an order: "We must be coming up on Brady Creek. We'll stop there." Mister Macalister just silently nodded his assent.

He was far enough ahead that I could ask without him over-hearing: "You think Mister Macalister's all right?"

A trace of a knowing smile eased itself across her face and a silent chuckle exited her nose in a puff of air. "He's a man, after all: stubborn, and thinks he's invincible."

She thought for a moment and then qualified what she'd just said. "Well, the truth is he's responsible for many, many lives. With all of them depending on him, he can't allow himself to show any weakness or indecision. I just worry that he'll push himself too far, and then all those depending on him might lose him altogether. Then where would they—*we*—be? Where would I?"

I could tell there was something else that concerned her but honored her impulse to either share whatever she was thinking or keep it to herself. Finally, she said, "Rye whisky is not the best dis-infectant around."

"So, you think he'll take your advice and stop at this creek up ahead?

"He'd better," she answered in no uncertain terms.

We continued on toward the creek—and eventually, I hoped, to Fort Concho. Mister Macalister looked back to rights, so I felt it'd be all right for me to urge Miss Luz to continue her story. "So Miss Luz, what *did* you do for shelter?"

"Further upriver I found a cave of sorts. It was more like a recession in an embankment, but it offered some protection from the rain—at least when the wind wasn't blowing directly into it. By that time the leaves were starting to change and there were a few days of cooler weather, so I skinned all the animals I trapped in the hopes I could eventually make myself a coat.

"I tried different ways to fashion some kind of door to close off the cave for when the cold weather came. First, I tried using sticks and grass, then mud from around the river to chink between the sticks, but it wasn't the heavy clay like we had in Mexico so the rain would wash it away; or if it dried, it crumbled away. Then I used pelts from the animals I trapped as coverings, but I had no way of tanning them at first, so when they got wet, they hardened and started to fall apart. Just like my coat.

"I finally went back to grass woven in branches held up by rocks at the base on either side of them. The rocks helped keep the rain somewhat from rotting the sticks too quickly. I could put the skins on the inside, but I had to leave an opening for the smoke to escape. As it got colder and colder, I was torn. I wanted to be as isolated as possible from the cold wind and weather, but to have a fire, well…"

"Did you ever find a way to cure your hides? There are oak trees we use in Poland that produce a lot of the chemicals you need for it."

"Yes. One time I'd harvested some pecans from a different tree. I had to break them open with rocks, their shells were so hard. When I tried to eat the meat of one it was so bitter that I had to spit it out. I tried boiling them, but they were still too bitter.

Then I got very sick; couldn't do much of anything for days. When I finally came to myself, I noticed that one of my pelts had fallen into the bitter *nogal* water. I threw out the water and hung the pelt on the door to dry. Over time, I noticed that it was the only pelt that didn't harden and fall apart. I had my treatment."

I tried to imagine being in a similar situation. The idea made me shiver. "Miss Luz, that must have been horrible—all by yourself, living in a cave."

"It was. My Spanish blood cried out for company. But it's funny: unlike most in our colony, I could entertain myself for hours just exploring, trying different berries and seeds I'd come across, naming the birds and animals I happened to see." She smiled to herself. "The others were afraid something was wrong with me.

"During my illness, I kept remembering how the adults back at the fort would talk about how unendurable life was there, isolated as we were; how much they missed their relatives and friends, how they ached for the fiestas, walks and socializing in the town squares with guitars and fiddles playing; how they'd give anything to be back in New Spain. For them, this solitude was pure torture. And in my situation at that time, I laughed to myself. They had no idea what true loneliness is.

"But yes, *hijo*, it was a lonely, desperate time. There were many nights I cried myself to sleep."

"So, how did you come to be a part of the Macalister family? Did they find you and take you in?"

"I found them, actually. I was constantly exploring. I found a better cave farther upriver and sheltered from the wind. It was a somewhat drier area and not so thick with trees. One time I was exploring and saw smoke. I assumed it was that other friendly tribe my people had mentioned back at the fort. I was still cautious, though. I guess I'd been on my own for so long by then, over a year anyway, that I was a bit shy of people—afraid even, for some reason. And I couldn't be certain that those Indians were really peaceful.

"But curiosity and just...loneliness, I guess, got the better of me. The next day I set out in the direction of the smoke. As I got near, I saw a boy in the distance.

She paused for a moment like she was reliving the experience. "I can't tell you what that feeling was like, after all that time completely alone and suddenly seeing another person, a fellow human being.

"He was different, this boy. It was the first time I'd seen anyone with yellow hair." I looked up at Mister Macalister. The hair he had was mostly gray, but there was still a bit of light-colored strands mixed in.

Miss Luz continued. "I don't know...maybe all that time alone had made me suspicious. It was like being split into two people: one that was afraid and the other that was starving for companionship. But I had no idea if these people would be friendly or hostile.

"I hid behind a tree and just watched him. Then I got the feeling that he became aware of me, of being watched. So I ran. I knew how to disappear without a sound or a trail so he couldn't follow me.

"The next day I went back, being careful not to be seen. When I got to the same area, I saw something on a big group of boulders. There were crows pecking at it. I waited a while, made sure no one else was around and went to investigate. It was food. The crows flew away at my approach, and I saw bread and meat. I hadn't had bread in such a long a time!

"I wasn't sure what was going on. Had the boy left this out for me? Was it part of a trap? Could it be poisoned? The crows didn't fly far hoping they'd get another chance at the food. They didn't seem to show any signs of illness—but what if it was slow-acting poison? Or they were immune somehow?

"I was tempted, especially by the bread, but I didn't eat any that time. I went back the next day and there was a new supply of food. This time most of it was gone as the animals in the area had already begun to investigate themselves.

"I decided that on this occasion I would take a small taste, thinking that if it was poisoned, it would only make me sick but not kill me. That's how I figured out what nuts, seeds and berries around the fort were safe to eat."

I could see the creek ahead of us and hoped Miss Luz would finish the story before we stopped. I had to know how it had turned out. "So, was it Mister Macalister leaving the food out for you? Was the smoke from their home or their camp?"

"Luz," Mister Macalister called out to his sister, "pull the wagons parallel to each other beside the creek. I'm gonna ride up to the top 'a that hill, see if there's any trouble ahead."

Miss Luz did as she was directed, and she and I immediately busied ourselves with undoing the mule team and watering them in the creek. She took care of feeding and hobbling them, and I went to help Camp Cookie with his team. There were a lot of other chores to do to set camp, so I'd have to wait until supper to urge Miss Luz to finish the story of her adoption into the Macalister family.

I was anxious to hear how it all came to be.

Chapter V

Sovereignty lies essentially with peoples and not with kings. The kings exercise it by consent of the people...And in the event of its abuse, kings can be deposed and war may be declared on them.

--Francisco Morales

I condemn the evils I have caused America, now the dream has been removed from my eyes, and my penitence has left me prostrate. From here I can see the gallows upon which I shall be executed, and with each moment I breathe out pieces of my soul, and before I die...I shall die a thousand times of shame for my excesses.

--Father Miguel Hidalgo y Costilla

Now I understand, José Necahuatl thought to himself. *That sense of uneasiness, it wasn't my imagination.*

He remembered his first stirrings of unquiet, even as far back as when he was still with his family. He felt it first from his father during one of his last few visits. Don José Sebastián just didn't seem as relaxed as he had been during previous visits. José Necahuatl realized on that occasion that it had been a long span of time, months maybe, since his father's previous visit.

He also now remembered that during that visit and the final two after it, his father didn't do many of the things he normally did: taking the family out for a picnic, mounting José on his horse and letting him ride. He just wanted to be with the family, there in the house he'd built for them. He'd held José's mother in an embrace even more tender than usual. In fact, he was more affectionate with all the family. It felt good, very good—but still, there was that vague sense of anxiety underscoring those gestures.

José yearned to know more about his father. What was his other family like that he always, and even more so lately, seemed sad when he had to return to them? The boy had tried and tried to find out more about this man who provided so well for him and his family, who was so very loving and gracious to José's mother and his siblings and, he thought, especially to himself.

The fact that his was an illegitimate family mattered not at all to José. There were so many like his own, a second family to a moneyed *hacendado*. The difference was that his own family was well provided for. And loved. The many other "second" *mestizo* families he knew lived in hovels and rarely had enough to eat.

The family situation had, however, by that time of the scarcer visits, taken a turn for the worse. The regular stipend that his father had so faithfully sent now began to wane and those that did arrive were less generous. José wondered if it were connected in any way with the feeling of unease he perceived—mostly in the way Indians and *mestizos* were treated by their superiors.

But José was aware that asking his father about it always made José Sebastián uncomfortable and the last thing the boy wanted was to spoil those increasingly rare visits. So, he contented himself with the knowledge that his father cared for this, his second family, and gave José, at least for a time, a better life than many of his peers.

Now after the hated years in the *obraje*, here José Necahuatl was, with Father Hidalgo and the rest of the rebel leadership. All the more than three years he'd spent working in the priest's workshop, during all the secret meetings the conspirators were so careful to exclude him from that disquiet had grown.

Even during his last year in the *obraje*, the manager and supervisors had grown increasingly brutal. Somehow José felt that it was a result of that, that strange disgruntlement in the air. If he hadn't been liberated by Father Hidalgo, who knows what his fate might have been.

Since the *Grito de Dolores*, Father Hidalgo's call to arms for the revolutionaries, the insurgents had had incredible success. They'd taken Celaya without a fight. Now here in San Miguel el Grande, the mass of peasants the rebellion had won over on its trek from Father's *Dolores Cry* had overwhelmed the meager forces the establishment had managed to muster. They were flush with success. It seemed nothing could stop them.

But something felt wrong to José Necahuatl, the *mestizo*. Certainly, the savage mayhem visited upon the peninsular Spanish by the peasantry was concerning—at times, repugnant. He was sympathetic to Don Ignacio Allende's call for discipline and demonstrations of compassion for the Spaniards and for the creoles who had remained loyal to Spain.

That sentiment had made him think of his adored father and hope that he had sided with the rebels—or, if not, that God would keep him safe from the brutal retaliations visited upon loyalists.

Father Hidalgo had called for all true Spaniards to be exiled back to Spain; or executed if they refused. José Necahuatl was puzzled by such an intemperate lack of mercy, yea of downright ruthlessness, from a man of the cloth—especially from one who had been so kind and generous with him. How can a man, even a priest, be so kind and generous with some and so brutal with others? It almost seemed like he was two different people.

Of course, there were other inconsistencies—could one even go so far as to say hypocrisies?—in Father Hidalgo's comportment. His vow of celibacy was, as best José could perceive, a mere suggestion, the priest having fathered several children, and by more than one consort.

José marveled at the contrast between the priest's benevolence and seeming respect for not only José himself but all *mestizos* and Indians and the little regard for the oaths he'd sworn to the Lord. He also found it curious that such—to be kind, indiscretions—did not detract one iota from the reverence and esteem in which he was held by the community at large. It seemed that those infractions were considered forgiven before committed—the normal behavior of any man. José wondered if perhaps they were.

How could a person be so decent and compassionate in one sphere of his life, however, and then be utterly merciless in another? For some reason, José thought about the power and influence of the church and therefore in those of its practitioners. Could it be power that corrupts? Or is it that the corrupt tend to seek power?

There was no question that the Catholic Church and its representatives held enormous influence in New Spanish society. José had perceived a mighty rivalry between it and the Spanish government in the person of the King and his representatives, always those born in the mother country.

Could this rebellion be simply a contest for power and influence?

There was certainly something beyond the brutality that troubled the young man. From the very start of the clandestine meetings of those disgruntled creoles, José Necahuatl had snuck behind doors listening, or caught snippets of muted conversations when he served the faction refreshments.

From the little he'd been able to decipher, he questioned its very purpose. He could find no ideological basis at its core. He'd heard no mention of the rigid class structure that kept people of talent and ability in positions of servitude. All their potential contributions to the advancement of Mexican society were cast to oblivion—or probably not even thought of.

José had managed to save a few of the books by philosophers of the previous century or rescued parts of them from the remains of the bonfires into which they were invariably thrown. There was one by a French philosopher named Jean Jacques Rousseau and another, fortunately in translation, by an Adam Smith concerning something about "Moral Beliefs or Moral Sentiments"—the rest of the cover was burned beyond recognition but a good portion of the text he was able to rescue.

In both cases, they were quite a revelation for the young man. They seemed to supplant divine revelation and hidebound tradition for reason as the arbiter of truth. He could see why the Catholic Church, with the full support and encouragement of the government, would condemn them as heresy and commit them to a public burning. Such theories would be a direct threat to their status and exalted position in New Spanish society.

José Necahuatl de Arreola had gotten the sense that almost to a man, the inflexible hierarchy of New Spain, as inherited from the mother country, was considered designed by God. It was itself the reflection of the divine order of Heaven. If the ability to reason or inherent talent rather than birth should determine one's station in the culture of a nation, it would overturn everything that formed the basis of their cherished beliefs.

In those very issues lay all of José's misgivings concerning the present uprising. The revolution's whole objective, it seemed, was merely to replace the peninsular Spanish with creoles, but keeping this stultifying hierarchical system in place—merely with a different class at the top. Was the talk of liberation merely a pretext for class envy? How the quest for power does seem to corrupt!

There had been nary a word concerning the manumission of slaves, of greater liberty and opportunity for the Indians and *mestizos* like himself to realize their personal potential. There were only sops, like better working conditions for the mineworkers or the suspension of the tributes the Indians had to pay. José wondered, however, once the creoles were safely ensconced as the ruling elite, how long those reforms would last.

No, he feared that all would continue as it was, with one's condition still determined by the accident of birth, merely supplanting one aristocracy for another. He'd heard that at the first sign of pregnancy of a Spaniard or creole that the wife (or mistress) was immediately put on a ship bound for Spain in order to claim peninsular origin.

Is it believed that merely being born in a particular place endows the child with some kind of magical powers? It defied all rational thought. It struck him that such a belief was a patent indication of feeblemindedness. *How ironic!* he thought.

However, it seemed equally ridiculous to José that having pure Spanish blood, as the creoles do, should endow one with a privileged position. That, however, was something he could never openly aver. He knew his place. He had carefully studied the interaction of the different classes during his time as ward and employee of Father Hidalgo y Costilla in his pottery workshop and as servant in the priest's home.

By exercising considerable discretion, he had managed after a time to at least have his suggestions considered concerning the marketing and packaging of the pottery ware. That for a long time he was not given credit mattered little to him since he found the work inherently interesting and challenging. Compared to the *obraje*, it was Heaven-on-earth.

Was he completely alone in recognizing the futility of this rebellion? The thought ate out his sense of belonging and left him feeling adrift in a boundless sea, no shore or ship to provide rescue or companionship.

So, he would keep his own counsel religiously, quietly observing and perhaps hoping that the movement would in time come to acquire some sort of ideological/philosophical core.

*A*nd now, here in San Miguel, José Necahuatl stood listening to the bitter argument between Father Hidalgo and Don Ignacio Allende from behind the parlor's closed door. He was at first distracted by the sounds of rioting and mayhem throughout the city. Stores were being pillaged and set afire, Spaniards humiliated, many murdered. With the Indians all-consuming hatred for their Spanish conquerors and no one to restrain them, the carnage was as predictable as the sun rising in the east.

As the debate grew more and more heated, however, and the leaders' voices rose in anger, he could hear their arguments more clearly. First came the strident voice of Father Hidalgo:

"No! No! These peasants have just endured two years of drought and famine, not to mention the villainous depredations of their Spanish lords! Was it the *gachupines* who starved, who heard the cries of hunger from their children and were powerless to stop their suffering? Was it they who stood helpless as starvation drained their little ones' lives away?"

José heard Don Ignacio try to answer Father Hidalgo's tirade, but apparently it was not yet finished. José could clearly hear the priest continue. "Their only motivation to fight is to finally have some reward, some relief from their crushing want, some...some share in the bounty of Mexico, and some opportunity to express their outrage! And they have every right to visit upon their tormentors just a taste of their years, their decades, their *centuries* of suffering!"

There were some cries of agreement and applause, followed by quieter voices of appeasement that José could only make out by their tone. They were quickly followed by the only slightly less fulminating voice of Don Ignacio. "Father, no one denies the suffering of the Indians, even of those of mixed heritage, but if we are going to replace the present government, we must show that we are capable of governing. This looting and pillaging, this chaos demonstrates exactly the opposite. And you cannot win a war, any war, without discipline!"

José listened to Don Ignacio's plea for order, for rationality, with sympathy. While he could not deny that this creole had had a considerable part in the breeding of that sulfurous animosity toward the occupying Spanish, he hoped that Father Hidalgo would be counseled. As a military man, Captain of the Queen's Provincial Dragoon's of Guanajuato, Don Ignacio had the experience in how to wage an insurrection, or at least of how to lead an army.

But José de Arreola was torn. He owed so much to Father Hidalgo: his rescue from the hated *obraje* and his introduction and instruction in the pottery craft, not to mention his patient education in academics.

Of course, there were years of suggestions José had offered that made the business thrive, nearly tripling its profits, for which no acknowledgement was forthcoming. Gradually, he began to receive at least verbal affirmations. It was only during that last half-year that Father had first made him a supervisor, and then put him in charge of marketing the workshop's wares. All that time, the priest had also devoted himself to José's instruction in religion, the sciences, philosophy, anthropology and languages—which José drank in like a tick on a dog.

Unfortunately, it seemed that in the present discussion, Father Hidalgo would not be easily appeased. "And who will fight this war without incentive?" he continued shouting at the top of his compass. "And what incentive have they if not to visit upon their tormentors some of the torment they have suffered? If not to take back some of that bounty stolen from them by their masters?"

Judging by the vehemence of the two debaters, José thought it likely that it would soon come to blows, signaling the death knell of the movement. Of course, he wondered if it were even worth saving in its present form. He still held onto the hope, however, of its eventual redemption, of the recognition that it was the system imposed by the Spaniards and accepted by practically the whole populace and not those who ruled that needed to be scrapped.

Notwithstanding his status in the pottery business, the enterprise for the time being having been suspended, he had now been returned to his former place as a mere servant and lowly mixed breed. So, what could he do? He wracked his brain for some pretext to enter the room, wondering even if he could, what he could do once there.

He looked around the antechamber outside the parlor, hoping for inspiration. After a moment, his eyes fell upon a keg of ale that had been "liberated" and brought here by the rioting forces. Yes, this had been one of his duties in Dolores for the parties and *tertulias* and soirées at Father Hidalgo's home after an evening's concert or play. He quickly filled as many flagons as he could fit on one tray. He gingerly tapped on the parlor door and entered.

He could feel the consternation at his interruption and wondered if his tactic would in fact exacerbate the problem rather than assuaging it. Throwing caution to the winds, he first went to Father Hidalgo whom he perceived to be the most choleric. Father's glance fairly pierced his eyes and exited out the back of his skull. José de Arreola's ploy had certainly stopped the argument, but would it also lead to his own doom?

As Father accepted the cup of ale, José knew it would be the height of presumption on his part to make his look one of instruction. While he knew he had this prelate's love and even a nascent respect, he also knew his place in the social order. Consequently, he certainly made the tenor of his interaction one of plea, not exhortation.

Though Father's first reaction was one of blistering irritation, the imploring look from his charge had the effect of at least interrupting and hopefully temporizing his fury. José counted on the affection he'd always felt from his holy confessor. As the two faced each other, he could feel Father's fury slowly begin to abate. He breathed a sigh of relief. He could also sense perhaps a tiny tinge of gratitude from the others in the room for the intervention.

José went directly to Don Ignacio and was careful to offer him his drink in a mate to the stein he'd served to Father Hidalgo. Though he'd met the captain and had served him often at Father Hidalgo's gatherings, he recognized that there was not the familiarity he had with the priest. He merely bowed slightly as the general took his drink.

As subtly as he could, José tried to keep himself between the two at some little distance to the side as he served the rest of the assembly. Fortunately, he had filled and brought more than enough cups to serve the entire assembly. He could feel the temperature in the room slightly attenuate. As it did, José Necahuatl de Arreola slipped as unobtrusively as he could out of the room.

He breathed a sigh of relief upon closing the door as the intrusion did seem to have the palliative effect he was hoping for. Father Hidalgo was finally able to speak in a somewhat more moderate tone so that José Necahuatl could barely make out the words. "Well…I suppose we can ask the…the troops to at least moderate to some degree their…their *ebullience.*

From the rest of the room, José could feel a sigh of relief.

Still, José Necahuatl de Arreola was troubled. What was it about Father Hidalgo's indulgence of the peasants' desire for vengeance, their flagrant indiscipline that bothered him so? He thought about all the many gatherings at the priest's house where the aristoi mingled with the commoners.

It seemed to José a heartfelt effort; the good Father was the only member of the ruling class who did such a thing, after all. The only function to which Indians and *mestizos* weren't invited were the literary soirées, as the vast majority were illiterate.

Did the classes really mingle, though? Was there more than token interaction between them? It seemed to José that all the guests quickly formed into groups of their own kind. What would an illiterate peasant have to say to the scholars, the merchants, the civil servants or even the military officials present? The awkward condescension of the latter any time they were addressed was glaring.

As José served the guests at those functions, he had observed those few tentative attempts at collegiality. They were all so brief and ill-fitting as to actually increase distrust and suspicion—at least in most instances.

In his own case, though he had advanced in the ceramic workshop and gained a considerable command of mathematics, science and philosophy, he was still relegated to service at Father's affairs. Beyond that, he even to this day felt some social wall between them, an unbridgeable gulf—between himself and all those of pure Spanish blood, peninsular and creole alike.

In Father Hidalgo's indulgence of the savagery evinced by the lowly born was contained the same fatherly indulgence in having them attend his many affairs. It was not truly an egalitarian impulse. While father had a genuine affection for the Indians and *mestizos* in his care... *In his care,* that was it! Though the fondness was genuine, it was the indulgence of a parent for a child, not that of genuine camaraderie among equals.

José suddenly realized that Father's purpose in having peasants attend those functions at his house was not to evoke a realization of some kind of common humanity, but rather to instill in those of the upper class a sense of *noblesse oblige*. Those of the lowly born were still considered—even by Father Hidalgo—as children to be cared for rather than as individuals capable of caring for themselves given the necessary opportunity.

Consequently, though José de Arreola's stratagem had succeeded in calming the turbulent waters of the revolution, the young man still had a feeling of defeat.

When the faction finally retired for the night, José was left alone with Father Hidalgo. The young *mestizo* was uncommonly quiet, which became a source of curiosity for the priest. "You've hardly said a word since the meeting, *hijo*. What's on your mind, boy?"

Though nineteen now and fully a man, José actually appreciated the address. He knew that *boy* was meant affectionately. Though it still had the savor of condescension, the feeling of familiarity for José far outweighed the sense of class distinction. Still, he hesitated. Who was he to question Father's judgment? And yet question it he did.

"It's the behavior of the peasants, isn't it?" Father pressed. "Go on, *hijo*. I'm curious to know your thoughts."

"Well...," José began with an uncomfortable sigh, "the...the wholesale slaughter, Father, it..." José was loath to continue.

"What? You agree with Don Ignacio? You don't think the people have legitimate grievances?"

Though he sensed Father Hidalgo's umbrage, José Necahuatl had a feeling that because, unlike Don Ignacio, he had no real power, no status in the movement, Father could tolerate his questioning of its direction and the wholesale mayhem that the priest tolerated—even encouraged to a degree. José could feel the condescension in that tolerance.

"Of course they do, Father. I'm...I'm only thinking of the long-term consequences of such carnage—of a policy of indulging the worst impulses in human behavior."

Now it was Father Hidalgo's turn to pause and reflect. He was struck by the sophistication of his young charge's argument. But he was hardly convinced. "I consider it necessary to send a message to those who oppose us—to let them see how their treatment of the lower classes has fomented such resentment."

He paused to give his pupil time to consider. "Speak up, boy. You have nothing to fear from me."

"The message, sir... Should we not be sending an indication that it is not the men we revile, but the social order whose rigidity keeps us—all Mexicans, even those of the aristocracy—in a kind of bondage? That ties us, that chains us, because of something as arbitrary as place of birth or parentage, to such a limited and implacable set of possibilities?"

It was here that José de Arreola lost his patron. Father frowned, not in condemnation but rather in lack of understanding as the true nature of the boy's argument went sailing over his head.

"But it is these men that have created this infernal system." Father Hidalgo paused in irritation. "At any rate, I disagree with your assessment, José. I'm not sure it's really pertinent, in fact. The social order is ordained by God. As He in Heaven rules the seraphim and cherubim and as the latter take their place above the saints and the saints above the common man, so God dictates to the Pope that he may rule here on earth in clerical matters. And, being inspired by God, the Papacy *infallibly* instructs all the bishopdom and priesthood. So we, God's chosen to spread Catholicism to the entire world, as shepherds direct this poor benighted flock of heathens on the path of salvation.

"In like manner, the Lord chooses the king and princes to rule in earthly matters and care for and direct their inferiors. Should we not, in our best, attempt to replicate the divinely inspired order established by our Creator?" Confident he had put to rest these unnatural ideas expressed by his charge, he simply waited and then challenged. "Well...?"

Here was the crux of the problem, José thought. Father's assessment took him back to the original planning of the rebellion amid furious debate. Because those arguments had festered deep in José de Arreola's spirit like a dirty infected splinter beneath the skin, he could still hear Father Hidalgo's dogmatic assertions at the faction's earliest meetings:

"No! I know these Indians. They will not fight for abstract ideas like independence or autonomy. Those concepts are meaningless to them. They will only join our crusade if we do it in the name of King Fernando, to restore him to his rightful consecrated place on the throne of Spain."

That conclusion, precisely for its inherent truth, stuck in José de Arreola's craw. The most pernicious element of this hierarchical system for him was the fact that almost all his fellow *mestizos*, together with those of pure Indian blood, accepted their place in this inflexible society. To the Indian, the king was, like God, a benevolent father who cares for them the way a doting parent cares for his children.

José de Arreola wondered why they could not see that it was that very way of thinking, of hoping for the "good and kindly father" to rescue them that kept them mired in that very misery they sought to escape. Such a people—those seeking a savior, looking to others for their salvation, are those easily dominated and controlled. It is the individual who undertakes his own deliverance who thrives and who thereby makes the greatest contribution to society as a whole.

He sought a manner of answering Father Hidalgo's question that would incorporate those concerns. "I…I wonder if we are imitating the form rather than the spirit of the Divine, Father. Did not our Savior take the form of a common man and lead by example rather than by fiat? Why did He not incarnate Himself as emperor of Rome if such rigid hierarchy is the true way?"

Father Hidalgo paused half in puzzlement and half in consternation. He seemed almost stupefied by his charge's reasoning. José had a sense of the quandary he'd put his patron in and so let the ideas he'd expressed marinate in Father Hidalgo's reflections.

After a moment, Father Hidalgo finally spoke. "You have an extraordinarily supple and subtle mind, José Necahautl de Arreola. You've given me considerable food for thought. I maintain, however, that someone must lead, and some have to follow. The idea that the necessary wisdom can be found in these unlettered pagans is absurd if not blasphemous."

José was quite cowed by the word Father used to describe his musings, but mustered the courage to share one more thought: "Were not the Apostles simple fishermen, Father, who became the founders of the Catholic Church? And were they not Jews?"

Father Hidalgo stared at his young adoptee for a considerable time in silence. José could sense his irritation but felt it stopped short of condemnation. Finally, the priest slowly said, "Yes. Yes, they were."

*I*n the end, however, little changed.

Chapter VI

The day the first insurgent is hanged,
Spain must give up all hope of holding
on to America.

--Carlos María de Bustamante

Government is an institution which prevents
injustice other than such as it commits itself.
It should be restrained to a minimum for, as a
necessary evil, it is the constraint of men by
other men.

--Ibn Khaldun

So much death and destruction, so much suffering and pain, José
Nicolás de Cos de la Portilla thought as he escorted the manacled
rebel leaders to the gallows. Finally, this stupid and bloody insurrection was over, the rebels killed or taken prisoner.

He had reluctantly joined his father on this campaign to, as the
patriarch said, "crush this swarm of rattlesnakes like the vile traitorous maggots they are." For young Nicolás not to have done so
would have showered his family with shame and condemned him to
humiliation and possible banishment. That possibility struck Nicolás
as even more hideous than this horrible war. He could think of no
greater punishment than being ostracized, excluded. Alone.

Now, amid all the horrors this bloody war had thrust on him,
only one filled him with the hate necessary to welcome these rebels'

execution: the death of his worshipped big brother, Antonio. On top of so profound a loss, it now left him the oldest male child, the inheritor and representative of the "de Cos" name. Not in his wildest dreams could he imagine ever feeling worthy. It was, however, another burden he must endure.

Every time he thought of his brother's hideous death, the hate for these jackals grew like a cancerous mole. *I should revel in their gruesome fate,* he thought to himself. *It was they who wreaked such havoc and misery in New Spain, they who are responsible for Tony's death!*

And yet... A competing, unarticulated sentiment seemed to invade and attenuate the joyful anticipation he felt at these rebels' coming extirpation. It sat like a blockage to the consumption of joy he would have at their demise. *Would I truly want to spare them?* he asked himself. *Why?*

Only now that the rebellion had been routed had he begun to accommodate the horrors he'd beheld: the spouting blood, the body-parts and brain matter strewn across the battlefield, the horrific screams of fellow soldiers and rebels as they writhed in pain and terror. The slow, agonizing deaths of the mortally wounded—comrade and enemy alike—tortured him every sleeping moment with nightmares of butchery and despair.

Even those horrors paled in comparison to the death of Antonio. His hero. His idol. Though mercifully quick, it was that single event that made him capable of the savagery that war necessitates. But would he ever become inured to its loathsome horror? Would he ever for the rest of his life be able to put his head to pillow without horrifying visitations and night-terrors?

Every reminder of the first time he had killed, and of every time after that, turned his stomach inside out and brought on the same urge to purge all that his entrails contained. Now, he must once again witness the agony of death by hanging.

Some of those condemned would be fortunate (as fortunate as one can be who is hanged): the blotches of blood in the face and eyes that showed the arrested flow of blood to the brain signaled unconsciousness. It was mercifully quick.

But then there were those not so lucky, who suffered death by agonizingly slow asphyxiation: the extended tongue, the bulging eyes, the dance of death as they struggled to find some footing, some support, to allow the passage of air to lungs burning in desperation; the excruciating terror as death approached.

And all, regardless of time or manner of death, had to suffer the indignity of a final opening of their bowels and bladder as life drained slowly into the pitch black of nonexistence. Or perhaps it was in terror of what was to come.

Which was worse: to watch one's fellow human beings slowly robbed of life, or to actually take that life on the battlefield? Each had its own separate torment.

José Nicolás' only hope was that these being the leaders of the rebellion, the wholesale slaughter could finally be brought to a close and some semblance of normality prevail. Buried in the depths of his soul, however, was the knowledge that those beings deprived of life would haunt him the rest of his days.

It is a truism that men can only do their duty in war by dehumanizing the enemy. To acknowledge the humanity of those you must kill paralyzes the will. The only escape for José Nicolás was to see these condemned as nameless traitors, to deny their place as children of God. He was unsuccessful, however, at transforming them into vile vermin, purged of all that made them men.

So, when the rebel at his side addressed him, "What is your name, young man?" he startled so that his horse shied. Dulcinea, his beloved mare, then reared, almost throwing him from his saddle. Once he regained control of her, and of himself, he made his best effort at ignoring the address. He trembled at the possible consequences of having intercourse with any of these traitors.

"Oh, I do so humbly beg your pardon for startling your mount. Please forgive me," the young prisoner abjectly apologized. "I merely hoped for some distraction for a brief moment from the reality of my coming fate."

Despite his discomfort, however, Nicolás was intrigued by this detainee. Unlike the others, he seemed to ride on his donkey to his execution with what looked like resignation, even courage. One would think it would be the priest two donkeys ahead who would not fear death, but Nicolás could sense the sheer terror through the prayers that Father Hidalgo continually mumbled. And that terror terrorized him.

This young man who'd spoken to Nicolás didn't even seem to mind the humiliation of being ridden through the town on the sorriest burros his father could find—displayed as an example of what happens to those who would challenge the established order. Nicolás was surprised that one so young—only a few years older than himself, he reckoned—could be among the rebel's leadership.

He finally gave in to curiosity. "I'm José Nicolás de Cos de la Portilla," he said as quietly and casually as he could, continuing to face forward.

"Oh, I'm José as well," the young man answered—to Nicolás' astonishment, almost cheerfully. "The rest of my name, however, is not nearly so distinguished. I'm simply José de Arreola."

Nicolás tried to inhibit his natural inclination to turn to his interlocutor and continued speaking under his breath as best he could. Arreola? Are you—"

"He is my father. But my mother is an Indian. Of course, they were never married."

"You are a caste, a *mestizo*."

"I am." José Nicolás was rather surprised that this mixed breed admitted his parentage without any sense of shame. His admission, in fact, seemed almost prideful.

"Then how comes it that you are among those to be hanged? Is it possible that..." Nicolás stopped himself as one of his father's lieutenants rode by. He was alerted by Arreola who, as soon as he noticed the soldier approaching, turned to face forward and acted the part of one dejected by the thought of his coming fate.

Nicolás was grateful for Arreola's discretion, so grateful that he continued the conversation. It was, in fact, a most welcome distraction from the unremitting malignance of the war and the coming executions he would have to witness. What he didn't count on was that the conversation would humanize one he had made such an effort to objectify as generic *rebel*.

"How is it that a commoner of mixed blood is among the very top leadership of this insurrection?"

"Oh, I was a servant and student of Father Hidalgo. I just happened to be with him when we were captured."

"Oh. Well...didn't you tell them? Didn't you explain your—your situation?"

"Oh, I tried," Arreola answered with a subtle scoff. "The result was as I suspected it would be. I'm resigned. This so-called revolution was bound to fail from its inception—even had it prevailed on the battlefield. It had as its short-sighted goal the mere substitution of one ruling elite for another. In the end nothing of substance would have changed—for Mexican society in general, at least."

Nicolás was completely disarmed by this *mestizo* and disconcerted by this unlikely situation. He found himself more and more drawn to this astonishing young man. But he was confused. "Well, isn't that what a rebellion is for? Is it not instigated by those who resent their betters?

"Unfortunately, that was exactly the sum and substance of this revolution. It is my belief that that is precisely why it failed."

"Well, what other purpose can there be?"

"Oh, in my opinion there can be higher ideals to be fought for, such as freedom and equality—equality of opportunity and treatment, that is—the unburdening of the people from the yoke of a system that imprisons them in an inflexible role for as long as they live. That of the United States revolution is as salient an example as I can think of. The French one started out that way before it began searching for guilty parties in every nook and corner and thereby unleashing its Reign of Terror.

"Pity that this one had such limited and selfish ends. Again, I believe that's why it failed, and was doomed to failure from the start."

Young Nicolás was flabbergasted that this young man could wax philosophic at this particular moment, when he was bound for his own demise. He was so perplexed by the fact that he had no idea how to respond. The nascent thought of saving him led Nicolás to flounder inarticulately. "Well, I-I don't...I can't..."

"Oh, there's nothing to be done. We all have to die eventually. Perhaps this early death is a mercy in disguise; it might be saving me from a life of misery as I had before being rescued from the *obraje*. Not that I want to die, mind you, but I imagine I would find it just as disagreeable at sixty as I do at twenty."

Notwithstanding the blithe attitude he affected for José Nicolás, José de Arreola very much wanted to live. That pretense was part of a whole stratagem he was confecting moment by moment to save himself. Some instinct or ability to read people, honed during his time as both debt slave and servant, had told him that Nicolás was his mark. He had sensed this boy's likely abhorrence of war and repugnance at the coming executions.

The ruse was successful. Nicolás sat bewildered atop his mount at this half-breed's aplomb as he faced his own horrific execution. Nicolás was so taken in, in fact, that he forgot about dissimulating his fraternization with the enemy. He thoughtlessly turned to address Arreola directly. "You know, you don't talk like an Indian—or even a *mestizo*. In fact, you don't talk like anyone I've ever known."

"Oh? And how are we supposed to talk? Do you speak Náhuatl?" At this, Arreola made his escort emit a tentative laugh.

"Nicos! What's going on here?"

José Nicolás had been so absorbed in the conversation with this apparently *accidental* revolutionary that he hadn't noticed his father pulling up beside him. "Oh, uh...Father, I uh... I know this man looks like a creole but he's really a *mestizo*."

"Good then, we'll shoot the purer part of him and hang the heathen."

José Nicolás knew he was courting danger in speaking up for any of the prisoners regardless of their role in the rebellion, but he'd been completely seduced by this young caste. "Well...I mean, as a *mestizo* he couldn't—he couldn't have been a leader, wouldn't have had any substantial role in the uprising. He was probably coerced as a servant to the priest."

"And?" his father bit off with contempt.

There was something working in Nicolás' feelings for this young so-called rebel that the boy was not even aware of. José de Arreola had an air of mastery much like Nicolás' big brother, Antonio. Although Arreola's proficiency was in very different spheres of competence, that sense of confidence and aptitude thoroughly seduced the young soldier.

Tony's loss was a gaping hole for young Nicolás that had left him rather lost at sea. His brother had taught him to ride, to shoot, what to do on his first sexual experience. Tony even made sure that his baby-brother was included in all the parties and dance events and that he had— Nicolás being painfully shy—appropriate female companionship. Plus, Antonio and this *mestizo* would be close to the same age, had his brother lived.

"Well, I—I just wondered," Nicolás hesitatingly said to his father, "if we...if we could perhaps spare him. I mean since he was really forced into service of the rebellion."

Though loath to show it, Nicolás' father might have had some inkling of what his son was feeling. Don José Maximiliano had lost his first born, after all, his greatest pride. As certain as he was that there was no place in this life for sentimentality, he knew how attached the boy was to his big brother—indeed, how he hero-worshipped him.

With good reason, Don José Maximiliano thought to himself. One dreams of having a boy like Tony. José Antonio de Cos de la Portilla was all that a man should be. He could ride with the best and almost always won whenever the *hacendados* of the region got together for races—often with the inferior horse. At his young age, he could drink older and bigger men under the table. And his prowess with the ladies was legendary. During this rebellion, he had been his father's ablest lieutenant.

And now, because of these ungrateful vermin, he was robbed of the most promising future Señor de Cos could imagine. "These miserable cockroaches are responsible for your brother Antonio's death, for God's sake!"

Ah, Arreola thought, *they are both in potent mourning. That might complicate matters. On the other hand, it might present an opportunity.*

"I know, Father. I know." Nicolás strived with every ounce of fortitude he possessed not to cry; it is so unseemly for a soldier. "But…"

"But what? As a half-breed mongrel he would only be a burden on Spanish society."

Arreola pounced on this opportunity. "Mi Coronel, I would never want to be a bur—"

"Silence dog! You've been given no permission to speak!"

93

Arreola was expecting exactly that reaction and knew how to play his part. "Your pardon, sir," he answered with the appropriate abject humility.

Now, he would go to work on this man in charge. The fact that he was the boy's father actually presented itself as a welcome turn of events. For beneath de Cos' implacable exterior, Arreola could sense his lacerating grief.

He knew the type all too well: no time for self-indulgent sentimentality, the Colonel was—or labored to be—all about business, with a potent concern for his image as a man among men. If Arreola was right about that, then this, his remaining son, would be even more dear to him, and the boy's sympathy might work in Arreola's favor.

Besides, those who have to work so hard at being hard often are trying to deny a potent sentimentality that they consider a despicable character flaw. So, Arreola would show the appropriate humility, maintaining silence for the moment, awaiting his next opportunity.

Then came a most welcome intervention. As the line of donkeys and riders neared the makeshift gallows, Father Hidalgo, two donkeys ahead, abruptly broke off his prayer recitation and addressed Don José Maximiliano. "If I may speak a word, my esteemed Colonel?"

Though a rebel and traitor and therefore meriting the severest opprobrium, Father Hidalgo still retained some respect as a man of the cloth, particularly as he was a creole of unimpeachably pure Spanish blood.

Colonel de Cos turned away and spat. "What is it you have to say, traitor?"

"Only that this young man is the son of José Sebastián de Arreola y Riaño, one of your compatriots in this war. He—"

"This *rebellion!*" de Cos cut him off.

"You pardon, sir: this…rebellion."

"And what is his parentage supposed to mean to me? His mere association with a butcher like you condemns him to a like fate. More than *three hundred* innocent peninsular Spaniards, *your betters*, beheaded and thrown like garbage into a ravine!"

"My honored sir, that was the work of one of my captains. I didn't authorize—"

"A captain you commissioned! Ah, why am I even arguing with the likes of you, a traitor, a heretic and an apostate?"

The vehemence of his father's indignation sat somewhat uncomfortably with José Nicolás. He remembered at the battle of Las Cruces where his brother had died. When the battle devolved into a stalemate, Nicolás' father had called for a parley, suggesting he might join the rebels.

José Nicolás was aghast. Could his father really mean this? Then he saw the two cannons that were hidden from view in the brush loaded and aimed at exactly the position the parley was to be held. He couldn't believe that his father would stoop to such a dishonorable deception. He went to him. "Father, what are you planning to do?"

"I'm planning to crush this vile *chusma* once and for all…and to avenge your brother's death!"

"But Father, he died in battle. I hate them with my blackest heart, but to use such deceit, it..."

"They've proven they have no honor, so why should we show them any?" he answered distractedly as he oversaw the preparations of his other artillery.

"Well...perhaps to prove that we're better than they?"

Don José Maximiliano turned on his son in a murderous rage. "We *are* better! Better in the way the king is better that a common beggar! And they have taken away the best of us!"

Nicolás was arrested by the vehemence of his father's response. Don José Maximiliano waited just a moment to make sure his son understood the depth of his wrath, then turned back to directing his artillery troops.

After that moment, Nicolás tentatively continued to question his father's apparent plan. "Well...I just wonder what purpose we serve when we stoop to such treachery."

José's father stopped the orders he was giving to his lieutenants to give full attention to his one surviving son. In a cold, measured but deathly manner he responded. "The purpose we serve is the perpetuation of this sacred system ordained by God and created to mirror the divine hierarchy of Heaven. Any tactic, any subterfuge is warranted to the achievement of that sanctified end!"

José Nicolás wondered if his father was being honest about his motivation, even with himself—if it was not in reality pure vengeance for the loss of his eldest son he sought. But young Nicolás was easily intimidated by his father's anger, and he'd never seen him with such seething hatred as he now betrayed. The idea of putting up any kind of formidable debate was beyond him. After all, his father had the experience, the position, the esteem of the royalists that had made him a colonel.

It was also true that young Nicolás lacked the attribute by which a man might step out on his own, regardless of the consequences. No, young Nicolás needed too much to be a part; the idea of being rejected, ostracized, was more fearful to him than death itself. It would be a living perdition.

So, when his father concluded with such certitude, he could only weakly stammer, "But have we no…no…obligation to, to…?"

"Our obligation, our *only* obligation is to crush this insurrection of pirates, to grind this rabble beneath our heels, that it be a lesson to all who would challenge the established order, the consecrated order of God!"

So, all young Nicolás could do is stand and watch as the rebel army approached, and his father gave the order for both cannons to fire. Then, as the rebels flew in a panicked retreat, Don José Maximiliano unleashed the awesome fury of all the remaining artillery.

The results were catastrophic: body parts exploding into the air, arms, legs and heads wrenched from torsos, and those split open, gushing blood like macabre fountains dyeing the field a hideous crimson that slowly turned a nauseating maroon as it dried.

Perhaps it was the memory of that massacre; perhaps it was some effort to atone for his father's sin that fed young Nicolás' passion to save this rebel—this unintentional rebel who bore his own Christian name. Nicolás was, after all, a like unwilling participant in a similar outrage.

He tried to think of some argument, some appeal, that might touch his father's heart—or at least make him consider the consequences. But all the many possibilities that flashed through his mind ran directly into the roadblock of his father's seething passion.

It was just at that moment that a sudden change seemed to come over Father Hidalgo. He again managed to stop his donkey which caused the rest of the train to do likewise. The transformation as he looked up at Colonel de Cos struck all present with a mixture of curiosity and irritation.

When he finally spoke, it was with sincere and honorable penitence—and perhaps, self-realization. "Your pardon, sir. You are absolutely correct. There is no defense for the evil I have committed, and I have died a thousand deaths of shame for all the innocents whose blood indelibly stains my soul.

"I have no right to ask anything of you, but I must humbly plead. This boy, this young man, José Necahuatl de Arreola, if anything, has the purest soul of all, loyalist and rebel alike. He in fact urged me to decommission and even put this bloodthirsty captain in prison. I will go to my grave forever repenting that I heeded not his directive.

"I found out later that this young mixed breed even formed a group to spirit those destined for execution to safety, putting his own life in dire peril. He is, in fact, a hero to you, the loyalists—and now, I realize all too late, to myself.

"I humbly beg you, Colonel, to spare his life. I believe him to be the true future of Mexico. Or at least, I hope he will be."

And so, José Necahuatl de Arreola was spared.

Chapter VII

Those who would give up essential liberty
to purchase a little temporary [security]
deserve neither liberty nor [security].

--Benjamin Franklin

Either both the choice and the risk rest with the
individual or he is relieved of both.

--F.A. Hayek

The West became the mainstay of American
power and vigor, the home of an Americanism
that looked down on the slightly decadent
Easterners who stayed behind.

--Amaury de Riencourt

After watering and picketing the horses and mules when we stopped at Brady Creek, the first thing we did was attend to Mister Macalister's leg. Miss Luz unhooked his pants leg that she'd previously split open and closed with safety pins. A worrisome redness spread out above and below the bandaged wound. It was apparent to all that the whisky had fallen short of its intended aim.

"That blasted Injun musta' soaked the barb, maybe the whole arrow, in somethin'," Mister Macalister said through gritted teeth.

"That could be," Miss Luz curtly answered. "The chiseled stone does enormous damage as it's pushed through flesh."

Though I could tell she was more than concerned, she went right to work with my mother helping as though it were routine. Little Amelia looked on as Miss Luz had my mother try to open up both sides of the wound so she could get in as much of the *antiseptic* as possible. She stopped for a second to hand a stick to me. "*Hijo*, whittle this down to a point; but not too sharp. And make it as graduated as you can, so it goes from wide to narrower over the whole length."

I wondered what the stick could be for but did like I was told. Miss Luz sure seemed to know what she was doing, and her orders were made to be followed. After a moment, she took a look at the stick I was whittling. "That's sharp enough," she said as she took it from me.

I hadn't carved it down to much of a point at all. I knew it had to have something to do with Mister Macalister's wound but wondered what it could be.

She first soaked the newly trimmed stick with the whisky. Then, she took a rag and got it good and saturated with the whisky as well. Now I had an idea of what she was going to do. She wrapped the rag around the stick and used the stick to push it as deep into both sides of the wound as she could. Again, I was amazed at how Mister Macalister just clenched his teeth and barely grunted as she did it.

The pain was evident to little Amelia though, as tears ran down her cheeks. "Why you hurting Papi, *Abue*?"

Abway? I wondered what that meant.

"Sometimes the only way to help is to hurt, Meli," she answered.

Camp Cookie had stayed after he brought the whisky. "You in pain, Mista' GP?"

"Ah…some," he answered dismissively.

"Mebbe we should put some peppermint oil on it, soothe it a bit," Cookie suggested. "'N' Mister Jacob got dat stuff he take."

The look that came from Mister Macalister at that suggestion pierced through Cookie like a pair of sharpened needles. He knew right away to walk the offer back as quick as he could. "Er mebbe jus' de peppermint oil."

I found it exceedingly strange that Mister Macalister's son was not helping with his care. In fact, I was surprised he was not jumping in ahead of everyone else.

Of course, he was behaving pretty much the same way as he did when we pulled the arrow out of his father's leg. He just sort of stayed around, looking uncomfortable, but again sort of unconcernedly so. When the process was over, he got right back up on his horse and rode back to where the cattle were. He seemed more comfortable with the other cowhands than with his own father. How in the world did that ever come to be?

Now I wondered what was in that flask of Jacob's that got such a severe reaction from Mister Macalister. I thought to ask Miss Luz, but again, I didn't want to pry.

Mister Macalister looked up at his sister with a penetrating frown. "Is it?" is all he said.

"Not yet," Miss Luz replied. "But we'll be at Fort Concho in two days. Sooner if we go round the clock."

I didn't know for sure but had a suspicion they were talking about gangrene. It worried me when she said, "not yet," as though something was inevitably coming, and I'd seen what gangrene can do to a body. I wished my brother Alexander was here. He might have some better notion of what to do.

We had a dry camp that night, without a fire. Miss Luz explained that we didn't want to advertise our whereabouts if there were other Indians around—or if the same pack that had struck us once decided to try again.

Mister Macalister seemed to rally a bit as we ate a cold supper of beef jerky and cornbread that had gotten stale and hard. I remembered that first year in Panna Maria and realized that there was many a night there I would have killed for what we were having now.

With Mister Macalister seeming a bit better, I thought it might be all right to ask Miss Luz to continue the story. "So Miss Luz, did you finally start eating the food Mister Macalister was leaving for you?"

Mister Macalister chuckled. "So she's been tellin' tall tales about our history, huh?" I thought the fact that he was able to laugh a little was a good sign. "Truth is I actually managed to trap her," he took up the story himself. "She just got careless as she came day after day fer the food I was leavin'. So one time I circled around back to her cave I'd discovered earlier 'n' waited behind a bush with a slice 'a' pie my mother'd made."

"I couldn't believe someone had got the better of me on a trail," Ms. Luz interjected. "When he came out from behind that bush, I immediately pulled my knife, but then he said something. Of course, I didn't understand, but the way he said it—the tone was… kind of soothing.

"I said, 'Whatcha' think I'm gonna do, stab you with a piece 'a' pie?'"

"I remember he held it out to me," Miss Luz continued the story, kind of laughing at herself. "But I don't know, all that time on my own, I'd gotten to the point of not trusting anyone."

"I took a bite and offered it to her again but she wadn't havin' it," Mister Macalister explained. "So, I just took another bite and put it down on the rocks around her campfire 'n' stood back a few paces. We just stood there starin' at each other for a while, me talkin' in as soothing a tone as I could. I could tell she didn't understand a word. Then she finally picked it up." He snickered. "You shoulda' seen the look on her face when she finally tasted it."

"I'd forgotten the taste of sugar, of sweet. It had been so long."

"So is that when you joined their family? Right then?" I asked.

"Oh no," Mister Macalister said. "It took over a week like that before she followed me home. I'd taught her a little English and she'd taught me a little Spanish, so we could communicate some with a lotta' sign language."

It was obvious that telling the story had exhausted Mister Macalister, so Miss Luz wrapped him in two blankets. That left us only two more and Mister Macalister started to take off one. This time, however, Miss Luz fairly ordered: "*Hermano*, we can double up. And our bodies will keep each other warm. Keep those blankets around you." Mister Macalister started to resist but this time Miss Luz prevailed.

My mother seconded her saying in her barely comprehensible German, "Yes. Stay with blankets. Cold wind."

My mother and I wrapped a blanket around our huddled selves and Miss Luz enclosed herself and Amelia in the other. The little one seemed accustomed and fell asleep right away. I marveled at how cold it can get in the desert at night when in the afternoon it gets pretty darn warm for the end of February. There were even some pretty warm days in the previous month. The temperature must've dropped thirty degrees by the system they use here: *farinhite* or something like that.

I said a prayer for Mister Macalister before drifting off myself. We were all completely worn out and the snoring didn't bother me a bit. The next thing I knew I heard birds singing and saw that day was about to break.

Boy, the land being flat like it is here makes for some pretty spectacular sunrises and sunsets, especially when there are a few clouds to reflect the sun. They first were a kind of purple to like the color of red wine. Then, as a little sliver of sun peaked out over the eastern horizon, they burst out into the richest gold I think I ever saw. As I went about my chores to break camp, I caught glimpses of them fading to a pale yellow before dissipating to nothingness.

I was about hitching up the mule teams with Camp Cookie when I noticed my mother and Miss Luz repeating Mister Macalister's treatment from the night before. I started over to help when Miss Luz stopped me. "Finish with the teams, *hijo*. We need to get to Fort Concho as soon as we can. We'll travel through the night."

Again, she tried to convince Mister Macalister to ride in the cart, but he would have none of it. I wished he'd listened as he could barely hobble over to his horse. It was kind of painful watching him saddle her, and the first time he tried to mount, he fell back down. I winced a little myself at the pain I could see it caused him, and even worse when he finally got to rights atop her.

We started off and I could sense Miss Luz's growing concern for her brother. Consequently, I didn't ask her to continue the story of her joining the Macalister clan. I guess she could tell it was still on my mind, though, as she started of her own accord. "What is it you want to ask me, *hijo*?"

"Miss Luz, I don't want to distract you from—"

"No, it's all right. I need to do something besides worry about Gerardo. I can tell that there's something you want to know, so ask."

"Well…I mean, you and Mister Macalister weren't really brother and sister. Did you never think about, you know, becoming man and wife?" I wondered if her disfigured face might've put the kibosh on that possibility.

Miss Luz was silent so long that I was sure I'd crossed the line. "I'm sorry, Miss Luz, that's really, *really* none of my business. Please, don't—"

"It's something you need to know, *hijo*. It's a story that will help you understand both of us. It will help you to know this land, and all the people that inhabit it. The whole story will give you some insight into your stepbrother, Jacob, and the two stepsisters you've yet to meet. And you need to know it to survive in this family—in this land."

The just…*heaviness* she said it with made me wonder if I really wanted to know. At the same time, though, it really piqued my curiosity. I started to hand her the reins, but she stopped me with a raised hand. "I'll guide you. Just head toward that uprise in the distance."

Then she returned to the story of her joining the Macalister family. "The Macalister farm must have been on the rich, fertile soil," she began. Her lips drew up into a gentle smile. "I remember how just seeing those thick green fields of corn waving in a gentle breeze gave me a sensation of comfort. It was a familiar bit of Mexico—actually made me a little homesick.

"Of course, that was the only thing in my new life that was anything like my Mexican one. I was still young, around eleven or twelve, and English came fairly easily. I suppose my calling my new brother Gerardo, when the whole family called him GP, might have been a personal quirk to hold on to a bit more of it."

"His family called him by his initials?"

"Yes. He was named after his father, Gerard Phillip, so the only other option was to call him 'junior'. They chose the former."

She took a good bit of time just looking out at the vast expanse of chaparral that surrounded us. A few little tufts of yellowed grama and buffalo grass, interrupted here and there with a lonesome mesquite or huisache tree—so vast and flat that it seemed if you went far enough, you could fall off the edge of the earth.

"It was probably a good thing that I had that time on my own," she continued. "I think it might have made it easier to adjust to an English-speaking, Protestant family. It was much more...what's the word I want...*formal?*...than in a Mexican Catholic family. There was...I don't know, less affection, less familiarity and...thinking about it now, more...individuality, maybe?

"But I adjusted very quickly. While there weren't the open demonstrations of affection like in a Spanish family, I came to see that there was no lack of love. Instead of saying the rosary at night, Mister Macalister would read from the Bible. He and his Misses expressed their love more in guidance and mindfulness, I came to realize. Although Mama, as I eventually came to call her, was more demonstrative than Mister Macalister."

My mother interrupted at that point, addressing me in Polish. "What is she saying about Catholics, Johann?" She even used my Polish name. "Nothing bad, Mama. Just that she was raised Catholic, and the Macalister family was Protestant."

"Not anymore," my mother said. "That was my one demand in marrying this man."

"I know, Mama. I know," I answered in English with a chuckle. I wondered how firmly Mister Macalister would hold to his promise to convert.

"Gerardo!" Miss Luz suddenly shouted. I looked to where she was looking. Mister Macalister was pulling himself up from almost the side of his horse. It looked like he had almost fainted and fallen right off. He righted himself and then just waved like he was saying he was all right.

"Should we try to talk him into riding in the cart, Miss Luz?"

She clenched her jaw at the idea and a dismissive puff of air escaped her nostrils. "If I thought we'd have any chance at success, I would. I think the number one cause of death in men is stubbornness." She seemed like she was considering that pronouncement for a moment. "Ah well, I suppose it's all part of life being a matter of trading one thing to have another."

"What do you mean?"

"That it was that fierce drive of my brother's that built the Lazy Eight—the third largest spread in Texas, probably in the country. Besides being his legacy, it's provided a good living to a lot of people, including myself. It's supplied beef and other products to a good part of the country, and thereby, I imagine, created good jobs all the way down the line.

"That's the good part of that kind of single-minded drive. We're seeing the bad part now. But I guess it just comes with the territory. My brother built the Lazy Eight by never giving in to defeat, to adversity, by braving territory that no sane man would consider, although many have tried. Some have been successful; most have not.

"I wonder what it is in men like him and like his father, that are willing to face constant danger and crushing isolation to build a life where no Mexican or Spaniard would ever willingly go—or certainly not without lots of company.

"Hah! I heard one man say about people like my brother and Scots-Irish Anglos in general that they fear God so much that they have no fear left for anything else."

We were both quiet for a while thinking about what she'd said. It did give me a chance to answer my mother when she asked what we were talking about. "About life, Mama. About what it takes to build one and make something of it, I guess—the risks being the price of the rewards."

My mother looked at me with a frown of bewilderment. "Like the risks we took, Mama. We could've stayed in Poland and barely eked out a living—or maybe not even that. We chose to take a big risk to come here. And I guess we paid a pretty high price."

I'm not sure I really made my mother understand, but she settled back with little Amelia who'd taken to her like a second mother.

I suppose Miss Luz was right about life being a matter of trade-offs. Like I tried to explain to my mother, our family had given up the relative safety of home and what we knew for the hope of a better life. I thought of my father and baby sister and figured I was right in what I'd said to Mama: we'd paid some pretty huge costs to do it. I guess there's no perfect choice, good and bad being a part of any decision you make. Thinking about our journey from Poland, it seems there was a lot of bad before the good came.

"So Miss Luz, how was it in your new family?"

"After being on my own for so long and after what I'd been through at the presidio, it was like heaven on earth. Of course, it took some adjusting from being on my own so long and making all my own decisions to being part of a family and following the rules of the house, but the rewards were more than worth it."

She paused rather ponderously, and it made me wonder if it was really so heavenly. Then she answered that question by continuing. "At first."

There was something ominous in the way she said "at first" so I hesitated to ask.

"No *hijo*, there was nothing bad in the family. From the very start, they treated me like I was one of them. Mister Macalister even told me that I could practice my Catholicism as best I could if I wanted to. There were no churches or priests where we were."

I got the feeling that something really horrible had happened, but I just waited for her to continue—if she decided to.

"It was a wonderful three years. I got closer and closer to the whole family but especially to Gerardo. We did everything together, work, play, exploring, whatever. Then Mama had a baby boy." Miss Luz had to stop, and I could tell it was because the story was just so painful to tell.

"Miss Luz, please...I—"

"I loved that baby like he was my own. Baby Daniel, named after Mama's father. I was fourteen or so when he came to us and knew right then that I would have many, many children of my own." There was another ominous pause that made my flesh tingle a little. "It...didn't work out that way."

I could tell she needed some time to collect herself before continuing the story. I respected it.

After a good few minutes, she took a deep breath and then sighed it out. "It was early the following year when they came. The Comanches. We'd been warned. That's why Papa, Mister Macalister, with Gerardo and I helping, was starting to build a kind of fort around the house. If we'd had a few more months, maybe even weeks...

"They came during spring plowing. Papa caught sight of them coming and almost got us back to the house before they descended on us—the little good it would have done. One of them caught him in the back with a spear. Papa still tried to fight them off and get us in the house.

"I wish that spear had killed him."

Miss Luz took a moment, which unfortunately made me wonder if a quick death would have been preferable to what did happen. What could that have been?

"While two of them grabbed Gerardo and me, others shot arrows into Papa and still others dragged my mother out holding the baby. They ripped little Daniel out of my mother's arms, and... They forced us to watch as they...as one of them threw him up in the air and landed him on his spear. The scream...! I will never not hear that scream."

This time Miss Luz couldn't go on. We rode in silence for what seemed an eternity and I was grateful because I didn't know if I could stand any more. Finally, I found the fortitude to speak. "My Lord in Heaven, Miss Luz, I—I can't imagine…"

"That was only the beginning. My mother and I were stripped naked. Gerardo was held and beaten, and his hands tied up with leather bands behind his back. Then they went to work on my father who was still alive.

"The first thing they did was cut off his…manhood. My mother and I kept trying to turn away, but they forced us to watch. They forced that…part of my father into his mouth. Then they scalped him. The only small mercy he received after that was a blow that split his skull open.

"They turned then to Mama and me. What they did to us is just unspeakable. I could not retell it myself. When they were at Mama, somehow Gerardo managed to slide his hands down his legs so they were in front. He grabbed a piece of wood and started beating the Indian who was on top of our mother. One of the renegades hit him over the head with a club and was about to spear him when the other Indian stopped him. That one, the one that Gerardo had beaten, must have been a leader because he was obeyed.

"After they were finished with Mama, the last one plunged a knife into her heart. I wish they'd done the same to me. But no, my brother and I were taken captive. We rode hard night and day with only brief breaks. I hated those breaks because the squaws would beat and burn me, and all the Indians would beat us with their bows. I was beaten senseless. I had to struggle not to drown in my own blood.

"We had nothing to eat and precious little water for five days. We were both fainting from hunger. I got to the point that I would welcome the beatings if they came with just a little food.

"Finally, we stopped, and they made camp. That night they had some celebration with cries and dancing. It seemed like they were proudly recounting the raid on our home. Our hands were tied behind our backs with braided leather bands so tight that they cut into the skin. We were put face down and our ankles bound the same way and then attached to our hands. The rope was so tight I was sure we would lose our hands and feet. That's why we both have these scars on our wrists and ankles."

I couldn't even look at her much less say anything. I was actually at the point of asking her to stop.

"Gerardo was adopted by the Indian who he'd tried to beat off Mama. I was just kept as a slave. I suppose that was because I was too old to be adopted. I was beaten and burned regularly. These scars on my cheeks are from the squaws putting live coals to them. That was just for fun. They laughed while I screamed.

"I suppose I got too ugly from the beatings and burnings for the men to have anything to do with me. That's when the most horrible torture came. The squaws tied me to four posts stretching me out by my hands and feet. They applied the same live coals to my body, but this time it wasn't to my face. The reason I couldn't marry is that those burns made me incapable of certain…wifely duties.

"…It makes other things difficult, too."

It was only a brief moment she paused before continuing. I think it was because she was ashamed at what she'd revealed. I just concentrated on the ground below us. "So for almost all of the three years we were captive, I was a slave. But since Gerardo was actually adopted into the tribe, he was able to put an end to the harshest treatment. Then one time the squaw I was slave to tried to beat me again.

"I was at the point that I didn't really care if I lived or died, so I fought back. I was surprised when the other Indians didn't intervene. They just watched, apparently enjoying the fight. I got her down and was beating her with all the fury I'd built up during my captivity. I wasn't going to stop until she was dead. Finally, she cried out for mercy.

"I heeded her pleas, and I don't know why. I expected ever more horrible treatment, but it was actually then that the beatings and torture stopped.

"Gerardo had grown into a young man and was accorded status as a warrior. He was probably fifteen or sixteen then. We bided our time, communicating in English, of which there were few Comanches who knew any at all. We talked very carefully in very sparse words of a plan of escape. I was so grateful that Gerardo played his part without succumbing to becoming totally Indian.

"One day, he went hunting with his Indian father. As he mounted his horse, he looked at me in a way that told me that this would be the moment. I guessed his plan correctly. When he and his father were away from camp and they dismounted to recover a deer they'd killed, Gerardo pulled his knife. He told me that his Indian father didn't even seem surprised.

"They made passes at each other cutting flesh here and there. Gerardo was losing some blood, but by then he was hardened in the

Comanche way. The fight lasted a long time, my brother said, until finally Nocona, his Indian father, managed to get him from behind with his knife at Gerardo's throat. But he hesitated for just a second, my brother said, perhaps out of affection for the boy. It was just long enough for Gerardo to turn and sink his knife into Nocona's heart.

"He grabbed the reins of his adopted father's horse and jumped on his own mount. I knew he would race through the camp and let me mount on the run, which is what happened. We rode all day and all night, only stopping briefly to attend to Gerardo's wounds. He'd learned all the Indian tracking tricks and he put them all to use. A lot of the Indians had been out hunting as well, so we had a good head start.

"After days of riding with brief breaks for sleep, eating on the run, we finally found our way to Fort Houston on the Navasota River. I felt so close to death I think I slept for three days, only waking to drink and eat."

Miss Luz sat back in the buckboard, and I could tell she needed a break from recounting her history. I was so completely stunned by the story that I forgot all about driving the mule team. They stopped, feeling no direction from me. Miss Luz was apparently likewise in such a state that she didn't even notice. I could hear like a faraway echo Camp Cookie call a halt to his wagon. There was only the sound of that constant wind, a lament of isolation and aching emptiness.

Suddenly Miss Luz called out, "Gerardo!"

As I looked up, I saw Mister Macalister just slide off his horse and hit the ground like a sack of potatoes. There he lay motionless, one foot still in its stirrup.

Chapter VIII

We'll be fighting in the streets
With our children at our feet
And the morals that they worship will be gone
And the men who spurred us on
Sit in judgment of all wrong
They decide and the shotgun sings the song

I'll tip my hat to the new constitution
Take a bow for the new revolution
I ain't freed by the changes all around
Pick up my guitar and play
Just like yesterday
Then I'll get on my knees and pray
We don't get fooled again.

--The Who

Finally, thought a battle-weary, leaden-hearted José Nicolás de Cos de la Portilla as he made his way from the final scene of execution to the safety and security of home, *finally an escape from the savagery and sickening treachery of war.*

Every league traversed atop his beloved mare brought with it a loosening of the tortuous knots in his neck and shoulders. Pale touches of color emerged amid the gray-scaled sameness of his war-hardened world.

How long had it been since he'd heard the sweetness of bird-song and swallowed the rich aroma of summer verdure? Where had gone the spirit-lifting, soul-filling rapture of a serene ride along a gurgling brook? Had he ever known a moment of coming upon a lush verdant vale and not seeing the sickening horrors of war: battle-hardened troops thirsting for the blood of those who foresaw a different way, fields strewn with the body parts and the lifeblood of his fellow countrymen, the sordid implements of war urging more death, more destruction, egging on the hate for those who disagree?

The only consolation he clung to in the pitch blackness of his war-calloused soul was the deliverance from execution of his namesake, José de Arreola. Why was that mercy almost never practiced by either side in this hideous conflagration? It was, in fact, the only time Nicolás could remember it ever being consummated.

Realized it was, however, and Nicolás strove with all the will he could muster to fix his mind on that one tiny luminescence in the Stygian darkness of battle-weary despair. He remembered the final words of Father Hidalgo y Costilla and fastened his own hopes upon those of the priest's: that a man of such courage and human decency as José de Arreola would be the future of Mexico.

Only then could men live without war and subterfuge. Only then could a system be established where differences were settled with words and not sharpened steel and cannonades. Only then could debate supplant spilled blood as the arbiter of governance.

The more José Nicolás fixed his mind upon those possibilities, the more the deadening, deafening weight that had plunged his shoulders earthward seemed to lift and lighten his body and soul in the saddle—the saddle of horse and the saddle of life.

Now, visions of peaceful days in the comfort of family, of community, dangled enticingly before him and ever-so-slowly began to melt away the rigidity and fatalism that war demands—demands at least for those who, like himself, recoil at the sheer bloody barbarity.

He could now slowly, painstakingly unhinge his thoughts from the drudgery and heartache of sanguinary battles and never-ending duplicity. Now he could almost taste the peace of home, the comfort of family and friends.

He dreamt of parties and dances, festivals celebrating the final end of strife and hatred, the consummate pleasures of music and laughter. How long had it been that he'd only heard the sardonic laughter of battle-hardened soldiers at jokes of death and dismemberment? How he ached to once again hear the laughter of mirth and gaiety! Even the mischievous chortles of his peers at a dirty joke or vaunted conquest appealed.

He longed for the dulcet mirthful gentility and consoling company of women. All the womanliness he'd known these years of war were the whores who traveled with the troops, their charms stultified by years of being solely objects for the pleasure and relief of battle-hardened soldiers.

He had at times taken advantage of their supposed charms, the horror of war making the sexual act an inevitable compulsion; the opposite of death is sometimes mere animalistic desire. He marveled at how empty each of those encounters left him.

Would those other men who survived this insanity be coming home from the war as well? Would they, like he, see their former laughing, feeling selves as a distant memory? As ones divorced and estranged from the men they'd become, someone they could not even recognize? He wondered if he would ever again be able to fully take part, to revel in the warmth of kith and kin. Oh, to know that joy once again!

At the thought, the tender, infectious laughter of Señor Arreola y Riaño's youngest daughter, Isabel, came so prominently to mind that it caught him by surprise. Nicolás also gloried in the fact that the young man he'd had a hand in saving was almost certainly Isabel's half-brother. He wished his namesake the peace and fulfillment he anticipated for himself.

But Chabelita! She must be fourteen by now, preparing for her *quinceañera*. And so, marriageable, he thought with a certain longing. (How long had it been since he'd had such airy impulses?)

He remembered her raven-haired beauty with big, bright eyes that bewitch and cheeks that dimple in the most charming way whenever she laughed or smiled. It was such a gentle, feminine chuckle.

Nicolás remembered her love of animals and how all the family's dogs and horses flocked to her wherever she set foot. He thought himself good with animals as well, better than with people, he realized, and that convergence of attributes filled his spirit with possibility.

Isabel was quiet like he but seemed so much more confident. Though he found that confidence a trifle intimidating, at least then, it made not a whit of difference to the pleasure he found in her company.

Now, with the experiences he'd had fighting this filthy war, he could think of nothing that might daunt him beyond a murderous charge or whistling rifle ball, the explosion of cannon fire and a mercilessly wielded saber. He made a firm resolution to call at her home as soon as possible after his arrival.

His arrival. Imagining that longed for event flooded all his being with hope. Such simple pleasures as a home-cooked meal and a family supper in the company—the *peaceful* company—of mother and father, brothers and sisters, grandmother and grandfather, perhaps cousins and aunts and uncles. Where he could recover from war's fearsome wounds, physical and spiritual.

He would insist on picnics beside the river. Perhaps he could invite Chabelita! Would Don Sebastián allow it? He patted Dulcinea's neck at the sheer rapturous memory of rides along the Lerma on her back. The river's soothing gurgle and florid surroundings wafted through his mind on a gentle autumn breeze.

Dulcinea seemed to sense the reason for the pat and gently nickered in answer.

He could almost smell the water's rich aroma of bulrush and opulence and hear the primal call of a hawk on the wing. His imagination then took him onto rides along the river in the splendor of the Bajío's graceful green fields with Isabel. An enchanted smile involuntarily spread across his face at the fantasy. He could see all her dogs following as being equally enamored of her simple presence.

But just to be home, enjoying friends and family, tranquility and grace!

*A*las, 'twas not to be. Again and again, as one insurrection was stifled, another, in another place led by some new adventurer, would rear its ugly head. Each time, the fear of promised ignominy for refusing the call grudgingly impelled young Nicolás to follow his father into the fray. *Will nothing satisfy these rebels? Will I— we—ever know such peace again? Will* I *ever know any?*

Most troublesome was that each new phase of revolution came closer and closer to achieving its goal. Each battle was fiercer, each victory more costly and evermore purchased with the currency of betrayal. From Guanajuato to Apatzingán, Chilpancingo to Puebla, it seemed there was more and more support for each revolution as it erupted.

José Nicolás, though he hadn't yet had the nerve to raise the question with his father, began to wonder if the only possible end was the rebellion's ultimate success. Then another terrifying thought reared its ugly head: If independence were to be achieved, would even that put an end to the slaughter? Might it simply usher in reprisal and sanguinary civil war?

Over the years, the horror of battle after battle, of death after agonizing death, had worked its perverse sorcery to harden the spirit of this most tenderhearted of men. It ever-so-gradually numbed him to atrocity and made moot questions of *why* and *when.*

Fellow-feeling, even for his comrades, was slowly smothered by the ineluctable dictates of conflict. Yea, human feeling itself went on holiday, and gruesome scenes of death and dismemberment became the daily routine of life.

He wondered, however, if it was really the horror of battle that had submerged him in apathy, in utter callousness. Perhaps more vexing still was the blithe acceptance of perfidy and subterfuge that seemed all too common on both sides in this hideous war—or wars. Could it in reality be that pervasive absence of honor that had snatched away all tender sentiment in him, all hope for the future of New Spain, of Mexico?

He came to see that there was no honor in these wars on either side. Individuals, and even whole armies, went from one side to the other depending on what was most expedient. Setting traps and feigning loyalty only to ensnare the enemy struck him as the order of every day.

It seemed he was living in a completely amoral universe where the only ethical rule was whatever artful ruse succeeded. It was like living in a moral fog, a land estranged from right and wrong—or one where right and wrong were as pliable and elusive as quicksilver.

There came a point for Nicolás before he'd become habituated to such freewheeling subterfuge that he was so bold as to question his father's tactics. "I wonder, Father, without honor on either side, what kind of country will be this war's product—if there ever comes to be an end to it."

His father answered without hesitation but perhaps with a tiny crack in his adobe-hardened certainty. "It will be as God intended and the Council of the Indies set forth, with King Fernando reigning absolutely. It will consist of defined classes guaranteeing the stability of the monarchical state. As the Council has stated, it will be a system of dependence and subordination that ensures the obedience of the lowliest peon to the authority of his betters. All may be sacrificed to that glorious, Heaven-inspired end."

José Nicolás wondered if it were this very lack of ethics that caused these insurrections. He remembered the words of the prisoner who had his Christian name, he who had escaped execution by the exercise of true nobility by his priest and leader in acknowledging his crimes. What was it he said? Something about its failure being due to its lack of a true moral grounding and the absence of…ideals, was it?

Or was it perhaps the perversity of the ideals they cherished?

As all his experiences in combat had imbued him with a self-confidence or lack of fear, he continued to challenge his father. "And have we no duty to God to achieve that end with the honorable, virtuous means the blessed church and the Bible teach?"

His father scowled. Was it only the questioning of their faction's righteousness in the manner in which they waged this war, or was there some recognition that his son's reverence and respect for him had begun to weaken? Don José Maximiliano trotted out the usual riposte to his son's doubts. "The methods I use are justified by their sacred ends: the restoration of God's holy representative on earth to his rightful place on the throne of the entire sanctified Spanish Empire!"

But was it delivered with the same granite-hardened assurance as before? Though young José Nicolás still questioned his father's moral reasoning, it was as best he could discern common as dirt throughout the ranks of both loyalists and rebels.

It was also true that the idea of pursuing his objections always fell before the overarching need to simply belong. Whatever his qualms, the idea of standing on principle even if it meant ostracism was too horrible to contemplate.

So, the young man's means of accommodating such perfidy was to shut off *all* feeling—to become an automaton, to make the killing of the enemy the simple swatting of a mosquito or crushing of an ant. Watching people hanged no longer roused the slightest disquiet in him. He watched with indifference, as though it were the shooting of a rabid dog.

Hah, he thought to himself, *there was a time I was repelled by the killing of a dog—even a rabid one. Have I changed so thoroughly?*

He finally even became inured to his father's treachery, promising amnesty and then, when this or that rebel group surrendered, imprisoning or executing them. Or Don José Maximiliano might revisit the deceit he'd practiced at Las Cruces, calling for parley and then slaughtering the enemy as they approached.

It seemed that such deceit was the steady diet of this war. Father Hidalgo and his crew, after all, were captured by a similar subterfuge at the Baján, the false promises of refuge cloaking arrest and execution.

Sometimes rebel group would fight rebel group, leaving royalist forces the job of simply mopping up the remains. Or one group of rebels would inform on another, setting them up for certain slaughter. At first, Nicolás was grateful for those times, as such cleaning-up operations were a welcome respite from the horrors of open battle. As time went on and his heart hardened, however, he began to be indifferent to any and all situations of war—welcoming none and regretting none.

The situation devolved so far that it became difficult to know friend from foe. Amnesty by the main forces in Mexico City became a turnstile where men would fight with the rebels, accept amnesty, fight with royalist forces for a while, go back to the rebels when it was convenient. Then again, they would take advantage of amnesty offered. Some would go back and forth like that many, many times.

*T*he final blow to José Nicolás' father and the loyalist forces in general came in the form of the defection of the supreme leader of the royalist cause to the revolution. It was accompanied by another egregious display of duplicity. Colonel Agustín de Iturbide, commander of the Spanish forces, once he had formalized his union with the main body of rebels, sent false notice to the Viceroy in Mexico City that he had at long last persuaded the one remaining rebel force to submit.

He was welcomed to the capital city with pomp and accolades, fanfare and ebullient gratitude, only to declare the independence of Mexico once in the seat of power. His announcement came with the option for those still loyal to the king and Spain to either join the revolution or be arrested and face exile, imprisonment or execution.

It was an easy choice for most.

But it was not so for Don José Maximiliano de Cos de Asunción. "Never! I will *never* submit to these treasonous pirates! The devil has taken hold of their blackhearted souls! How can men nursed at the hand of Spain commit such treachery?"

How can they not, José Nicolás thought to himself, *when it is the steady diet of this civil war?*

"Help will come from Spain," Nicolás' father continued, "and when we emerge victorious there will be no amnesty. There will be no trials. They will all be hanged as the worthless scum they are! None of them even deserves the dignity of a firing squad!"

His father's rants had become more and more desperate, sucked dry of the confidence with which he had once uttered them. In his anguish, he sermonized to the troops, not even noticing how their numbers had fallen nor the ambivalence and even world-weariness with which they listened.

José Nicolás tried to take stock of his own thoughts and feelings about this astonishing and at the same time unsurprising turn of events, as routine as they'd become. He wondered how both reactions could be simultaneously a part of him.

Was he really not surprised? How could he have these joyous feelings of relief and at the same time a profound sense of loss, an insidious desire to be simply through with life? Now death struck him as nothing more than a final rest from the heartache and drudgery of life.

He even wondered if it were worthwhile trying to reason with his father as to the hopelessness of their position. "Father, don't you think that if it were worth it to the mother country that the Cortes would have sent someone other than General Juan O'Donojú, a noted liberal republican?"

"It can only be a trick, a feint to put these murderous rebels at their ease, so that the blow of the monarchy will catch them unawares! The glory of Spain will rise again and banish to hell all those who have befouled their oath of loyalty!"

One change in himself Nicolás had become aware of was that he was by this time no longer intimidated by his father's bluster. He wondered when that had come to pass. Was it simply the ennui that had overwhelmed all care and concern for life—his own and others'? Was it that nothing really seemed to matter anymore? Monarchy or republic, empire or independence? Of what possible importance could it ultimately be since every civilization, as each individual, is bound in the end to pass away and be forgotten?

So, when his father would declaim "O'Donojú, peninsular or not, is a traitor to his king and to his sacred oath! He was imprisoned by Fernando VII and with good and righteous reason. I will never *ever* concede the dissolution of the Spanish Empire, this glorious power on earth, commissioned by God to spread the truth of the most holy Catholic religion! I will fight with my last breath for it!"

Nicolás didn't even bother to answer his father's rantings, sounding as they were more and more those of a man who had lost touch with reality.

In a last desperate attempt, his father gave the order to return to San Miguel el Grande, so certain he was that there, in the Bajío, the heart of New Spain, he could raise an army of decent, faithful Spaniards.

It would have been sad to Nicolás, if he could feel anything at all, to watch their retinue grow smaller and smaller as they made their way. Even by the time they started the journey, Don José Maximiliano's army had shrunk by half. With each league traversed, troops seemed to dissolve into thin air.

Offers of amnesty for surrender arrived from Mexico City almost daily, threatening confiscation of land and wealth if they were refused. By the time the pitiful assembly reached the outer frontier of the Bajío that army of twenty thousand had shrunk to fewer than so many hundreds. With San Miguel finally in sight, there remained only Don José Maximiliano and Nicolás, the rest numbering in the tens.

On a hill overlooking the town, Nicolás' father dismounted, dropped his horse's reins and stood gazing below, silent and immoveable. José Nicolás turned to the few ragtag, starving troops remaining and with just a nod of the head dismissed them all. In ones and twos they noiselessly shuffled away, leaving father and son never so alone as now they were.

Though birds sang in dulcet euphony and the river merrily gurgled, José Nicolás found his ears proof against their soothing timbre. The rich, heartening aromas of catkin and bulrush could not penetrate the viscous levee of his despair. Father and son gazed hopelessly at the land and riches taken from them for a father's faith in a faithless future past.

Chapter IX

Every individual is continually exerting himself
to find out the most advantageous employment...
But the study of his own advantage naturally, or
rather necessarily, leads him to that employment
which is most advantageous to society. He intends
his own gain, but he is in this...led on by an invisible
hand to promote an end which was not part of his
intention.

It is not from the benevolence of the butcher,
the brewer, or the baker that we expect our dinner, but
their regard to their own interest.

--Adam Smith

In the Founders' understanding, whoever says
equality of liberty thereby says inequality of outcomes;
whoever says equality of outcomes thereby says
inequality of liberty, because only the unequal handi-
capping of the superior will prevent their capacities
from manifesting themselves.

--Martin Diamond

Rescued from the hangman's noose, José Necahuatl de Arreola began the long and perilous journey back to the Bajío. In addition to the dislocation caused by the rebellion, a severe famine had spread across the length and breadth of Mexico occasioning the deaths of thousands. Without a penny to his name, he wondered how he would sustain himself en route.

His greatest concern, however, was for his family. He'd been unable to send remittances or even a letter home during his imprisonment and subsequent trial. Now, his trek from Coahuila province might add a similar stretch of time to his absence. He trembled for their health—indeed, for their very lives.

All his time in Dolores, first as mere servant to Father Hidalgo and then tasked with the upkeep of the pottery workshop, he was able to send a small allowance once a week to his family outside San Miguel el Grande. Then, as his contributions to the business began to be noticed, his remittances grew more and more generous.

He wondered why his father, who had been so solicitous of the family during José's early years, had come to abandon them. Had he had a prick of conscience about having two families? That would be quite unusual, since it seemed to be a widespread practice among the aristocracy. The *hacendados* frequently had even more than two families, fathering children with many of the peasant women on their properties.

What he couldn't have known is that Don José Sebastián de Arreola y Riaño had not died in battle. In reality, he had not fought in the revolution at all—not in any of them. No, while his death was ruled as natural causes, what had actually led to his demise was the gradual poisoning by his legitimate wife. She evidently was not so sanguine about her husband having a second family.

She was pure Spanish, after all, born and raised in the mother country while Don José Sebastián bore the diminished esteem of mere creole origin. The marriage had been nothing more than a business merger engineered by the fathers of both husband and wife, Señor Arreola y Riaño de Llano seeking the status of peninsular origin and the bride's father relief from debts and eventual penury.

Knowledge of these facts would have gone a long way toward explaining to Arreola his father's gradually dwindling visits and his disinclination to play with José and his sisters or give them rides on his horse when he did manage to get there. The youngest, Luisito, he had never even had the opportunity to know.

So, all José de Arreola knew was that he was his family's sole support as little brother Luisito was still too young to be able to help in any substantive way. Arreola only hoped that his mother had had the foresight to save some of the money he could still send before his imprisonment and trial and aborted execution. If not, he feared the worst.

Fortune (or God) was with him, however. Just one day out of Monclova where the trials and executions had taken place, he happened to come across a mule train on its way to San Luis Potosí and from there to Guanajuato. It would pass through the heart of the Bajío.

The caravan had just stopped for the night and supper was being prepared. Arreola had not eaten since the previous morning and the succulent aromas of corn tortillas, pinto beans and boiling corn on the cob set his gastric juices flowing like a tidal wave. He found the owner, a Señor Tomás Sánchez, and begged him to exchange a meal for work.

Don Tomás, having acquired the wisdom of many years lived and many characters dealt with, looked on the young man with a tinge of paternal indulgence. "And what do you know how to do, *joven*? Do you know anything about the care of mules, of loading and unloading merchandise, the servicing of wagons and carts?"

As hungry as he was, the thought of exaggerating his abilities swept briefly through Arreola's mind. He quickly dismissed it, sensing a certain uprightness in the old man.

"Sir, I must confess that I know very little of horses, mules or donkeys, but I learn very fast. As far as how to handle merchandise, I was once manager of a pottery workshop and know very well how to pack even fragile items for transport—and to unpack them safely and expeditiously. I also know what materials and foodstuffs to include for an extended journey and to barter and trade, if those skills would be of help."

José wasn't sure why he had to add a caveat to the last skill he mentioned. Perhaps it was that probity he sensed in Don Tomás. Whatever it was, he felt compelled to elaborate: "I feel for some reason, however, that I should tell you that in the pottery business I always tried to give my clients a fair deal for their money or trade, even when I knew I could milk a better deal for myself."

Don Tomás was impressed by the young man's honesty concerning his skills and lack thereof—and especially by his last statement. Moreover, he had acquired over his years in business an incisive ability to size up character upon the first meeting. His every instinct about the boy was favorable.

Fairly confident about that positive assessment, he was already considering how Arreola might contribute to his business in the long term. He had recently lost an employee to the rebellion. Or perhaps they were just bandits; often they were indistinguishable. The integrity he sensed in this boy was rare in his experience, and he also divined a wisdom beyond this young man's years. "It might very well," he tersely concluded.

He then turned and pulled a tin bowl and spoon from his wagon and started to usher Arreola over to the victuals.

"Oh, sir, I must do the work before taking advantage of your hospitality."

Again, the old man was impressed but unmoved. "I find that all my workers perform better when they are not starving to death. You have that look."

Arreola hesitated. "But…"

"*No hay pero que valga.* Go on. Eat." So José Necahuatl did so, and with gusto, impressed himself with the old man's solicitude. That positive assessment of character and competence was mutual.

Once he finished, and that was in a mere breath of time, he immediately presented himself to Don Tomás for duty. He learned that very night how to unharness, water, feed, brush down and picket mules, being very careful to commit the process to memory. (He was already maneuvering to extend his time in the employ of Don Tomás.) Afterward, he inspected the old man's merchandise and suggested ways it could be better secured with less binding that would facilitate unpacking and repacking.

Don Tomás was delighted with the suggestions, and now doubly impressed by the immediacy of Arreola's grasp of that aspect of the muleteers' business. "I imagine in your management of the pottery concern you mentioned that you've had to deal with those who cheat and steal."

"In the production, the transport and the sales, unfortunately."

"Hmm, yes, one must be very careful as to that. I have quite a bit of experience with unscrupulous workers and clients."

"As do I."

So was José Necahuatl hired for the entire journey; and so, a binding friendship was forged. In Don Tomás, Arreola found a new father figure, his own he'd only lately been misinformed as having died in battle early in the uprising—a gracious lie to honor the man's memory.

There was nothing in Don Tomás Sánchez's pedigree that was anything like that of his real father. However, Arreola sensed an integrity, a probity of character like his father's that was, before God, truly ennobled.

As they made their way south, José de Arreola peppered his new-found mentor with questions about every aspect of his business: how he was contracted, what items he merely transported and which he sold directly and to whom. He soaked up the information and slowly began to make himself indispensable.

While initially hired on a shelter and board basis, Don Tomás quickly realized that Arreola was saving the enterprise precious time and effort—and therefore, money—by inventing more efficient procedures across all aspects of the business. As far as sales were concerned, he could already sniff out a scam as well as Don Tomás himself. He could often turn the swindle back on the prospective swindler.

Consequently, after a few weeks and over Arreola's protests, the old man started paying Arreola a commission on any sales he made above a certain minimum. His admiration for the young man increased dramatically when he watched him send every last penny he made to his family in San Miguel el Grande. Don Tomás sincerely hoped that the money was not disappearing along the way.

When they at long last arrived at Guanajuato, Don Tomás had to fight José to get him to take a small bonus before he flew off to find his family. "José, you have saved me untold amounts above the added sales you made. Who knows how much of the money you sent to San Miguel actually got to your family, if any? And if not, you'll need this if you're lucky enough to find them alive. I'll be passing this way after a short trip to Valladolid. I'll find you in San Miguel or Dolores or wherever you end up. In the meantime, *take the money!* You'll be no use to me dead or mourning your family."

So, José Necahuatl grudgingly acceded and set off immediately for San Miguel el Grande.

He walked day and night. In the dark, stumbling his way by a moonlight diffused and dissipated by diaphanous clouds, he reflected on his incredible fortune to have made the acquaintance of so fine a man as Don Tomás Sánchez. It was truly a gift from God. It might very well have saved his life, and that of his family in the bargain.

How rare a man he was, dealing with everyone, employee and client alike—even with his stubborn mules—with the utmost fairness and compassion. *What a society we might have if everyone behaved with like honesty and respect*, he thought. But the recognition that such rectitude was in painfully short supply there in New Spain weighed heavily on his heart.

The moon finally emerged free of clouds, casting an attenuated watery glow that allowed him to avoid the worst stumbling blocks in his path. The soothing white noise of wheedling crickets combined with a more sure-footed path allowed his mind to freely cogitate.

A strange thought struck him: Don Tomás was like this welcome moonlight, a faint glow of probity in the darkness of deceit and subterfuge that seemed so pervasive in New Spanish life, that so often thwarted successful enterprise.

He contrasted it with the underhandedness he'd known in his life: the virtual enslavement of Indians, blacks and *mestizos* in the *obraje;* the involved machinations he had to go through as manager of the ceramic workshop to avoid being cheated—how it added to operating costs!

Above all, there was the casual double-dealing in the war: the deceitful ruse that led to their own capture; Father Hidalgo's wretched treatment of the enemy; even in the blatant disregard for his vow of celibacy as a priest, fathering so many illegitimate children.

How can a society exist with such cynical situationism, such an egregious lack of trust? The thought of such a paucity of honor among men saddened and disgusted him. How can anything be accomplished when no one can, with any surety, predict an outcome? Thank God for people like Don Tomás Sánchez. Pity the country where such honor is so rare.

When José de Arreola found his family, his worst fears were realized. Forced from their home for nonpayment of interest, they'd been living on the streets of San Miguel for over a month, reduced to begging for their livelihood. Adding to their woe was the fact that, due to the famine and the dislocations caused by the rebellion, few had anything to give.

In fact, there were many in the same condition, competing for the meager alms from the few who could afford to offer them. Had Arreola been another month delayed, he might not have found his family at all.

Their gradual convalescence was only due to the generosity of Don Tomás. They all had the haunted look of approaching starvation, with empty eyes and sunken cheeks, skin sallow and diaphanous.

This was particularly true of Luisito, his baby brother, who, though considerably advanced in years since the last time Arreola had seen him, wasn't walking any better than when José had left. He noticed that his legs were rather bowed, he was irritable and between those fits of pique, he seemed rather dull and listless.

Arreola had learned through his experience of going from the measly sustenance of the *obraje* to the sumptuous meals at Father Hidalgo's that a body unaccustomed to a rich diet will at first reject it. Consequently, he started them off slow with the liquid from boiled pintos and corn, gradually including a few beans and kernels to let their bodies adjust, before graduating them to solid food.

He scavenged the town and countryside for cast-off materials—which were almost non-existent. With persistence, however, he was able to procure enough to build a crude shelter. Of course, it leaked horribly when it rained and was of no great help in a strong cold wind, but it was better than nothing.

Now, before the money Don Tomás had provided was used up, he had to formulate a long-term plan. He would definitely join the old man on his next junket, but he had to find a better situation for his family. He wondered what had become of Father Hidalgo's pottery workshop in Dolores. Perhaps he could persuade Don Tomás to make a slight detour on their coming enterprise.

First of all, the workshop might provide shelter for his family while he was away with Don Tomás. Then again, he wondered if he could find some way, if it were simply abandoned, as many businesses and structures across Mexico were now, of restarting it. Perhaps Don Tomás might be interested in investing in it. That would kill two birds at one shot.

When he went to send a letter to one of the artisans he hoped was still in Dolores (and still alive), he had the happy occasion of receiving one from Don Tomás. The old man would be in Guanajuato in two-or-three days' time, he wrote, and from there he had contracted for a delivery to San Luis Potosí. From San Luis, he would head to Mexico City to pick up a large consignment of merchandise and take it to Acapulco for shipment to the East.

Perfect, Arreola thought. Dolores is on the way to San Luis, so he would be able to see for himself the condition of the ceramic workshop. He hoped to hear from his friend and former employee in Dolores before having to leave for Guanajuato. If the factory wasn't abandoned, he would have to take his family back to the miserable shelter in San Miguel while he was working for Don Tomás.

As is so often the case when we make plans, we can count ourselves lucky if even part of them turn out as we'd hoped. He was reminded of the saying, "If you want to make God laugh, tell Him your plans."

The workshop was indeed abandoned, but it was now owned by a local Spanish merchant who had no interest in backing a common *mestizo* to take it over.

José was disappointed, but discouragement was not any part of his constitutional makeup. He actually counted himself quite blessed. While there was hunger and despair throughout the land, he had gainful employment that would provide for his family as well as himself.

He addressed his employer: "Don Tomás, I'll have to take my family back to San Miguel as there would be no time to find or build shelter here in Dolores. If I hurry, I might be able to catch up with you in San Felipe, or at least, San Luis."

"Nonsense, boy. What you will do is bring your family with you."

"Oh, but Don Tomás, I couldn't impose on you that way."

Don Tomás smiled. "What you will not deprive me of is the extra help your family can provide. They will work for food and shelter. If they're half as industrious and smart as you, I'll make out like a bandit on the deal."

And so, a lifelong friendship, even a family, was forged. Arreola's younger brother and sisters came to see and even to love Don Tomás as a kindly grandfather, loving but in no way overindulgent; he had little patience with Luisito's temper-tantrums. But he, Arreola observed, came to treat them with the love and concern of a nurturing patriarch.

Arreola's mother and sisters came to make vital contributions to Don Tomás' business, learning the tricks of the trade almost as fast as Arreola himself. His mother and eldest sister, Veronica, made themselves indispensable with all domestic chores, cooking and cleaning and generally making the journey more pleasant for everyone. His younger sister, Patricia, like her elder brother, had a quick mind for care of the mules and keeping the books for Don Tomás.

Luisito, on the other hand, was quite an irritant. He contributed little to the upkeep of the train, he had a gunpowder temper, and it was obvious with his legs so bowed as they were that he could not keep up with the rest. Luisito was approaching manhood and Arreola was concerned that his disagreeableness was not something he would grow out of.

Don Tomás, in his bounteous generosity, quickly put Luisito on the buckboard with him and taught the boy to drive the mules. Luisito occasionally rode with Don Tomás' son, Alfredo, driving the second wagon in the train. Fortunately, Alfredo had inherited his father's patience and disciplined the boy only by taking away the reins and letting him stew in his own juice.

During stops for their two meals of the day, Arreola learned that the old man had had a family of his own, losing his first-born in the famine of 1785-86, then his wife and youngest girl and boy to the cholera epidemic some decade later. His last remaining son, Alfredo, was almost taken by highway bandits that were so prevalent during the rebellion years and would always be a plague. Arreola and Alfredo became fast friends, the former never feeling the least bit of jealousy from the latter.

Arreola wondered how, amid such horrible tragedy, Don Tomás maintained his integrity and optimism. "I have my son, Alfredo, and now God has blessed me with a new family to replace the one He, in his infinite wisdom, took to dwell with Him in His glory. Always remember, we are entitled to nothing, José Necahuatl. That is the only way to live this life with any sense of peace and fulfillment, so that, whatever we do have, we may be ever thankful for."

That would be a lesson that Arreola would take to heart as Don Tomás' enterprise, which little by little became their enterprise, flourished as never before. It would take less than two years' worth of these excursions to amass the funds, with the help of a loan from the church—the principal source of such credit in Mexico—to rent and rehabilitate the ceramic workshop in Dolores.

On inspection, Arreola found only one still-workable potter's wheel and another capable of being repaired, which he immediately set to accomplishing. Remembering Don Tomás' wise council, he gave thanks for that. It was a good start.

He immediately sought out an Indian artisan, Tlayolotl, who had created the most beautiful and interesting designs of useful pottery and even intricately designed works of art before the first revolution. Unfortunately, this talented artisan had died in the famine that started before the latest war and lasted the better part of three years.

So it passed with many of the Indian and *mestizo* artisans that Arreola had hired before the war; so many of them lost to famine or disease. He began to feel a twinge of desperation, as his own artistic skills were meager.

The Talavera pottery was recognized throughout the Bajío, however, and he knew all it would take is one competent artisan to start to rebuild the market. The brand was known as far away as Mexico City, Guadalajara and Acapulco—even as far as Spain itself.

One day on an excursion to San Miguel to try to locate just one of his former employees, he came upon an adobe hut with some quite beautiful designs etched and dyed in very tasteful colors adorning its exterior. It even had a door of sorts, obviously scavenged and merely propped against the entranceway. He knocked on it.

A middle-aged woman answered, emaciated and with the sunken eyes of the ever hungry. He had to help her move the door aside. Arreola addressed her first in Castilian. He could tell that, while she understood, she was not comfortable enough to respond with more than a simple *Buenas tardes*. That being the case, he tried Náhuatl. He could immediately feel a thawing in the atmosphere, and the lady's eyes slightly brightened.

He asked her if she were responsible for the beautiful designs on her home. Looking past her into the house, he was able to make out ollas and cups made of the same clay as the structure. The lady answered that she and her daughter were. "And the ollas and cups I see on your shelves?"

"The same," she answered.

"Could I ask what kind of potter's wheel you have to make those fine designs?"

She looked blankly at him. There was no word in Náhuatl for potter's wheel and he'd had to use Castilian. "What is *potors huil?*

142

she asked. He described the device. She again looked confused. "We have no *potors huil*. Only our hands."

The menacing clouds on Arreola's horizon suddenly evaporated. His face beamed like the risen sun. The Indian woman smiled in kind back at him, a little befuddled.

He tried to explain in terms she could understand that he wished to hire her and her daughter to work in his pottery workshop. She was at first perplexed. "Hire? You mean to pay me?" she asked with big, rounded eyes.

"Yes, to pay you and your daughter." He explained that at first it would not be much, but that with time and success it would almost certainly increase. She was still skeptical. He asked her if she had known of Father Hidalgo and his Talavera pottery.

"I have heard, but I know nothing of *potors huils*. Nor my daughter."

"I will show you. Believe me, it makes the production of pottery, the variety of designs so much easier. You and your daughter will love it. Please, can you and your daughter come with me to my workshop in Dolores?"

She looked at him with wide-eyed wonder, so certain that with so little to eat, the thought of making a trip anywhere was not within the realm of possibility.

He recognized the look of astonishment and took some pesos he was carrying and passed them to her. "Please have no fear, Señora, I will provide transportation and sustenance. Can you leave tomorrow?"

She stood in bewilderment looking down at the money. He closed her hand around it. "So you and your daughter can come with some food in your stomachs." Again, there was no word in Náhuatl for earnest money. "Oh, my name is José Necahuatl de Arreola."

Her eyes brightened further at hearing his middle name.

"I am called Papaplotl."

Chapter X

*Man everywhere has an unconquerable
desire to be the master of his own destiny.*

--Calvin Coolidge

*Democracy extends the sphere of individual
freedom, socialism restricts it. Democracy
attaches all possible value to each man,
socialism makes each man a mere agent.
Democracy and socialism have nothing in
common but one word: equality. But...while
democracy seeks equality in liberty, socialism
seeks equality [of outcome] in restraint and
servitude.*

--Alexis de Tocqueville

By the time we got to Mister Macalister, he was already trying to get himself up. When he tried to put weight on that right leg, however, it seemed like it just wasn't working somehow, and he crumbled back down to a sort of sitting, kneeling position.

"Gerardo," Miss Luz called out in as commanding a tone as I'd ever heard, "stay down until Cookie and John Michael and I can carry you back to the wagon." My mother was already on his other side.

Mister Macalister tried to protest. "Nah, Luz. Just lemme' git back on my feet and I can—" and again he tried to rise, but this time couldn't even get one foot under him.

"Not now, *hermano*! You are riding in the wagon until we reach Fort Concho."

Mister Macalister tried to push himself up with his hands but again, it seemed like he just couldn't get that leg to respond to command. I could see he was shivering though it wasn't even cold, and he sounded kind of short of air when he spoke.

Camp Cookie finally got to us, and behind him at a little distance stood Jacob, looking on with the queerest aspect. Best I could describe, it was one somewhat of concern but feigning indifference.

A couple of the cowhands came to see what the problem was, but Miss Luz told them she had everything under control and to mind the cattle. Cookie and I placed ourselves on either side of Mister Macalister's torso, with my mother and Miss Luz helping with his head and feet. "Relax head, GP," my mother was actually able to blurt out a command in English from her position holding Mister Macalister's head, "I have." We lifted him up and carried him over to the cart, a rather foul odor seeming to come from him.

Miss Luz opened up the pants leg and the full stench of rotting flesh made me gag. I could see the effect of it and of the dark reddish-black color all around the wound on the others. For the first time, I saw just the briefest glance of fear flash across Miss Luz's face. She recovered in a heartbeat though, and I could see her coldly sizing up the situation.

Before she could give orders, Mister Macalister just said, "How bad?"

"Bad," is all she answered.

"I can smell it myself," Mister Macalister noted.

Miss Luz then looked at the rest of us. "We continue on, not stopping for the night. With luck, we'll reach the fort sometime tomorrow afternoon."

My mother had already checked Mister Macalister for fever and had wetted her kerchief to apply to his forehead. "I ride in back, care for him," she said to Miss Luz in her broken German. "You drive. We go...now!"

Surprisingly, Jacob had made his way up to the side of the cart. I couldn't believe how unconcerned he was—or seemed, at least. He took his flask out of his coat pocket and reached it down from his horse over the side to his father. "GP, this'll help with the pain. Take a swig. You'll feel better."

Why all of a sudden is he showing concern for his father, I wondered. Beyond that, it seemed like the care he offered was given like you might do to a co-worker—or even a stranger. And what on earth could be in that flask that could help with what I was pretty sure was gangrene?

Mister Macalister looked up at his son with a cold-blooded scowl and addressed him almost menacingly, "Son...you get that stuff away from me. I will live my life beholdin' to nobody 'n' nothin'." He then turned to Camp Cookie. "Gimme that bottle 'a' whisky, Cook."

I found it odd that Jacob didn't react in any particular way to his father's refusal. He just looked down at his father with...I don't know, a sense of satisfaction, maybe? Then he took a good swallow himself and made his way back to where the cattle were. Strange.

My mother arranged some of the grain sacks around Mister Macalister. I thought at first it was to block the wind. Then she said in German, "put on top—softer." Miss Luz seemed to understand and directed us to lift Mister Macalister onto the grain sacks. My mother then put one blanket on top of him. The last one she put around little Amelia and held her close. I wondered at that since it just didn't feel cold at all to me. Of course, I've always been pretty warm-natured.

It then struck me why she'd taken over the mothering of the child almost completely. She'd lost her youngest child, my sister, on the ship that brought us to this land. Amelia was close to the age Elzbieta was when she died.

I sure miss that little girl, my baby-sister. Maybe I could be a big brother to little Amelia. She sure is a good child, hardly ever getting fussy. I was curious about her origin and her place in this family. I guess Miss Luz will eventually get around to that. I sure hope so.

My mother periodically moistened her kerchief and put it on Mister Macalister's forehead, hoping to break or at least minimize his fever. I didn't envy her right next to him getting the full force of the smell coming from his leg. But I'd never heard my mother complain…about anything, and she certainly didn't now.

We started on the trail again, this time with Miss Luz driving the mules. I felt kind of useless sitting on the buckboard with her, but I couldn't think of any way to help. And I sorely wished I could.

As usual, Miss Luz somehow knew what I was thinking. "There's nothing anyone can do at this point, *hijo*—besides pray. And I ask that you do that."

Sensing a grave concern and even a growing feeling of fatalistic grief in my—foster aunt, I guess I could call her—I tried to think of some solace I could offer. "I sure admire a man like Mister GP Macalister."

Miss Luz let loose a kind of sad little close-lipped grin. "Everyone does. You'll never find loyalty among a crew of ranch hands like the ones on the Lazy Eight. You'll never see the kind of respect the other ranchers and everyone else who knows him has for him." She said it with absolute conviction, but like there was some little burr beneath that confidence that rankled. I wasn't going to push her to elaborate, curious as I was. It turned out I didn't have to.

"Except for his only son; the only one he had before you."

It felt kind of good Miss Luz considering me his son. I felt like her saying that sort of gave me permission to ask for that elaboration. "You know, Miss Luz, I been wondering about that. I never seen a boy—a man—act toward his father the way Jacob does. Is there somethin', uh…?"

"Yes, *hijo*. There is something…something very sad. To understand it, though, you need to know the rest of our history."

She was driving the mules at a quicker pace than usual. I assumed that's why she'd taken over as she knew just how hard she could push them nonstop without breaking them—or at least not break them before we made it to Fort Concho. Plus, I had no experience with driving the mules in the dark, nor any idea where Fort Concho was.

She let out a sigh that seemed to hang in the air like a dense fog. It wasn't one of sadness so much as just…fullness, I guess is the best way I could describe it. I could hear Mister Macalister in the back of the wagon mumbling that poem or prayer he'd recited when we'd pulled the arrow out of his leg.

"I hated the Comanches," Miss Luz began. "I hate them now. I hated them even more than Gerardo. With the last breath of strength in my soul, I will always hate them. So when my brother offered his services as a scout for the army, I did too." A sniff of amusement escaped her nostrils. "The Colonel did everything he could not to laugh. The idea of the U.S. army hiring a woman for anything besides cooking and cleaning was something nobody had ever heard of—couldn't even imagine."

"'Well ma'am, I do appreciate the offer,' he said, 'but we got some Tonkawas providing that service.'

"My brother jumped in. 'Tonkawas 'er good at followin' trails, and they'd love to help wipe out the Comanches, but they don't know Comanche ways like we do.'

"The colonel chewed on that fact a moment. 'I'm sure that's true, and we'd welcome your help, Mister Macalister,' he answered, 'but the idea of the army letting a woman face that kind of danger is a pretty tall order.'

"I jumped in there. Showed him all the scars on my body modesty would allow, opened my mouth to show the missing teeth from the beatings. He could already see the front bit of my nose burnt off. Then I told him how many miles I'd ridden with Gerardo in four days' time. 'And I never asked for more rest than we both knew was prudent,' I finished, then asked how many of his soldiers could do the same.

"What finally convinced him was when Gerardo told him to take on both of us or neither."

"Wow, so what was it like scountin' fer the army?"

"We didn't do it for long. Of course, they wouldn't listen to me, but even Gerardo couldn't convince them, at least at first, that to dismount to fight Comanches is signing your own death warrant. They had always done it that way, so that was the way it would be done. And the colonel kept getting orders from the government to try to make peace with them, get them to sign a treaty."

Miss Luz dismissed that with a sarcastic scoff. "Comanches have no idea of peace or what a treaty even means. Their whole culture is based on raiding, killing and torturing. To them, peace would be utter pointlessness. It would be death."

I thought about the situation back in Poland, with the Prussians having control over us Poles, while before the partitions, it was ours. "Well, I guess they figured they were defending their land."

"They have no idea of owning land, *hijo*. They look at any people outside their tribe as prey—just like buffalo or deer. Although they don't torture animals. They took over the area by killing off the Apaches, the Tonkawas and other tribes, who had killed or scared off other tribes before them.

"But it wasn't the army's stubborn refusal to change their ways that finally convinced us to quit. My brother had finally prevailed on them to fight mounted."

"Well…what was it?"

She quietly sighed. "I suppose it's understandable. When you see homestead after settlement with all the people—or at least, all the adults and babies—naked, violated, tortured, scalped…it hardens most people with a hate that turns them into creatures who'll do the same in vengeance.

"One time we came upon a Comanche camp. The men were mostly gone, hunting or raiding. There were only old men, women and children." She paused, considering. "I guess the soldiers had reached that point of hate that Comanches were just not human to them."

She stared out at the surrounding vastness before us that seemed to stretch to infinity, silent for what seemed like hours. I just knew somehow to keep quiet, the power in her silence feeling inviolable.

Finally, she spoke. "And after what I suffered at the hands of Comanche squaws, I have to admit that I wasn't overly sorry for what the soldiers did. At least, not at first. When it came to the children, though, that was a different thing altogether.

"When I saw Gerardo knock a soldier off his horse who was about to bayonet a child, that brought me to my senses. The soldiers had enough respect for him that eventually he was able to stop the slaughter. As soon as we got back to the fort, he resigned. Of course, I did too.

"When you've seen such butchery over and over, it takes a rare man to not respond in kind."

"So, what'd you and Mister Macalister do?"

"Some of the non-military volunteers actually asked Gerardo to lead them and break off on their own. They brought in relatives and friends, too. They were all young bucks, with no concept of their own mortality, looking for adventure—some of them just looking to kill Indians. Gerardo made it clear, though, that anyone caught killing squaws or children, except in self-defense, would be hanged without trial."

"Wow. Did any…?"

"No, he never had to. Everyone took my brother at his word.

"He taught them how to ride like Comanches, took some Indian ponies on one early raid. They were smaller, quicker and hardier beasts that could forage in the open prairie. He drilled the men over and over so that they could do like the Comanches and fire a pistol hanging over the side underneath the horse's neck. He trained them to shoot a post at a full run and then even a ring on that post with their rifle, then ride straight on and hit another post some yards further on with one pistol. Then they'd ride to a third and shoot it under their horse's neck with their second.

"They were called 'Range Men', then. It eventually shortened to 'Ranger'."

"So, did you ride with them?"

"I did. I had no prospect of marrying and having children. What else was I to do?"

"The other men, they, uh…?"

"Yes, most of them were skeptical at first. When they saw me ride those drills better than most and learned to shoot at a flat-out run at least as good, I was accepted. I guess I was kind of a curiosity."

"Man. And you both survived. Were either of you ever wounded?"

"More than once. For me, after what the squaws had done to me, I was pretty impervious to pain. Gerardo was just as tough from his days as a Comanche warrior."

Knowing Mister Macalister was a Texas Ranger made me curious about how he got to where he is now. "So why did Mister Macalister stop doin' that and become a rancher?"

"The independence movement got in the way. It began to swell right about that time."

"Oh, did Mister Macalister sign on right away?" I was glad to see her lips curl into a smile that spoke of a pleasant memory.

"No. As a matter of fact, he tried to avoid it until he just couldn't anymore."

"Oh." I was curious about that, but I was even more interested about the question of her loyalties. I wondered if I had any business asking her about something like that. "Uh, Miss Luz, how'd you feel about that, bein'...you know...?

"Mexican?" She didn't seem at all offended and answered right away. "It was not just Anglos who fought for independence. There were many with Spanish names who died at the Alamo, and at the Goliad massacre. Your stepfather was almost one of them."

"He was at the Alamo?"

"If he had been, would he be here now?"

I felt kind of silly. "Oh no, 'a course not."

"That was General Antonio López de Santa Anna's big mistake. He thought by giving no quarter, executing all those martyrs, he would scare the Texians into submission. He had the lesson of the Comanches, how with their savagery they chased all other tribes and even the powerful Spanish army out of their territory. He thought he could do that with the independent-minded Texans. He didn't count on it just making them mad and hungry for revenge.

"No, Gerardo was with me at Goliad. Or I was with him, rather. I would follow your stepfather to the ends of the earth." Again, it felt good hearing her call Mister Macalister my stepfather.

She broke off for a second to ask my mother, in German, how Mister Macalister was doing. I wondered how on earth she and Mister Macalister knew German. Before I could ask, my mother answered her in her own limited German. "Not good. Say prayer over and over."

Miss Luz turned to me. The solemn way she looked and spoke sent a chill through me colder than that west Texas wind. "*Hijo...* you need to be prepared. When fever sets in from gangrene, the chances are...not good."

I knew she was right, but the respect I'd felt for Mister Macalister had grown into something more like fondness. The idea of losing him hung a hefty weight on my shoulders. And how could my mother take losing a second husband? And so soon? "I, uh..."

"Just so you know, *hijo.*"

Miss Luz and I were quiet for a while considering the possibility—really the likelihood— that I might lose a second father so soon after finding him. While I wasn't so attached that the loss would be devastating, I wondered what it would mean for my mother. And for me, I suppose. What would be our place in the household? Would we even have one? Well, I guess we'll cross that bridge when we come to it.

During our silent contemplation I turned from her, and the western sky seemed to burst into a rich yellowish-orange glow as the day inched toward dusk. Then, as the sun began to creep behind the western horizon, it took on a reddish cast and tinged the few puffs of white above with radiant golds gradually melting into maroons to purples to pinks at their outer edges.

When the sun finally disappeared from sight, the dark descended like a giant curtain slammed shut across the sky. A three-quarter waxing moon rose in the east. It shed a pale silvery glow that I hoped would help Miss Luz steer. That moon was the only interruption in a blanket of starlit wonder so thick across the coal-black sky that it gleamed like one of those Mexican dresses with all the sparkles and spangles.

I really wanted to know about Goliad and, as usual, Miss Luz seemed to sense it.

"What happened at Goliad was something I thought only Comanches were capable of. If the massacre at the Alamo stiffened the resolve of the Texians to pursue independence, Goliad turned that resolve into a crucible of hate. It dissolved to dust whatever residual feeling I had for the land of my birth."

I couldn't imagine anything worse than what she'd described of her time as a captive of the Comanches. I just sat back and waited for her to continue.

Chapter XI

Idealism, that gaudy coloring matter of
passion, fades when it is brought beneath
the trenchant white light of knowledge.
Ideals, like mountains, are best at a distance.

--Ellen Glasgow

Scratch the surface of most cynics and you'll
find a frustrated idealist—someone who made
the mistake of converting his ideals into expectations.

--Peter Senge

If our bodies were as lasting as this painted
effigy who would be afraid of death? But I
have to die and only this memory can remain
of me.

--Moctezuma, at his image carved on
Chapultepec Mountain

José Nicolás de Cos de la Portilla: now that name meant nothing—worse than nothing, for it was a name now tainted with the unpardonable sin of treason. It was one stripped of all the worth that lands and wealth and influence had once given it. It was a name carrying the stigma of disloyalty, of seditious refusal to recognize the sublime sovereignty of the Mexican Empire and the sanctified monarchy of Agustín Iturbide, now Agustín I.

That most others had done so only weeks or even days before the proclamation of independence (and many even after) mattered little. Was it too late for the family to do so now? He only had to look at his father to know the folly of such a thought.

It seemed appropriate enough, that impression of nothingness. For the horror of war had sucked from Nicolás all sense of self. The casual slaughter, the deceit and duplicity, the random shuffling of loyalties had left him without faith not just in the world that surrounded him, but in his very identity. The thought of starving to death or being hanged as a traitor held no terror for him. Death for him now was simply an escape from the insults and shocks of an unbearable existence.

He thought bitterly of this whole charade: loyalty to Spain and the King, rebellion and resistance, independence that only engendered a new king, one of the Mexican Empire with Agustín as its emperor, simply supplanting the arrogance, the gluttony and the corruption of the Spanish with more of the same.

What difference had it made? All the death and suffering, the loss of friends and comrades, the hate and recrimination? What did the loss of his cherished older brother count for now? All continued as it was. Emperor Agustín dissolving the congress when it went the slightest step away from his wishes. His ostentatious display of wealth that gobbled whole the greater part of the treasury. The congress plotting his assassination or exile.

What had changed? He could see no honor in his father's refusal to capitulate, a choice that had driven him semi-catatonic. José Nicolás witnessed the same treachery, the same promises never kept, the same backstabbing and disloyalty. What point could there be to any of it?

The only sentiment that kept him from complete surrender to apathy was the plight of his family. A kernel of concern for them still found restless harbor in his soul. It was for that residual scintilla of humanity that he acquiesced in his mother's plan to seek the succor of her sister, María Imelda de la Portilla de San Román.

So often during periods of famine had Nicolás' father saved the San Románs from destitution. So many times had he rescued Don Eleuterio San Román from financial ruin, paying off his debts incurred from gambling losses or ill-advised financial schemes. Don José Maximiliano de Cos de Asunción at times had to ignore his own affairs in order to set the San Románs to rights.

And each time, Don Eleuterio San Román de Ulúa would find someone, *anyone,* else to blame for these—never *his*—financial setbacks. It was always a cheating or incompetent associate, unreliable clientele, a trick of fortune or simply bad weather.

So it came to pass that with much solicitation and promises, Nicolás' family was allowed, and only grudgingly so, to take refuge on the San Román ranch outside Dolores. While his experiences in war had shorn José Nicolás of all pretensions of pride, he could see the effect of being a poor dependent relative had on his father. The old man had gone from only speaking when asked a question to now not uttering a word, only moving when prompted and staring blankly at nothing.

For Nicolás, however, this opportunity might very well have saved his life. For beyond the threat of poverty and want, what he could not ever endure was exclusion, ostracism. To be shunned from Mexican society was torture enough, but to be without the womb of family, of hearth and home, and to continue to exist in such utter desolation was beyond his ability to conceive, much less to endure.

Would God understand if I were to take the ultimate escape? he wondered. *Where would my family be then?* Added to that, the thought of ending his torment by his own hand violated the most fundamental precept of his Catholic faith: that life was a gift from God and only He can take it away. A bitterly ironic laugh escaped him at the thought of this life as a gift—it struck him now as an intolerable curse.

He was certain, however, that the suffering in this life would be a mere pinprick compared to the agony in the next for those who by their own hand snuff out their existence. He wondered what form his own eternal damnation might take. He imagined an utter and abject solitude, sans any person or even a lesser being to provide companionship—only the hollow sound of absolute silence, the haunting privation of light, of touch, of smell…for all eternity.

The thought of such a hideous fate carved all substance from him and left him an empty trembling shell in human form. It would always stay his hand and keep him struggling in this vale of tears. Or so he thought at the time.

His mother and sisters collected those few possessions left them, and the family made its way to a life dependent on the charity of relatives. He wondered what effect such dependency would have on each of them. He already knew what it had done to his father.

He thought little of himself. All measures of hope had dissolved into thin air with the progress of the wars.

Of his sisters, Consuela and Caridad, he was more optimistic. Consuela, the eldest, was of marrying age and had several suitors— at least so she had before the family's fall from grace. He hoped some among them might take her without a dowry and despite the ignominy of a traitor's brand.

Caridad had already had her *quinceañera*, so she was not far behind. Besides, she seemed to have inherited her mother's streak of independence and resourcefulness. José Nicolás envied that strength of character in his mother, who seemed to be taking this reversal of fortunes even better than he expected—and much better than he himself.

As for his father, however, Nicolás trembled. Don José Maximiliano seemed imprisoned in his own private hell. He stared absently into space, ate almost nothing, and continued only moving when directed. Efforts to get him to take an interest in the family's future were met now with not veritable but true catatonia. He only drank, trying to silence the demons reminding him of his dull, aching purposelessness.

The truth was that for José Maximiliano de Cos de Asunción, his possessions, his status as *latifundista*, his absolute dominion over his fiefdom and all who lived by it, was the major part of his identity. It was his sacred place in the ideal society, the reflection of the Heavenly Order, with each of God's creations in its predestined place that truly provided him purpose, belonging and a sense of wholeness. Shorn of that, he was a simple shell bereft of all that made him a man. The only thing that could fill the emptiness, or make him forget his own insignificance, was the worm at the bottom of a bottle of mescal.

Even after they were settled, however uncomfortably, in the home of Don Eleuterio San Román, his father displayed little to no life at all. As months grew into years, he merely sat the whole day on Don Eleuterio's ample front porch on a rocking chair, saying nothing, his activity limited to raising glass to mouth and refilling it once emptied. After a very short time, he dispensed with the glass.

After bottle after bottle of tequila, he finally began to betray the yellowed eyes and sallow skin of organ failure. He was saved from that slow, agonizing creep into oblivion only by true alcohol poisoning, his brain a reservoir of alcohol-infested spirits and nightmares.

A few months or perhaps a year later, Don Eleuterio San Román found an elderly widower to take Consuela off his hands. Nicolás was grateful for that, for as of late, his uncle's resentment against his dependent relatives was becoming more and more openly expressed.

Nicolás' eldest sister was always the most compliant member of the family and quickly resigned herself to her fate. José Nicolás marveled at how modest expectations seem to endow one with an enviable equanimity. The growing taunts and slights visited upon her and the rest of the family by Don Eleuterio never seemed to dismay her.

From the beginning of their stay with the San Románs, José Nicolás found himself wishing he could borrow some of that composure from Consuela. His experiences in war had whittled away at the fuse of his temper. Any sudden movement or noise he was not anticipating stiffened every muscle in his body. The report of a rifle or even the cocking of a pistol set his nerves to reeling that only hours of quiet isolation could assuage. Night terrors wrenched from him screams of horror that upset the whole household. It was so disruptive that within a few months of the family's arrival, his uncle had banished him to a room off the hayloft in the barn.

At first, that kind of social isolation exacerbated his anxiety. The horses, with their unique perception of human temperament, sensed his pulsing angst and responded with suspicion and resistance. Only Dulcinea, his faithful companion through the war, now old and sway-backed, somehow seemed to understand what war's horror had done to her master.

There was another animal, though, that worked even greater magic in his redemption. An old dog, Coqueta, had been confined to the barn and yard when her hunting skills had begun to wane. So grateful was she for human companionship that she absorbed all Nicolás' fits of pique, his angry outbursts and moments of sullen rejection. Always, when they were over, it was for Coqui as though they had never happened, her canine devotion as constant as the orbit of the earth. Nicolás' screams of terror in the night only elicited her loving concern and desire to comfort.

So, the consoling affection of dog and horse ever-so-slowly began to soothe José Nicolás' fractured spirit. His moderating distemper worked in synergy with the increasing comfort the other barn animals felt in his presence to gradually heal his war-shattered soul.

It began to manifest itself in his intercourse with others. More and more he could tolerate a sudden noise or brusque movement without his nerves fraying. Even his night terrors moderated.

That toleration ended, however, at the treatment of his mother and sister Caridad by his uncle.

Don Eleuterio's penchant for gambling and investing in propositions that were at best, questionable, had, if anything, been exacerbated by the absence of his brother-in-law's moderating influence. But Nicolás' uncle again was one who could not conceive that any hardship or obstacle on his way to riches might be of his own making. He was of pure Spanish blood, born in the mother country, the cradle of civilization, and assumed that that mere fact entitled him to success in all his endeavors.

No, it was always that his Indian peasants didn't work hard enough, they cheated, they stole; partners were incompetent or deceitful; his family didn't support him; even God was against him. Now, he had the perfect scapegoats.

Don Eleuterio's resentment at having to harbor his wife's family was, from the beginning, palpable. It went beyond the natural discomfort at having his household disrupted. There was actually a deep-seated contempt that was hardly veiled. It began with the fact that Don Eleuterio was a native Spaniard and his wife and wife's sister and brother-in-law creole. That resentment only grew each time he was rescued from financial ruin by Don José Maximiliano.

In addition, there might have been a subconscious sense of shame on the part Don Eleuterio that while he and his brother-in-law had both begun the rebellion as staunch loyalists, once the tide had shifted, it was only the latter that had never capitulated. Don Eleuterio had sensed the prevailing wind and shifted accordingly.

He had only grudgingly acceded to his wife's pleas to allow her sister and family to find sanctuary in his home. At first, his ever-increasing hostility expressed itself in off-handed sarcasm that, while in the beginning was delivered to his wife in privacy, soon came in the presence of her sister and family. As they increased in frequency, abetted by a coldly expressed contempt, they began to sting more sharply and come to the attention of his nephew-in-law.

So, with years of mounting financial straits and dependents whose very presence he mightily resented, that umbrage finally erupted. It was the day after the most recent and devastating investment loss Don Eleuterio had suffered.

"It was since they came to live with us that everything has gone to hell!" he bellowed at his wife, of course within the hearing of Doña Anastasia and Caridad. "They are traitorous leeches, sucking the life out of all the fruits my pure Spanish hand has created. And they need to know it!"

Although Doña María had herself begun to feel the pinch of providing for her destitute relatives, especially with their dwindling resources, she still had the virtue of hospitality and the discretion not to let her growing resentment be aired. "Teo, please," she tried to calm him, "not in the presence of—"

"No! They need to hear!" he fairly bellowed. "I don't care if they're your family. It is our harboring of treasonous pirates that has dragged us down, dragged *me* down. They live off all my hard work, making no contribution, sucking up whatever pitiful bit of—of good I can squeeze out of our possessions! *Our* possessions."

"Husband, they cook, they clean, they work in our garden, they make their own clothes. Things they've never had to do before. Nicos cares for your stock—"

"And does a terrible job! My horses are skittish—wild! My cows hardly produce a third of what they did before he came."

"That's because you've sold so many to pay off our debts, Teo."

It was at that moment that Nicolás entered the house to see what all the shouting was about.

"Oh yes," Don Eleuterio continued, "take their side because they're your family. I don't even have the support of my own wife!"

"My husband, I am only asking you to be reasonable."

"No! What you are asking is for me to dig our family's grave in order to cater to your sister's wretched family!"

It was at this that Doña Anastasia tried to intercede. As she did, Nicolás moved beside her for support. "Eleuterio, the idea of being a burden is repugnant to me. We have tried to be as little disruptive to your lives as possible and to contribute as best we can. But if our presence here is intolerable for you, we will find some alternative. I ask only for some few weeks to find other accommodations."

Perhaps because in some darkened corner of Don Eleuterio's mind Doña Anastasia's quiet dignity marqueed his own childish petulance, it enraged him even further. After a fuming moment where smoke might have escaped his ears, he replied with mordant sarcasm, "Yes, by all means, find someone else to leech off of."

"Eleuterio!" Doña María exploded in indignation.

Almost simultaneously, Nicolás' open hand made violent contact with Don Eleuterio's left cheek. For a moment, Don Eleuterio was stunned to paralysis, unsure of how to react. When he finally came to himself, he went directly to his collection of guns on the wall of the drawing room and advanced toward Nicolás with a loaded pistol.

"Teo, *no!*" Doña María cried, trying to interpose herself between husband and nephew. He easily brushed her aside and as he cocked the pistol, he brought it up to within centimeters of his nephew's forehead.

José Nicolás stood as a wall of stone, taking one short step forward to place his forehead firmly against the pistol's barrel. Though once more reconciled to life and loath to foster its untimely end, Nicolás had a sense of his uncle's cowardice that made him doubt Don Eleuterio would follow through. "Go ahead, Uncle. You'll be doing me a favor."

For a breathless moment, all stood frozen in place: Don Eleuterio in paralyzed fury, uncertain how to respond to such a provocation, Nicolás affecting a cold, steel-hardened challenge, and the rest afraid to move or speak lest such a gesture produce the unthinkable.

Somehow, Nicolás' glacial response penetrated even Don Eleuterio's rage. After a moment, he lowered the pistol and addressed his nephew and family in quiet but fulminating passion: "You will be out of this house tomorrow at daybreak. There will be no period for you to find alternate lodging. Be gone tomorrow." And with that, he put down his pistol and retired from the room.

*A*nd so, the de Cos family's sojourn into hell began.

Despite Doña María's nightlong desperate pleading, Don Eleuterio was proof against all entreaty. The only thing she could do the morning of her sister's departure was to try to pass along her now considerably reduced monthly allowance and promise that wherever the family happened to find harbor, she would send along the lion's share.

Now it was Doña María who was deaf to all her sister's insistence that she keep the money herself, Doña Anastasia assuring her that the family would be all right. She was certain that they would find refuge with Consuela and her husband.

Doña María had a difficult time hiding her skepticism concerning that possibility, and when her sister again refused the money, she surreptitiously slipped it into José Nicolás' threadbare bag.

"Please sister, once you find permanent residence, write me. I can at least give you some support." She cast a significant glance at her nephew, silently communicating her insistence that if her sister failed to follow through that he would be sure to do so.

With that, the de Cos family made its way to the estate of Don Felipe Plutarco Castañeda and his new wife, Consuela de Cos de Castañeda in the city and state of Querétaro. Doña María, estimating the time it would take for them to arrive, waited until she received her next allowance to send the pittance of it she could afford, figuring that it should arrive around the same time they did. Unfortunately, that was one of the last times she could do so, as Don Eleuterio discovered the subterfuge and quickly put a stop to it.

Once Nicolás and his family arrived, they were greeted in much the same way. Despite Consuela's pitiful entreaties, they were not even admitted into Don Felipe's elegant home.

"No!" Consuela's husband roared, "I have debased myself enough, marrying the daughter of a traitor! To harbor the rest of his family, and especially the son who followed him in his perfidy, would consign my reputation to the depths of a starving street mongrel!"

Consuela, accommodating soul that she was, could only quietly beg her elderly husband. "Don Felipe, could we not let them stay in one of your other houses? Or the ranch outside San Miguel, maybe? Not even in the main house; perhaps one of the ranch hands' quarters. They would be far enough away that no one would know."

Don Felipe exploded with a scoff. "No one? Everyone! Everyone would know in a heartbeat. You've no idea how fast gossip travels throughout the provinces! I'm being considered for a seat on the Congress in Mexico City. Nothing would dash those hopes faster than the harboring of royalist traitors!"

So the best that Consuela could do, which was for her a monumental step outside her character, was to recover the diamond necklace that was her wedding present from her husband and, through tears, pass it off to her brother.

Months later, when Don Felipe discovered what was to him an unpardonable insult to his honor, he confined Consuela to her bedroom for a month. She, governed by a cheerful stoicism, found it not a great hardship as she whiled away the hours looming tapestries, reading and practicing needlepoint, all activities she enjoyed immensely.

The only abiding ache was concern for her erstwhile family. Fortunately, she had a sympathetic lady attendant, Beatriz, and the two became best of friends. Being considerably older, Beatriz eventually adopted the name "Nena" for her charge. With a potent dislike for Don Felipe, Beatriz aided her "Nena" in locating her family, surreptitiously posting letters to them, normally containing what money Consuela could procure or, when she could not, another piece of jewelry or other valuable knickknack that Don Felipe would not notice was missing.

José Nicolás had at first thought of taking his family to the town they knew best, San Miguel el Grande. But the de Cos name and family, now shrouded in ignominy, were too well known there. So, in consultation with his mother and sister, they made their way to Guanajuato, hoping that its larger population might afford some measure of anonymity.

He found a rooming house in a modest corner of the city and rented a room for the three of them, using the simplified name of José Portilla and hoping that it was only the "de Cos" appellation that would betray the family's origin.

For a considerable period that stretched the better part of two years, the stratagem worked. Living off the remittances from Consuela and the exceedingly rare ones from Doña María Imelda, the family strived in everything to be as invisible as they could manage. How many of those monetary transfers were interdicted in transit was an unknown.

It was odd, after all, for a family so clearly of the aristocracy to find themselves in such pitiful circumstances. It was fortunate that the owner of the rooming house was only concerned with being able to collect the rent without disruption.

José Nicolás wracked his brain for some way to augment the funds from family that seemed to gradually diminish in amount and arrive with ever-decreasing regularity. Apparently, it had become in-creasingly difficult for Consuela to evade her husband's vigilance.

A letter from Doña María finally arrived without funds, ex-plaining that the San Románs had finally gone bankrupt, and that Don Eleuterio had committed suicide in response—ironically, with the same pistol with which he had threatened Nicolás.

Doña María had sold off a good portion of their ranch to pay off the family's debts and was now, herself, edging toward destitu-tion. She would welcome them back to her home but knew that her days as owner were numbered.

As Nicolás pondered the possibilities of finding employment, he was struck with the fact of his decided lack of saleable skills. The art of war he'd learned and learned to despise as hell on earth. The prospect of being accepted into the army with his history was laughable.

He'd of course accompanied his father in his duties as *latifundis-ta*, but what marketable abilities had that experience endowed him with? Could he risk seeking employment on one of the area ranch-es? Looking pure Spanish as he did, the *latifundistas* would imme-diately be suspicious, wondering what a Spaniard or creole would be doing without a ranch or enterprise of his own. Only traitors found themselves in such a situation.

The mortal blow came when, distracted, Consuela had forgot-ten to eliminate the "de Cos" name from one of her letters. It was probably the result of having gone so long without writing as Don Felipe had dramatically increased his supervision of his wife's activ-ities. Only the wily ingenuity of her servant, Beatriz, had allowed this most recent letter to be posted.

The oversight was answered with a series of misfortunes visited upon the family as word spread of their true origins. They were immediately informed by their landlady that their presence in her rooming house had become intolerable and would have to make other arrangements.

As word of their true identity spread, however, finding an alternative became more and more elusive. They might encounter lodgings for a few months, weeks, days, or even only a few hours, until their host or hostess was apprised of their history—and those landlords or landladies rarely returned the money.

As their situation became more and more desperate, human vultures moved in for the kill: knowing they had no standing to appeal to the law, whatever remittances from family made it to the city were appropriated by those providing postal services.

The family's home now the streets of Guanajuato, alongside Indians and *mestizos* only a few short steps from starvation, José Nicolás once again pondered the unthinkable. What alternative had he? Could he bring himself and his family to the depths of dishonor by begging? Could he move them to another city or town? The trip itself without money or sustenance might very well be a death sentence.

There would be no more honoraria from sister or aunt; financial ruin and Consuela's husband's vigilance had seen to that, not to mention local pilferers. No one would hire him; and what skill had he to offer even if someone might? The care of livestock, the art of war? He would even submit to the latter if there were any possibility of being accepted as a soldier in the army of the now

Mexican Republic. He even considered joining a cadre of bandits, if he could find one that would accept him.

One late autumn day, with a whistling wind carrying on its back a hint of winter, he returned to his family on the streets of Guanajuato after a fruitless search of area ranches and local business concerns for employment. His mother's sunken eyes and sister Caridad's trembling from cold and hunger pierced his manhood with aching shame.

In the midst of absolute despair, his sister Caridad told him of a solution to their predicament. Nicolás was momentarily flooded with a sense of relief. But then he wondered why, if this were truly the answer to their plight, his mother seemed, if anything, even more distant than ever.

"A local *latifundista*, Don Francisco de Aranjuez, will let us stay in one of his houses on the road to San Miguel," Caridad said. Nicolás wondered why she said it rather tentatively, not with the feeling of relief or even joy he might have expected.

He was immediately suspicious. "In exchange for what?" he asked. "I recently approached him about trading work for lodging and his reaction was, if anything, contemptuous."

Nicolás' concerns were heightened by Doña Anastasia's determined withdrawal from the conversation as she stared into the distance, taciturn. "Cari...?" Nicolás simply looked at her for an explanation, a rising tide of ill-feeling creeping into his viscera. "What does he propose, Sister? Is he asking for your hand in marriage? I wasn't aware he was a widower."

When Caridad said, "Not...exactly marriage," and lowered her eyes to the ground, the realization of exactly what the proposition was flooded him with a such a hot flash of nausea that it tore away his equilibrium. The humiliation that overcame him as he realized the hideous state to which he'd allowed his family to descend sucked from his body whatever paucity of strength remained.

"And did you spit in his face?"

At this, a tear rolled down his mother's drawn, haggard face. Doña Anastasia was quite elderly now and these years of insecurity and now months of homelessness had made war on her health. Caridad merely kept her head bowed, eyes upon the ground in mortification.

José Nicolás staggered back against the wall of the building behind which they'd taken refuge from the chilly north wind. Staring straight ahead in despair, his mind searched desperately for some alternative, some escape from this hideous devil's bargain. Perhaps he would learn to steal. That might usher in his acceptance to a gang of highwaymen. The thought of escaping this humiliation by death, and not only his, was among the alternatives that danced with abandon about his brain. In the end, that might be the only one possible.

He slowly sank down and adopted his mother's vacant, hopeless stare. His mind darted in search of some manner of painlessly saving his sister and family from such unspeakable disgrace: poison? Strangulation? Was he capable? Where might he procure a pistol and ball and powder for three when he couldn't even secure life-sustaining food? Could he steal them?

That horrible phrase of "death before dishonor" rattled rudely about his brain. He cursed Don Franciso. He cursed Mexican society. He cursed his father for bringing his family to this odious state. He cursed all the hypocrites who changed loyalties with the inconstant wind. He cursed his miserable self that had brought his family to this despicable end. He cursed God.

Just before he started to rise with the manner of death chosen for each of them, a voice from his past sounded from somewhere above him: "José Nicolás de Cos de la Portilla."

He looked up.

Chapter XII

The few who do are the envy of those
who only watch.

--Jim Rohn

I cannot help fearing that men may reach
a point where they look on every new theory
as a danger, every innovation as a toilsome
trouble, every new advance as a first step
toward revolution, and that they may abso-
lutely refuse to move at all.

--Alexis de Tocqueville

From the very moment he conceived of the idea of resurrecting Father Hidalgo's pottery concern, José Necahuatl knew the resentment he would face at the first sign of success. He was also certain that as the enterprise flourished, as he was confident it would, the threat to the area aristocracy would metastasize. Who was this uppity half-breed? In order to entice the owner to rent the space to him, he actually had to offer more than the asking price.

He had heard the sentiment expressed all too often, most succinctly by a creole member of Agustín de Iturbide's army: "If you can't be better than a damn Indian or half-breed, then what the hell are you?"

Arreola wondered about the fate of that soldier, once Agustín de Iturbide was established as Agustín I, monarch of the empire of Mexico and then deposed and exiled.

Consequently, as Mexico had gone from empire to republic, and rebellions and coups sprouted like weeds in a garden, he took great pains to conceal as best he could the astonishing success the business was enjoying.

With Papalotl and her daughter Axochitl fashioning the most exquisite designs and Don Tomás delivering the goods, it was less than two years before Arreola's biggest problem was simply keeping up with demand. He'd by then paid off the loan from the church that had financed the first three months' rent and all the materials needed for the endeavor.

In an effort to maintain as much anonymity as such astonishing success would permit, he kept his family lodged in the workshop. He also implored Papaplotl and Axochitl to stay there as well, hoping the crowded quarters would further dissimulate the concern's prodigious growth. They readily complied, so thankful they were for their newfound luxury, i.e., having enough to eat and not living under the constant threat of homelessness.

His mother and sisters understood the need for such discretion. The unfortunate exception was little brother Luisito. Suffering the residual effects of rickets, Luisito's irritability and peevishness had only grown as he approached manhood. It produced in him a profound melancholia that he self-medicated with the only remedy then readily available, alcohol.

He chafed at their cramped living quarters and regularly disobeyed Arreola's admonition to feign penury about town. In addition to his constant ill-humor, Luisito was hyper-sensitive about his deformity, which was even greater in his mind than in reality.

It wasn't long before Luisito was spending more time in cantinas than at the workshop. Arreola had mixed feelings about this state of affairs. He was, of course, saddened by his brother's alcoholism and particularly by his hair-trigger temper that led to many altercations—disputes that José had to often indemnify with cash payments to avoid reprisals and lawsuits.

The drain on the family's savings was of considerable concern for Arreola. He was certain that the envy of those higher on the social ladder would eventually lead to the concern's demise, and those payments to Luisito's victims were more unwanted publicity of the family's wealth. However, it was also true that the workshop ran much more smoothly and efficiently without his brother's ill-tempered presence.

Arreola wondered how long it would be before one of those altercations ended in a knife in his brother's back or a homicidal blow to the back of his head. He upbraided himself for the thought of the peace such a happenstance would provide the rest of the family. He still loved his little brother, and even felt a considerable measure of guilt at not having provided the family with the nourishment that would have avoided Luisito's condition.

Amid these worrisome events, orders came in from all parts of Mexico. As the years ground on, demand from Spain and even from Acapulco for shipment to the East kept Arreola and his artisans quite overwhelmed. Arreola had to find many surreptitious ways of hiding the bounty such success was producing.

Another perplexing problem was how to expand without exacerbating the envy and perceived threat to the privileged classes in Guanajuato State—and now, even in surrounding areas.

Fortunately, he had Don Tomás as his confederate and together with his son, Alfredo, the three were able to sneak in two more potters' wheels in the dead of night.

The even greater challenge was finding another talented artisan. Papaplotl, however, managed to locate a cousin with similar artistic skills so that, after a short time of patient instruction, at least three of the wheels were kept in operation. A happy bit of serendipity was that when one of the wheels needed repair, the fourth was ready for use.

This cousin's wife, who didn't have quite the artistry of her husband's family, was at least able to facilitate their work supplying clay and water and paints as needed, and then firing the finished products in their kilns—which she learned to do quite well. Thus, the workshop could, with delays, at least approach satisfying demand.

Now a new challenge presented itself. Adding the new potters' wheels considerably diminished living space—room that was already in uncomfortably short supply. The wear of crowding was beginning to be felt more generally than by Luisito alone. While depredations by the jealous elite cut into profits, irritability over cramped living quarters threatened the smooth functioning of the workshop.

With considerable circumspection, Arreola was able to find an out-of-the-way dwelling on the edge of town for all save his immediate family. Breathing space was agreeably restored, as was good humor—in all, unfortunately, save Luisito.

Now Arreola's lingering threat was the mounting resentment he could feel from those of pure Spanish blood. Over the years, raids on Don Tomás' mule trains had begun to increase at a worrisome pace. With the old man's encyclopedic knowledge of the country's geography, he was at first able to forge alternate routes and keep the seizures at an acceptable rate. When even that stratagem began to fail, the two partners suspected that there was an informant among them.

At first, the bandits took merchandise and any money their prey happened to be carrying. After a time, however, they began to take great pleasure in destroying whatever they couldn't carry off—visiting that destruction particularly on the pottery. Arreola and Don Tomás had no doubt that this was a directive from the area swells.

It was also possible that Luisito might have been the source of information on routes and schedules. He had a dangerous penchant, especially when drunk—which he normally was—for bragging of the family's wealth and success, not to mention its shrewdness in evading banditry. This tendency was spurred on by his exaggerated sensitivity and self-consciousness about his bowed legs and stunted intellectual growth. He also spent freely and, when not fighting, freely treated those around him.

Arreola had once tried to cut off his brother's allowance, but the resulting eruptions of rage and exacerbating bouts of drunkenness made that unendurable. Where he had gotten the money to continue his self-medication, José had no idea.

At the beginning of the concern's fifth year, other acts of sabotage began to make their appearance. Clay shipments were interrupted or tainted in route. When Arreola started gathering and fashioning his own clay, he would find his sources despoiled.

Orders also began to dry up, signifying that the efforts to undermine his and Don Tomás' enterprise were spreading across the country.

A curious development between Arreola and his landlord had come to pass over the years of their business dealings. While the owner, a creole by the name of Don Porfirio Calderón, had at first been quite loath to rent to this *mestizo*, he had come over the years to more than tolerate him. Arreola, unlike many of his tenants, always paid his rent on time and never flaunted his wealth. In fact, Don Porfirio was quite impressed by his enduring humility, affected though it might be.

José could sense that the recent sharp increases in rent, which had now grown usurious, were not of Don Porfirio's desire. He had discovered, through diligent attention and a few sympathetic creoles, that his landlord was a member of a masonic lodge, the York Rite Masons, who were nascent liberals. He was one of the few in Dolores.

The majority of the aristocracy were of the other main masonic faction, the Scottish Rite Masons, who were, if not monarchist, certainly centralist and embryonic conservatives. As such, they were without question the most threatened by this pretentious parvenu. Arreola had circumspectly observed how the majority of those of pure Spanish blood had pressured Don Porfirio to make the maintenance of the Arreola family business as difficult and expensive as he could.

Despite all these pernicious attempts to undermine the workshop, Arreola somehow managed for a time to continue squeaking out a small profit. His sales became clandestine transactions with clients who insisted on their anonymity. Don Tomás kept his transports mainly of non-pottery cargo and what pottery he carried was camouflaged and carefully hidden away.

All these measures of the jealous elite began to undermine the concern's continued success, however, and in short order that small profit became a worrisome loss. Between theft, vandalism and payments to Luisito's victims, those losses mounted. Now approaching middle-age and seeing the writing on the wall, José Necahuatl immediately began brainstorming alternatives.

Plus, his ability to keep the workshop alive, if moribund, made the aristocracy even more resentful and determined to wipe Talavera pottery off the face of the earth—or perhaps, take it over from this arrogant upstart. When all their heinous machinations again and again failed to completely destroy the enterprise, their measures became truly life-threatening.

On one of Don Tomás junkets to the capital, bandits not only robbed and destroyed their merchandise—including the non-pottery type—but also threatened the old man with a gun. When his son tried to protect his father, they shot him in the shoulder. It was a non-mortal wound, although the damage a ball fired from a pistol does to human tissue made Alfredo's left arm almost permanently unusable.

Shortly after, Luisito was beaten and stabbed to death after a drunken brawl in Papa Gallo cantina. The family had little time to mourn as the coup-de-grâce immediately followed in a trumped-up criminal charge against José de Arreola. It seems there were numerous witnesses alleging that he had participated in the brawl leading to Luis' death. In fact, he had been one of the main insti-gators, they claimed.

José Necahuatl and Don Tomás huddled together one Sunday afternoon as the former awaited trial under house arrest to try to devise some plan going forward, both knowing that their time as entrepreneurs was at an end.

"You will lose this case, *hijo*," Don Tomás pronounced in no uncertain terms.

"That is a foregone conclusion," José answered without a trace of defeat in his demeanor. "I've been brought before a tribunal one other time in my life and know the outcome is never really in doubt."

"What shall we do?" the old man asked.

José Necahuatl de Arreola took a deep breath and let out a sigh more of contemplation than of concern. He walked to one of the two windows in the workshop and looked out at the burgeoning city. "It's sad, you know," he observed more in curiosity than in sorrow.

"It's more than sad, *hijo*. It's criminal."

He turned back to his partner and virtual foster-father. "I'm not talking about my particular plight, as desperate as it is, nor even that of my family. My distress is for all of Mexico, Don Tomás. You and I have, by creating this flourishing enterprise, given good, meaningful work to people all over this country—even, with ex-port and import, to others abroad.

"Of course, we did it in our own self-interest, but in doing so, we've created wealth that has been invested and spawned other concerns that likewise have provided employment and hope to so many—even to those perennially excluded from such opportunities. And now, because of the accident of our birth, and simple envy, the country will destroy such promise. For all Mexico, as I can't imagine we're the only ones."

After a moment, Don Tomás said simply, "Ah, that."

"And beyond such uncharitable waste, why can this country not seem to be able to govern itself? We are a sociable people, Tomás. We crave company and live for our celebrations and gatherings, and yet we go from a monarchy, dysfunctional from its very establishment, with conspiracies to topple it and establish a republic. Then there are counter conspiracies to dissolve the Congress and proclaim royal absolutism—or simply to replace one *caudillo* with another.

"Now, we have a so-called republic with a President who hides away from his obligations on his hacienda in Veracruz.

"Why can such a gregarious, genial people not find a way to govern themselves? And why can we not—not just allow, but actually *champion*—those supposedly low-born but of talent and industry who create and provide such opportunity for others? Why must their vital, thriving creations be destroyed?"

Don Tomás had wondered about similar issues himself but had never heard them articulated so clearly. He took a moment of silence in awe of the questions his partner and adoptive son had just put forth. "Those are very good questions, *hijo*. But I must confess that I have all that I can handle with much simpler…perplexities of this life: like how we're going to save you from these false charges."

José Necahuatl, however, was waxing philosophical. "And now, who is colonizing our northern territories, Nuevo Mexico, Texas?

It's the Anglos from the United States. I've even heard that there are movements to secede from Mexico and declare a republic. Why aren't Mexicans flocking there to take advantage of free land and no taxes being offered to colonize those territories?"

"Perhaps for the very qualities you mentioned inherent in the Mexican soul: we crave company. We're shun solitude. To strike out on our own—there are a few willing, but most of us have too strong a need for fellowship."

"Then why can we not govern ourselves? If we are so sociable, so communal, what gets in the way of the establishment of a stable government? One that would allow mestizos like ourselves to…to just to make our own way? To have our creations honored?"

Don Tomás could feel the piercing ache that these thoughts germinated in his partner, friend and foster child's heart, but had no solution or even words of solace. "Ah *hijo*, you ask questions beyond my old brain's ability to even consider."

So was a plan hatched to spirit Arreola and his family out of Dolores and far from the state of Guanajuato. It took the form of a disinformation campaign, allowing a rumor to seep out that the business' next foray would be to Mexico City. Further misinformation was furtively dispersed that it would contain little pottery since the capital had ceramic enterprises of its own.

Arreola and the old man had by that time identified the informant supplying accounts to the area ruling class concerning merchandise and routes. This time they used him to their own ends. Included in that misinformation was a report of the commodities to be transported: textiles, a plethora of pelts, clay tiles and household goods, among other items. Notably left out was Talavera pottery.

They kept the plan strictly between the two of them that they would hide all the pottery they could manage beneath the copious pelts and other commodities. The trip's destination was also a ruse. Taking as many alternate routes as possible, they would veer off to Veracruz, shipping as much of their merchandise as shipping companies would take for markets in Spain and other eastern destinations. That included a newly found market in New Orleans.

The plan covertly disseminated to the public was that the mule train would leave the day after Luisito's funeral. In reality, in the dead of the night before that sorrowful event, as much of the pottery as they could fit was loaded with all the family's savings, paltry as they'd now become, contained in most of them. By morning, when suspicious eyes were upon them, they were placing the other cargo atop the ceramics, well camouflaged beneath mountains of pelts and other items. They would actually depart in the wee hours the night after the funeral.

As they packed, they created the hiding places for Arreola and his family they had previously planned. Their theory worked, with minor adjustments, perfectly.

The two disagreed about telling Papaplotl and Axochitl. Arreola prevailed, explaining—which of course Don Tomás understood—that he could not simply leave them in the lurch. When he did inform them, they begged him to take them with him. Quietly ardent was Axochitl, who had fallen in love with José Necahuatl during the time he taught her Castilian.

In truth, the attraction was mutual. Axochitl appeared to be a *mestiza* like he, although even if she were pure Indian, it would have made absolutely no difference to him. Her mother was almost certain that the man that had engendered her was none other than José Maximiliano de Cos de Asunción, the master of the hacienda on which she'd lived. Although it could also have been his eldest son, José Antonio.

This Indian maiden had the commanding quiet of those who have little doubt of their own abilities. By the end of the very first day, she sat at the potter's wheel as though she had been born there. Her concentration as her delicate hands with long, all-embracing fingers sculpted the clay drew from José Necahuatl his first twinges of affection. As their feelings for each other blossomed, Arreola found her all-encompassing focus and sensual handling of the clay truly erotic.

In part, José's reaction stemmed from Axochitl's passion for her craft. As her hands and fingers alternately caressed and firm-ly molded the spinning clay, the tactile concupiscence of it wove fleeting phallic images that, until she could distract herself, began to affect the vase or olla or cup she was fashioning. The process even engendered in her ephemeral uterine sensations she struggled to control.

"That will be exceedingly difficult," Don Tomás regretfully explained in reference to the two women's request. "The hiding places are already set for the family, and any suspicious eye might very well ferret them out. Any more would be too obvious, and if they visibly joined the train, it would immediately betray our scheme."

Arreola, however, was already brainstorming how they could manage to include the two. "Don Tomás, we are down one man for treason. We have arranged for all your wagons and mules and your two ponies for the journey. Could we not put one of them on the horse that Alfredo doesn't ride since it's now free? The other could ride on the buckboard without raising suspicion."

"Not raise suspicion? They're women!"

"Not if we dress them as men. Besides, we'll be leaving in the early hours when most will still be asleep. They would raise no alarm on the way, either, if they stay disguised."

Don Tomás quickly acquiesced with a smile, as he'd become suspicious of the amorous feelings shared by his adopted son and Axochitl. "That might very well work."

*T*he journey went surprisingly well with only one assault between San Juan del Rio, where they turned off in the direction of Veracruz, and Pachuca. The bandits carried off all they could handle but the members of the train were, at least at first, unharmed, the pottery undiscovered.

The women had been instructed to always wear their wide-brimmed sombreros and ponchos to cloak their feminine attributes precisely in anticipation of such surprise assaults. Arreola was now riding with Don Tomás on the buckboard as he would hardly be recognized this far from Guanajuato state. His sisters and mother were confined to their hiding places in three different wagons.

It turned out, however, that the stratagem concerning Papaplotl and Axochitl was unfortunately contravened. When the train was just starting to resume their journey, Axochitl, this journey being her first experience on horseback, inadvertently startled her pony. Perhaps it was out of fear of being discovered or relief at having escaped detection that her kick was more forceful than was needed.

The horse bolted forward, allowing her poncho to fall back against her chest. The bulges there exposed alerted the bandits' leader to her true gender. He immediately gave the order to his men to halt the train and then dismounted and pulled Axochitl from her horse, wrenching away her poncho and thereby revealing her femininity for all to see.

"Ah, *Señorita*," he lasciviously muled, "why do you hide your lusciousness from me?"

Arreola immediately reached for his pistol hidden in the buckboard of the leading wagon. Don Tomás stopped him with a hand on his wrist. There were almost twenty in the group of highwaymen, all with loaded rifles and pistols in their belts. Don Tomás would use his negotiating skills with the leader, whose intentions were obvious.

"Please sir, she is not a *señorita* but a *señora*, married to my foster son, José here," he said, taking the gun himself and surreptitiously hiding it beneath his poncho. He was gambling that the leader valued his life above the satisfaction of his prurient urges.

He went to the back of the wagon, lifted up the pelts it carried and reached into a secreted olla, taking from it a wad of bills. "Now," he said showing the money and revealing the pistol as he approached the lustful bandit. He trained the pistol directly on the leader's heart. "If I kill you, your followers will of course kill all of us. But then, you would still be dead. Not a pleasant prospect," he said with a smile.

All the other bandits had aimed their pistols at the old man. "Your band could shoot me first, of course, but let me warn you, my pistol has a very light trigger and I have been shot before and still my aim was true and deadly."

"On the other hand, I have here almost one hundred pesos that I would offer in exchange for the girl. That way, you would still have your life and you would be considerably richer: a decidedly more pleasant prospect. Would you prefer being alive and rich or abjectly poor as the dead invariably are? And no one in the history of man has been able to satisfy those masculine urges from the grave."

Utter silence reigned as the leader considered his options. In the time Don Tomás had stopped his foster son from the suicidal act he was about to perform, the leader had put down his own pistol with the intention of satisfying his lecherous intentions upon Axochitl. Don Tomás exchanged it for the money he had offered, leaving the latter in place of the pistol, and now had two pistols trained on the bandit's heart.

The bandit looked into the eyes of the old man who responded to the gesture with an aspect of ice-cold determination. The bandit recognized in that look that there could be no doubt that this old man would follow through with his threat without the slightest hesitation. He started to pick up the money and head for his horse.

"Ah, ah, ah!" Don Tomás cautioned, "Once you're out of danger I know you'll sick your men on me. Therefore, if you accept my offer, you will have to send your men away first, and *far* away, before I can let you go yourself. I trust you understand," he said with a deadly close-lipped smile.

The head of the cadre of bandits looked up at his men. "*¡Váyanse!*" he ordered his troops to skedaddle. "Take the treasure back to our camp. I'll follow once this *valiente* keeps his end of the bargain." They hesitated a moment. "*Now!*" he issued the order in no uncertain terms, and it was immediately obeyed.

After the band of thieves were clearly out of sight, its captain smiled menacingly at Don Tomás. "You have quite a pair of *huevos* old man. If we ever chance to meet again, you can be assured that I'll repay this little trick of yours."

"Then it is my fondest hope that that unhappy event will never occur. Now, take the money and be off with you." The bandit did so, mounted his horse with a snicker and followed his companions.

Don Tomás turned to his partner and foster son. "Now, we make tracks!" And off they went, galloping the mules and horses until they reached Pachuca, stayed there in relative safety for a few days, poorer by ninety-two pesos—a considerable sum.

*T*he partners had thought it more likely that they would be assailed somewhere between Pachuca and Xalapa or from there to Veracruz. Bandit gangs know there are easy pickings from mule trains going to Veracruz with shipments bound for the East. Instead, the only difficulty they had to deal with was a fierce storm coming off the Gulf. It did some damage to the top layer of pelts, but the rest were salvaged in saleable condition.

Once in Veracruz, they stopped at the market figuring they might be able to peddle some items retail. At the docks it would be wholesale, at prices much below those of the central plaza.

While they were in the midst of setting up their goods for trade, an event occurred that changed the fortunes of them all. A fight broke out between two of the other vendors, presumably over territory—whose stall was whose.

Arreola and Alfredo moved to break it up just as one pulled a pistol out of his belt. The other quickly followed suit. The one who fired first thankfully missed his target and all the others there, owing to the fact that all had hunkered down from the moment the gun was pulled. Apparently, such altercations were not particularly uncommon.

Unfortunately, the report of the first pistol caused Axochitl's horse to rear and, having little experience as an equestrian, the rider was thrown back to the ground. Both Arreola and Alfredo went immediately to her aid. As she was assuring them that she was quite alright, the second *pistolero* let loose with his weapon, again missing its target by a wide margin. That was all the other horses and mules could stand.

Arreola managed to keep Axochitl's horse from bolting and Don Tomás and Alfredo with their years of experience were able to quickly gain control of the mules. A horse and buggy with a very dignified and obviously rich doña and what looked to be her daughter, however, took off in startled fury, yanking the reins from the *dama*'s hands.

The two ladies' screams of terror aroused Arreola's sense of chivalry and without a thought, he jumped on the horse that had thrown Axochitl and went headlong after the runaway buggy. It was a considerable stroke of luck that he had learned how to handle a horse during his years of rebellion with Father Hidalgo and then working the mule train with Don Tomás.

Pushing the horse at breakneck speed, he managed, after a hair-raising few minutes, to pull alongside the buggy's horse. At first, he tried to grab hold of the reins, but could only manage to take one in hand. It quickly escaped him.

He then put his left foot up on his horse's saddle and managed to jump onto the runaway horse, almost falling beneath it to what would have been a fairly certain serious injury or even death. As he pulled himself up, he felt something strange about his right ankle, but his attention was completely focused on stopping the horse.

He managed to find the reins and gently pulled on them, trying not to spook the horse even more. At the same time, in as soothing a voice as he could manage with adrenalin coursing through him at a feverish pace, he called "Whoa, boy, *tranquilo*. Eeeasy. Whoooaah."

It took a dash of more than a hundred meters, but finally the pony began to slow and gradually come to a stop. Arreola spent some time ensuring the horse was completely calm, stroking its neck and soothing it with a loving tone of voice. The ladies in the buggy—a quite well-appointed one with cushioned seats and sides—were in a state of shock and merely held onto each other as Arreola dismounted.

When he landed, he was suddenly made aware of what that odd feeling in his right foot was. It and he crumbled to the ground like a sack of potatoes. The ankle was broken. He sat a moment on the ground trying to decide how he might be able to hobble his way over to the two ladies to check on their condition.

Before he could rise, they were on either side of him. The daughter threw her arms around him and hugged him so hard that for a moment she cut off his breathing. On his other side, her mother was examining the ankle. "Your ankle is broken, *caballero*. We will take you to our hacienda and pick up the doctor on the way. Are you in much pain?"

As he looked up to answer, Alfredo and Axochitl came up beside them. With one look, she could see the condition of José's ankle and immediately went in search of pieces of wood that could be used to stabilize his lower leg. Alfredo instinctively joined her, and they quickly found suitable props.

Despite the pain rather dominating his attention, Arreola sensed an air of authority in the elder of the two ladies he'd just rescued. "In the back of our buggy there are bolts of cloth you can use to wrap the splints," the elegant doña advised Alfredo and Axochitl.

In two steps Axochitl was at the buggy. "But...this is all brand-new material."

"We just bought them at the market. And I can think of no better use for them. Bring them."

So, while the ladies set about tearing the cloth into suitable strips to secure the splint, Alfredo tried to find the most comfortable way he could lift Arreola's leg for the procedure. "Does this hurt too much, *hermano*?"

"No, no. It's...fine," he answered with a wince.

His leg stabilized, Arreola was put in the back seat of the carriage. He had once or twice seen a buggy with a back seat but never one so richly cushioned in such finely polished leather. And with a roof, no less!

"You saved my and my daughter's lives, *Señor*. My husband will reward you handsomely."

"Oh please, *Señora*. Anyone would have done the same. I—"

"But no others did, and if they had, very few would have been successful. You will stay on our hacienda until you're completely recovered. You will have the best doctor in the state of Veracruz—maybe the best in all Mexico. My husband and I will see to that."

"As will I," her daughter added. "I'm María Josefina López de Santa Anna. And you, sir?"

"De Santa Anna? Your father is…?"

"Antonio López de Santa Anna, yes," the *dama* answered.

Chapter XIII

The central conservative truth is that it is culture,
not politics, that determines the success of a society.
The central liberal truth is that politics can change
a culture...

--Daniel Patrick Moynihan

This Constitution is likely to be administered for a
couple of [hundred] years and then end in despotism...
when the people shall become so corrupted as to need
despotic government, being incapable of any other.

--Benjamin Franklin

I woke up shivering a bit even though I found myself covered with a blanket. How'd I get back here in the...? Then I remembered: I'd started to fall asleep up in the buckboard and almost went over the side. I was only saved by Miss Luz's vice-like grip on my shoulder pulling me back up.

She pretty much ordered me back here in the wagon to sleep. I tried to get her to let me stay with her up front, feeling kind of bad her being all by herself driving the mules. She's sure got a commanding way about her, though. "I have enough to do driving the mules without having to worry about you going head-first onto the ground—or worse, into the mules. Go on, sleep. *Now.*"

So that's what I did. There were sacks of grain to use as a sort of pillow. Then I noticed that my mother had taken the idea of using the bags of grain as a sort of mattress for Mister Macalister for herself and little Amelia. There were just enough of them for me to do the same—a lot nicer than the hard wood floor of the cart.

The only thing that I could think of that could bother my sleep was that horrible smell coming from Mister Macalister. But nah, as soon as my head found that grain sack, I was out like a light. I imagine it was my mother who must have woken up during the night and put the blanket over me. I wonder how she managed that tending to little Amelia and Mister Macalister at the same time.

It was predawn, but as I rose up and looked over the side of the wagon, a soothing peel of reddish-orange glow sleepily peeked out above the eastern horizon. I felt like I was wrapped in a blanket of birdsong, with peeps and cheeps and warbles of every kind you could imagine. I wondered where they all came from and where they roost, this part of Texas being so dry and bare.

I saw one, a blackbird with a garish yellow head and neck. It's song, if you could call it that, sounded like a singer with laryngitis, a hoarse and scratchy, "ee*yeoww*" like. Then there was the champion singer Miss Luz told me was called a mockingbird, because it imitates the songs of all the other birds it hears. She even heard one imitate a horse's whinny, and even the squeaky wheel of a wagon. She says that during the spring, when they're trying to find a mate, they'll sometimes sing all night.

Boy, I know that feeling. I wonder if I'll ever meet a gal for me. I'm sure rarin' to go.

I guess I must've gotten somewhat used to the smell coming from Mister Macalister's leg during the night as it didn't seem to be bothering me as much as it had been. I sleepily turned around and there was my mother, wide awake and smiling down at me, little Amelia snuggled in her lap, the little one's head barely poking out from the tightly secured blanket of love and tenderness wrapped around her.

It again made me think of my own little sister, Elzbieta, poor little baby-girl. I do miss her. Perhaps little Amelia was a gift God sent to my mother and me as a replacement. I could tell Mama had already made the child her own. And from the way little Amelia lay so safe and secure in her arms it seemed the feeling was mutual.

"Good morning, Johann," my mother said to me in Polish.

"*Dzien dobrze*," I answered her in kind.

"*Buenos días, hijo. Guten tag*, Rosalía," came from Miss Luz up front. "Are you hungry?"

"Oh boy, hungry ain't the word for it," I answered for both of us. We hadn't stopped for even one meal since we put Mister Macalister in the wagon.

"Look here in my bag," she said as she passed a canvas bag that looked like it had seen better days back to us. "There's beef jerky and a food called pemmican I learned from the Indians. Not a Camp Cookie hot meal but something that will stick to your ribs."

I handed some to my mother first. "Oh, what's in it?" I asked Miss Luz.

"You should probably try it before I tell you, but fat, dried meat and whatever else is handy: dried fruit—I use mesquite beans, prickly pear fruit—nuts, corn flour, and wild onions when I can find them."

I took a small taste. "Hey, it ain't bad."

"It's better in a stew, or fried up with onions and potatoes, but if you can't stop, it will fill you up till you get where you're going." She tried to look back in the wagon. "Is my brother awake?"

I looked over at Mister Macalister. "Uh no, he don't seem to be. He's even snoring a bit."

"Good. See that your mother and Amelia eat some of whatever's in my bag."

I saw my mother put some of the pemmican aside for Amelia when she wakes up as she hungrily attacked some herself. "My mother's eating some now, and Amelia isn't awake yet. But Miss Luz, what about you?"

"I ate during the night. I'm fine."

"You got to be pretty tired, though." I crawled up onto the buckboard with her as I ate. "Why don't you get some rest and let me…" I stopped myself, realizing that I had no idea how to get to Fort Concho.

With smiling eyes, probably knowing that I recognized the folly of what I was going to suggest, she said, "I'm all right, *hijo*. I appreciate the company, though. You can help keep me awake. I'd hand you the reins but driving the mules helps me stay awake as well."

"How soon do you think we can make it there?"

"I'm hoping by mid-afternoon." She was quiet a moment, but I felt like she had more to say. Then, she softly added, "I just hope it will make a difference."

The way she said it made me feel like she wasn't particularly hopeful, and I was surprised by how sad that made me feel. It even scared me a little, and I wondered why that would be. I mean, I was always a bit concerned about how I'd fit into the family. What would be my place? But without Mister Macalister in charge...?

Of course, Miss Luz had made me feel welcome from the get-go—like I was a member of the family. Mister Macalister was more reserved, but I got a good feeling from him without words. It was the way he showed me how to shoot a rifle, ride and care for a horse, service a wagon and mule-team. There was like a *care* in it.

There was nothing sentimental in the way he taught me, though. Matter of fact, he was pretty direct telling me when I messed up, but...I don't know, I could just feel that there was concern in his teaching me the skills I needed to have to be able to survive out here where we're going—where we are.

I didn't mind, either. Judging by that Indian raid I could see that things out here need be done right, right from the start and lots of times without even having to think about it. I remembered the way Miss Luz positioned the wagon and got me to cover like it was pure instinct.

I turned back to look at Mister Macalister. I was sure hoping that Miss Luz was wrong fearing the worst. Maybe the doctor at Fort Concho might know more what to do. I sure wish my brother Alex was here. He always seemed to know a lot about medical issues. Maybe he'll become a doctor.

"It's kind of ironic, you know," Miss Luz said out of the blue. "All the injuries my brother has suffered—and he's been in constant pain as a result of them—the torture at the hands of the Comanches, the wound after wound he suffered fighting them, and most of all what happened to him at Goliad, that that one arrow in the side of his thigh..."

She stopped herself, and I had a feeling as to why, so I didn't need her to finish. I tried to think of something to ask her that might get her mind off Mister Macalister's condition. "Miss Luz, uh…when you first came to Texas it was a Mexican territory, right?"

"Spanish. It only became Mexican after Mexico gained its independence."

"Well…how'd that change? I mean, did the United States just take it over? Was there a war?"

Miss Luz let out a kind of ironic "Humph" and then thought for a while. I just respected the silence, figuring it must be a complicated subject—maybe even a painful one.

"From the very first Anglo who set foot in Texas territory, even accepting Mexican citizenship and promising to live as a loyal Mexican, the project was bound to fail. Just the fact that they would come to such an isolated, desolate and dangerous place of their own free will and by themselves… It was evidence of a culture so different from the Spanish/Mexican that Mexico's sovereignty was doomed from that very moment.

"I had a unique experience, being raised in both cultures. There was no possibility that people so independent-minded could adapt themselves to the hierarchical Spanish system. The Latin culture is one of deference to authority, of membership in the hive, of rulers and ruled. All ideas that didn't come from the top were discarded as worthless. No, they were actually never even considered.

"To the Latin mind, self-governance was next door to anarchy and the state of brute animals. There was a recognition that that independent spirit, that tendency toward self-governance was a threat, a very potent threat, to Mexican sovereignty. How do you keep a people capable of governing themselves loyal to another to whom deference to a superior was as natural as breathing? It was so different from the Anglo way.

"Spain first and then Mexico tried in many ways to colonize Texas, to populate all the territories they both claimed as part of their empires. Because there were so few volunteers, they forced convicts and deserters from the army to establish colonies or add to the population of existing communities.

"Eventually, almost all of those conscripts found their way back to the populated areas of Mexico. Many of those that did not of course went back to their old ways and were imprisoned for various crimes. There were exceptions, certainly, but even the Mexicans who stayed tended to stay in the cities: San Antonio, Nacogdoches, Goliad, where there were many of their own kind.

"There were some who tried to form a self-governing republic, both when it was Spanish and then Mexican territory. But when the culture of such deference is so pervasive, the need to belong so powerful, there just wasn't that...what's the word?...necessary mass to achieve its spread."

"What do you think made the two people so different?"

"I'm afraid that's beyond my abilities to say. Was it religion? Philosophy? Geography? Something in their physical makeup? I just know that I felt more like the Anglos than the Mexicans—or, than most Mexicans. Even though I ached at being all alone after the massacre, there was still a hint of pleasure at the adventure. I found some...excitement in it.

"Is it inherent in the Latin nature to balk at striking out on their own? Or did centuries of iron-fisted rule, like the Inquisition, the absolute monarchies, just drive the spirit of daring out of them? Was it the difference in climate? Who can say? There were the conquistadores, but even they came as a throng to conquer for the glory of Spain.

"What was it in the Anglo culture that impelled so many of them to strike out on their own, no matter the danger? It's obviously not in all Anglos as there were certainly those who stayed in the safer areas of the country. It was just, again, that critical mass."

It looked like Miss Luz paused to ponder the questions she'd just laid out, so I tried to figure them myself. I'm sure Alex would have a thought or two about it. That reminded me. "My brother Alex told me that there was a war for independence. Did Mister Macalister join the movement?"

"Not...right away." Miss Luz smiled at the thought. "That was the one time my brother surprised me. When the resentments and conflicts started to bubble up, I think Gerardo was tired of fighting. He'd fought other tribes and gone on raids with the Comanches, which I know he hated. That's part of the reason he escaped the first chance we had—that, and to save me. Then, we fought not just Comanches but the Apache, Kiowa and other tribes. Comanches were the most barbaric, though.

"I think he was sick of it—sick of the killing, sick of young bucks under his command being killed—even though he knew that there are times when it's necessary...unavoidable, really. And he never hesitated when it was.

"We had gone to a new settlement called Liberty in the eastern part of the state—well, it was a Mexican province then, seeking a parcel of land to farm and ranch. It was there that an incident occurred that made Gerardo want to avoid all conflict and, ironically, made it clear he could not."

"How's that, Miss Luz?"

"Just at that time, the Mexican government decreed that there could be no more immigration from the United States and its Territories—specifically, no more Anglo immigration. People from other countries were welcome.

"But it was too late. Texas was now predominantly Anglo. They had their own schools. They practiced their own faith although they'd also sworn an oath to convert. I think people naturally revert to their own religion. They organized themselves according to their own standards, which were directly opposed to the Spanish way.

"There was a lot of mutual...what's the word...*disdain*, even hatred. To the Anglos, the Mexicans were haughty on the one hand and disgustingly slavish on the other. To the Spanish culture, the Anglos were barbarians with no sense of place, of order and propriety.

"So the Mexican government sent in the army to enforce the order. From that point on, war was inevitable. Families with members still in the United States waiting to emigrate were now to be eternally separated. It was also disastrous business-wise, as growth meant more commerce, the lack of it, stagnation.

"There were meetings, petitions and protests. To the Anglo mentality those actions are as natural as breathing. I believe that that was how the United States was formed. To the Spanish/Mexican mind, however, which knows only subservience or armed rebellion, they were subversive, traitorous. 'Who were these rebellious ingrates? They were here solely because of the generosity of the Mexican State! They should show respect and gratitude to their gracious hosts!' That was the general point of view.

"When the military came, they came with that attitude. They had no experience with self-governing peoples and saw it as a threat. They were right, too. Self-governance is a major step on the way to independence—at least, in any Mexican territory.

I think it comes from the individual being the main unit of society rather than the collective. As a group of individuals, you impose rules on yourselves. Bees in a hive have no individual choice; everything is done for the sake of the hive.

"I saw first-hand in Liberty how the Mexican officers swaggered about issuing arbitrary orders, arresting people for minor offenses, even for not showing the respect and deference they felt was their due. They declared martial law on a whim. All of this was common practice in Mexico. For the Anglo, though, it was an outrage. Especially since the majority considered the Mexicans an inferior race.

"Ironically, the officer the Mexican army sent into liberty was an Anglo who had taken on Mexican citizenship, a Captain Juan Bradburn. I wonder if it was because he was Anglo that he was particularly cruel. Was he trying to prove himself a more loyal Mexican than those native-born? Or did he just have the sort of character that made him fit neatly into that rigid, hierarchical system?

"When he marched his troops into Liberty, he immediately abolished the settlement. He ignored all civil authority in the region and redistributed the land grants himself. I watched how he treated all the civilians—including the Mexicans—with utter contempt. Any protest or petition was met with public whippings, even hangings.

"One time he'd just come back from the coast where he'd gone to enforce the newly instituted customs duties. A girl was attending her father who was chained to a whipping post in the town square. Who knows how long he'd been there? She had given him some food and had just filled a cup from the town pump and was letting him drink.

"Bradburn broke from his troops and ran his horse right at her as she turned. He actually knocked her down, knocking the cup out of her hands. I started to go help her, but Gerardo stopped me and went himself. He helped her up, dusted her off and, looking straight at Captain Bradburn, refilled the cup at the pump. Then he gave it to her and escorted her back to her father.

"I was very concerned. People were being hanged for less. Sure enough, Bradburn angrily dismounted and started toward the girl. My brother stepped in the way. I and everyone watching held our breath. No one had ever stood up to Bradburn. Even minor offenses were punished as this girl's father was.

"Bradburn stopped, and he and my brother just stared at each other for the longest time. I was sure the captain would have Gerardo arrested—if not just summarily shot.

"But something happened. You know how powerful my brother's look can be when he's angry. The mistreatment of women was something that made him seethe. As they continued their stand-off, I could sense a hesitation in Captain Bradburn. Was he afraid of my brother? With his whole platoon behind him? Did Gerardo's intervention somehow shame him into acknowledging that he had been a cad? Was there that tiny bit of honor left in him?

"Whatever goes through a bully's mind when someone finally stands up to him, Bradburn, without a word, just withdrew and mounted his horse. As he continued on his way with his troops behind him, he trained his gaze forward, never glancing back at Gerardo or to the side at the crowd.

"'*Danke. Eh, tank you,*' the young lady said to Gerardo. She started to go back to her father but stopped herself as my brother tipped his hat and just looked into her eyes. I think most young girls would have been shy about holding a man's stare, even one who'd just saved her from certain punishment. But she just stared back into his eyes with her lips curled up in the tiniest smile.

"'You're welcome ma'am,' my brother answered. 'Please let me get you some more water for your…is this your father?'

"*Ja,* he is,' she answered."

A broad smile broke across Miss Luz's face as she recalled the scene. "Gerardo just stood there for a moment, kind of mesmerized. When he finally came to himself…It was the first time I'd ever seen him so awkward. "'I'll, uh…I'll be right back,'" he kind of sputtered out. "'It's, uh…it's just right over here. I'll just, uh…'

"It struck me right then that I'd never known my brother to ever stammer or be unsure of himself in any situation. I don't think there are many men in this world who could get the best of him." At this, a satisfied chuckle escaped Miss Luz. "But I could see with this girl that he'd finally met his match."

I smiled myself thinking about that. It was hard to imagine Mister Macalister thrown off his horse like that.

"We used some smithing tools to unchain the girl's father," Miss Luz continued. "He was, of course, boundlessly grateful, and with his daughter translating, insisted that my brother and I go back to his home and have supper with them."

"You said the girl first said, '*danke*.'" Was she and her father German?"

"They were. They were German immigrants. Mister Bauer had actually gotten his land grant because he wasn't an Anglo."

"Well then, why'd they whip him?"

"For signing a petition. I doubt he even knew what he was signing, since I'm sure it was in English. Even if Edeline translated it for him, I don't think he really could've understood what it was about, or what the results of signing it would be. Edy could speak English pretty well but learning to read a foreign language is a bit different.

"So, her father already had his league of land. We hoped Bradburn wouldn't take it back as a result of Herr Bauer signing that petition. I guess it turned out he thought the whipping was enough.

"Gerardo and I agreed that I would apply for ours and the title would be in my name. I used my original Spanish name and as a result we got some of the best land available."

"Oh, so is that how you 'n' Mister Macalister came to speak German?"

Her lips curled up into almost a smirk. "I would say I learned enough to hold a conversation. That was probably because I already had two languages—three including Comanche, so another came fairly easily."

She let out a light chuckle. "My brother has many talents. He's a great leader, tracker, hunter, Indian fighter, a fairly good farmer and an even better rancher. His ability with a foreign language, however, was I would say quite limited—and that's being as generous as I can be. He did learn Comanche, of course, but he was still young then."

"I guess you can't be good at everything."

"No, you certainly can't. We each of us have our strengths and weaknesses." She let out a puff of mirth. "What was particularly hard for Gerardo was the pronunciation. At first, Jakob—Herr Bauer—couldn't understand Gerardo when he tried to speak to him in German."

Miss Luz then smiled a *sweet memory* kind of smile. "Edeline always seemed to, though. She was patient with him but never hesitated to correct his mistakes. I think she appreciated the effort. Most people expected everyone to learn English, period.

"And you know, I think that's actually for the best. For every Mexican in Texas at that time there were many, many Anglos. If you couldn't speak English, you really had a hard time doing business, finding a way to make a living and just being part of the community. The lowest classes were always Mexicans who didn't learn to speak English. Those who did, did better. For one thing, they could negotiate with both groups so they could have a larger clientele to do business with or work for.

"I think the inability to communicate breeds distrust, too, and keeps people separate."

"So how'd Mister…Bauer, did you say?"

"Yes, Bauer. You're going to ask me how he managed without learning English."

"Yes, ma'am, I was."

"San Antonio was majority German at that time, so he was able to make his way pretty well without English. As Edeline learned, he could depend on her. I think it gets harder to learn a new language as you get older."

"So did this German gal become Mister Macalister's first wife?"

I wondered why Miss Luz, though smiling at the memory, looked like the happiness was tinctured with a hint of an ache. "Yes, she did. I could tell during that supper with the Bauers that that was pretty much a sure thing. I knew it when we started to excuse ourselves to let Mister Bauer rest. He was falling asleep at the table and manners wouldn't allow him to go to bed with company still there.

"Then Edeline had a rather sharp discussion with him. Although I couldn't understand a word, I had a good idea what it was about since at the end of it Mister Bauer excused himself.

"So I did the same. Gerardo started to get up with me, but I grabbed him by his belt out of anyone's view and held him down. He got the message and stayed. He didn't get back to the rooming house we were staying in 'til the wee hours."

Miss Luz broke into another smile, but again it seemed to have a tiny stitch in it. Maybe she missed her sister-in-law; I imagine she would. "Edeline was perfect for him. She was quiet but no shrinking violet, kind and supportive but firm in her convictions. She actually did most of the accounting and negotiating for all the concerns we were involved in."

"Oh, did you go into business together?"

"We did. It was pretty obvious from the start that Gerardo and Edeline were bound for marriage. So, when we found out our land grants were close to each other, we did a little horse trading with another grantee and got our lands bordering each other and worked them as one farm.

"Jakob was a sharecropper farmer in Germany, Edeline had a good head for business and my brother and I, with Jakob's direction, worked the farm. Edeline, Edy as we called her, told me that her mother, along with a little brother and sister, had died of scarlet fever back in the old country. She and her father had heard about the opportunities in America, and that there was a sizeable colony of Germans in Texas. So, they snuck away and found their way here.

"We built a crude shelter at first with a dog-run between two rooms. We started right away on an extra room for when the families were to be united in marriage."

"Well Miss Luz, how'd you...uh..." I stopped myself, wondering if it was appropriate for me to ask.

She smiled with what looked like a bit of nostalgia. "...How did I fit in?"

"Well...y-yeah," I answered kind of shyly since I felt like I was butting my nose where it didn't belong. "If you don't mind my asking."

"Like a hand in a glove. I finally had some female companionship, we weren't having to fight and kill anymore, and we were far enough east that we were out of hostile Indian territory. With Herr Bauer's knowledge of farming and Edeline's business smarts, it was barely two years before we had a growing concern.

"Of course, there were disagreements here and there—Gerardo was more interested in ranching than farming—but those years were as close to ideal as you can get in this imperfect world."

There was still a distant ache in the way Miss Luz remembered those times which made me curious. Plus, the Macalister ranch was now out west in Comanche territory, so I wondered what had caused the change. "Well, how'd all that change, Miss Luz? What happened?"

Now I was sorry I'd asked because I could tell that discomfort I sensed in Miss Luz now turned into a deeper pain. She was quiet for a long time, and I respected the silence, until finally she just said with a puff of air out her nose,

"The Alamo."

Chapter XIV

The casual right to usurpation and pillage has
enthroned itself in the capital of Mexico and in
the provinces of the Federation. ...allied with
General Santa Anna, the most perverse of mortals.

--Simón Bolívar

Those who dare to undertake the [governance] of a
people must feel themselves capable...of changing human nature,
of transforming each individual...into a part
of a much greater whole...of altering the constitution
of a man for the purpose of strengthening it.

--Jean Jacques Rousseau

We cannot change the Nature of things and
of men, but must act upon them [as they are]
the best we can.

--Edmund Burke

José Nicolás looked up with starvation-exacerbated hate at the man who'd addressed him. The stranger had used his full name, the name that had brought his family to ruin and himself to the most profound dishonor. At first, Nicolás could not see past the uniform. He immediately assumed that the Mexican army had finally come to put an end to his earthly travails.

He considered that possibility with a potent sense of satisfaction, even elation. The thought of death, and not at his own hand, he welcomed with relish. Gone would be the scathing ignominy of his failure as a man to provide for his family. Final relief there would be from the traitor's brand, the hunger, the beggary, the public shame and exclusion from Mexican society.

For his mother and sister, however, this was not so. His death would leave them with the hideous Devil's bargain his sister had so shamefacedly described. To forestall that heinous fate, he would fight to the death.

However, as his gaze came to rest upon the soldier's face, he noted that it was remarkably free of the bitter contempt he expected to find. Indeed, there was rather a kindness totally at odds with his military habiliments. Nicolás then realized that there didn't seem to be the hostility in the stranger's address that would normally accompany such animus.

"What has become of you, José Nicolás, my savior?" the stranger asked.

Savior? thought the now middle-aged José Portilla. *What on earth can this mean?* He wondered if this creature before him might be a hunger-induced hallucination, a palliative trick of the mind to soothe the way toward death by starvation.

But it seemed so real. Somewhere in his debilitated mind there was a vague sense of familiarity with this...apparition, if apparition it was. Nicolás scoured his past for some idea as to the stranger's identity, if he indeed was real. That he used a name Nicolás had abandoned so many years and torturous thoughts ago meant that their paths had to have crossed in the distant past. Try as he might, however, identification remained a mental fingertip out of reach.

"You obviously don't recognize me," the man or spirit continued. "I certainly can't blame you. We met in another lifetime. Perhaps if you picture me not astride this mighty steed but rather on the sorriest burro imaginable. See me not in this officer's uniform but in peasant's attire with my hands bound behind my back."

José Nicolás frowned in confusion as aching hunger and weakness made memory a grasping of the morning mist. There was some vague sense that he should know who this is. The hints the stranger gave seemed to spark some recognition that swam in the muddy swamp of his famine-debilitated mind.

The stranger now dismounted and spoke as he pulled some stale tortillas and jerky from his bag and a blanket from beneath them. "How can you forget the young rebel whose life you saved from the hangman's rope?"

There was little pride left in any of the three members of the de Cos family and they greedily gnawed off, barely even chewed and swallowed the bits of food the soldier provided. The stranger enfolded the two shivering ladies in the blanket and then provided more food for the three.

"I entreat you to slow your consumption of my pitiful offerings and chew them thoroughly before swallowing. You have the look of those who have lost true acquaintance with regular meals, so I fear your stomachs will rebel at only partially masticated victuals."

Gradually as he wolfed down the stranger's offerings, totally ignoring his warnings, José Nicolás' memory began to haltingly coalesce. He cocked his head trying to bring the recollection of this, their deliverer, into focus. *Upon a donkey*, he thought, *with hands bound behind his back.* That would have to mean a procession of rebels, on their way to their execution. That would have been so many years, nay decades, ago.

Finally, the incident pieced itself together into a recognizable form. "At Coahuila!" José Nicolás exclaimed, "at the end of the first rebellion. You were part of the train with Father Hidalgo y Costilla, on its way to their execution. You were the only one in peasant's clothes. But I forget your name. No, wait... It was José, like mine."

"Yes, it is José, like yours. I am José de Arreola, now a colonel in the army of President Antonio López de Santa Anna, preparing to march to the province of Texas in an attempt, which I fear will be futile, to put down a nascent independence movement—which my leader calls a rebellion of pirates."

"So you did join the rebels. After you were spared."

"No, I actually did not. How I got to be a member of the army of General López de Santa Anna is a tale to be told over a real meal, at the house where my wife and I are staying."

"What are you doing in Guanajuato?"

"I am tasked with mustering troops for the adventure in the northern province—a duty I find quite distasteful owing to my pessimism concerning its chances of success. But a soldier must carry out his orders, disagreeable as they may be. I owe my life and the lives of my mother and sisters to the general and president."

"How did that come to be?"

"I will gladly tell you the story, my whole story from the time of my thankfully thwarted execution, but you and your mother and sister, as I presume these to be, need genuine sustenance.

Come on. Our rented apartment isn't far, and it's almost time for supper."

"You actually went to the capital as the President's representative?" an astonished José Nicolás asked.

Supper had just ended and Axochitl was clearing the table. Doña Anastasia and Caridad had risen to help, but the lady of the house insisted that as guests they remain seated and enjoy the conversation. It was the first full meal they'd had in a while, so it wasn't exactly sitting comfortably on their stomachs.

Arreola answered with a rather ironic smile that covered a darker sentiment. "I did, for all the good that came of it."

Caridad, who'd always had an interest in the law and governance, pounced on Arreola's statement. "You weren't successful? What were you trying to accomplish? And why did you leave?"

Arreola smiled sadly. "I left to save my life, and so that my wife and children would have a husband and father."

"I told him it would be safer to be a soldier," Axochitl interjected, very aware of the irony.

"You were threatened? Why?" Caridad continued with what was almost an interrogation.

Arreola sighed. "I think that question goes to the heart of everything that keeps our country so dysfunctional. One can have a polity based on persuasion and if you are outvoted, your recourse is to reconsider your position or modify your message.

"On the other hand, if your concern is a cynical desire for power, the logical stratagem is force, violence or subterfuge—or some combination of the three. How many of our leaders have been assassinated or exiled? How many of them gained the presidency by their own rebellions or acts of sabotage?

"I think it is the result of short-term thinking. In the immediacy of violence or deception, one may attain one's immediate goal. It creates in its wake, however, a generalized state where such behavior may be turned on the original offender—and at any rate makes effective governance impossible."

Arreola sighed. "I don't know. Perhaps it is as the *Libertador* has said, 'There is no good faith in America, not among nations. The treaties are papers, the elections are combats.'"

"And why do you think that is, Don José?" Caridad pressed.

Arreola took a deep breath and paused in an effort to organize his thoughts. "When I went to Mexico City as a representative of our president, I went with all the political philosophy I'd learned at the hand of Father Miguel Hidalgo. Hah! even in that name I find a problematic aspect of Spanish culture. It means—it is short for—'*Hijo de algo*', 'the son of someone of worth', someone that matters—as though all other children are somehow lacking value or importance.

"And beyond that, it is a signal that one's worth is not in what one does, but in who he is, and more to the point, who his parents were and the very fickle fortune of where he was born. I think that legacy of a person's merit being determined by the accident of birth—as opposed to character, ability and accomplishment—is the central toxin that rots the very soul of Mexican society.

"Without some sort of meritocracy, where people of talent and intelligence can realize at least some of their potential—and in the process, benefit all society with their contributions—they learn to cheat. That, I believe, is especially true as they see their supposed betters making a total mess of things and cheating at every turn."

"Could you find no others to join you in working for the good of the country?" Caridad asked.

"Oh, there were true patriots—quite a few, actually, to differing degrees. But the critical mass…while they'd listen and agree when I quoted Montesquieu on the separation of powers or Madison or Wilson on finding the right balance of those powers, once on their own, most would revert to their old ways, their narrowly conceived self-interest; most certainly as they saw others doing the same.

A moment of silence ensued as each member of the gathering considered Arreola's words. It was broken by an incredulous José Nicolás. "Something I don't understand, Colonel Arreola. How can the president's own representative be threatened? Did not such an exalted position provide you with an air of protection?"

"Nicos, my friend, I think you've hit upon the very core effect of what ails this country. It is true that President López de Santa Anna stays in Veracruz on his hacienda because he loves to rule, to wield power, but finds actual governing supremely boring—annoying even."

Axochitl jumped in with a warning for her husband. In order to keep it private, she delivered it in Nahua: "Be careful what you say about the President, husband."

Arreola acknowledged her caution in Castilian. "Yes, my love, thank you for reminding me." Then, in Nahua, he added a brief "But I believe it's safe considering our guests' history."

He then continued with his assessment. "In addition to that proclivity of our president, I have the suspicion that he also recognizes the potent danger in actually taking up the reins of government—exposure to rebellion, even the prospect of assassination. And if the President himself is not safe, then pity his lowly representative."

"So, how did you manage to avoid the plot?" Nicolás continued. "And how were they planning to avoid the wrath of our president? Surely he would have avenged your assassination."

"Hmm, perhaps. But I don't think you realize how expendable we factotums are. As to my escape, I was warned in advance by a like-minded member of the constitutional convention. He just happened to have a spy among an opposing faction.

"The plan was to make it look like a simple case of robbery. I often walked home at night, sometimes quite late, to clear my head after a day, often a very long day, of persuading, cajoling, inveigling—insisting, when I thought I could get away with it—and generally pounding my head against a stone wall."

"But you succeeded in creating a constitution, did you not?" Caridad demanded.

"Yes. It was one based quite closely on that of the United States. I had high hopes it might lift us out of the mire of constant rebellions and coups and counter-coups."

"Perhaps it will," Caridad said a trifle defensively.

"Yes, hope must spring eternal, I suppose. However, I fear that even with the most perfect document in the world, a society must have a critical majority willing to live within its precepts. Remember that, irony of ironies, the Republic was recently overthrown in the name of the Republic!"

"And yet you follow our president to Texas. You muster troops for him, despite your pessimism as to its outcome. Why?" Nicolás asked.

"A very good question, my friend. When we arrived in Veracruz, we had only our wares, and precious few of those owing to banditry and bad weather. Our host went beyond whatever he felt he owed me for saving his wife and daughter. He gave me employment on his hacienda, eventually making me foreman."

"He listened when you suggested he actually pay his workers," Axochitl pointed out. "And consequently, increased his own wealth to a considerable degree."

"He also sent you to Mexico City as his representative," Doña Anastasia added.

"So it is a debt you feel you owe him?" Nicolás pressed.

"That is...part of it." Arreola seemed to gaze far into the distance in a moment of introspection. "My mind tells me the expedition is ill-fated, but... I must confess a perhaps irrational attachment to Mexico and its people and, right or wrong, an impulse to come to its aid."

"Why are you so doubtful of its success?" Caridad questioned. "Texas is ours, is it not?"

"By legal principle, yes it is. However, when a people of a culture so different from ours come to dominate an area, and it's my understanding that for every Mexican there are ten Anglos there, the principle becomes muddied."

"How did that come to be?" Doña Anastasia asked. "Did the United States government send them? Why did we allow that?"

"No, actually. Our own government invited them, on the condition that they adopt Mexican citizenship and convert to Catholicism. Because we could get so few of our own to settle the land. And they came totally on their own, with no help from their government."

"Then they are Mexican citizens. And traitors," Caridad averred.

"Technically, I suppose that's true. But remember that Mexico, until very recently by historical standards, was a part of the Spanish Empire, as the United States was a part of the British."

"And why *is* that, Colonel? What is the difference between us that they settled the land that we could not?" Nicolás pursued the topic.

Arreola took a deep breath and let out a profound sigh. "Another excellent question, José Nicolás. And I struggle to answer it." He took a moment looking up in an effort to gather his thoughts. "I wonder, ultimately, if it is a question of the power of individual initiative. All of those Anglos came as individuals or individual families, facing isolation, estrangement from their kind, risking failure and even death in the hopes of creating something of their own.

"Where does that adventuresome spirit come from? I have no answer for that. But I think that to us, Texas is a piece of land, a part of the Mexican empire. To them, it is their home. And even the lowliest animal will fight for his home."

At Arreola's seemingly final assessment, a gray cloud of silence descended upon the table. Axochitl was more aware of the physical and mental state of their guests than her husband and took advantage of the interlude. "Doña Anastasia, Caridad and Don José, I can only imagine the exhaustion you must be feeling as a result of your recent troubles. Why don't you take advantage of our parlor and retire for the night? I've already put out blankets and pillows for your comfort.

Doña Anastasia was quite surprised, even shocked, at this further offer of hospitality. "Oh, but Axo…" she started, but then, in a sudden recognition of her own prejudices, corrected herself, "… but Doña Axochitl, we have already too much imposed on your generosity. We cannot—"

But she was cut off by Arreola, "Yes, Doña Anastasia, you can. If it weren't for your son, Don José Nicolás de Cos de la Portilla, I would have had the majority of my life cut off at the tender age of twenty—and, I might add, in a most…*disagreeable* manner. I would never have met my beautiful wife or had the enormous pleasure of seeing ourselves reincarnated in the gift of a child."

"We insist," Axochitl said with a finality that permitted no resistance.

José Nicolás then stood to deliver the following: "Don José de Arreola, you have saved us from a fate worse than death. Whatever debt you felt you had in my favor I consider paid a thousand times over."

There was a sense that Nicolás' statement was a prelude to something. "I have no earthly right to ask any more but ask I must: Now that the final war for independence is, I at least hope, a fading memory, is there any possibility that your commander, our President, might allow me to join his army on this campaign in the north—even as the lowliest soldier?"

There was an enigmatic look on Arreola's face as he answered. "No, my friend, I'm afraid that would be altogether impossible."

Axochitl frowned, wondering why her husband had to deliver the bad news so brusquely.

José Nicolás was not in the least offended or even surprised. His only thought was that his employment as a soldier might save his mother and sister from the devil's choice between starvation and—in his mind—a fate even more unthinkable.

However, the brief and tentative wind in his sails provided by his benefactor's rescue suddenly reversed itself into a contrary gust that pushed him back into the doldrums of despair. The feeling then coalesced into a leaden ball in the pit of his stomach that he fought valiantly to keep from exiting its rebellious setting.

Doña Anastasia sensed the pike of hopelessness that pierced her son's entrails and reached for his hand. It now lay cold in unbridled despondency at his side. She squeezed, hoping for some reciprocal gesture of consolation, but it lay as flat and moribund as the future they both foresaw for themselves.

But José de Arreola had not finished and the stern look with which he had delivered the initial message softened into a gentle smile. "As my adjutant, however, a man of your character and military experience would be an invaluable contribution to my retinue."

For a moment, Nicolás was not sure he had heard correctly. Then Arreola's cheerful demeanor finally drove the message home.

It was as though the whole room inflated to bursting with such an airiness that each could feel him- or herself slightly lifted off their chair. Axochitl smiled and gently shook her head at the little game her husband had played on their guest.

Nicolás had to fight back tears of relief and gratitude. For an embarrassed moment he could not speak. Then finally gaining some control over himself, all he could manage was a guttural "General Arreola, I am speechless before your generosity."

"Not generosity, sir. It is purely self-interest that prompts me to seek an experienced soldier that I can trust by my side." Before any of the three could respond further, Arreola managed to put an end to the evening: "And now as my dear wife has made me aware, I can see that the three of you are at the point of falling asleep in your chairs. Please do as she so wisely suggests and take your rest. It's a far cry from luxury but it at least is sheltered from the wind and weather. We won't be far behind."

*I*t was not long after Arreola joined his wife in after-supper chores, that he could hear the steady breathing and even mild snoring from their house guests.

The first time he engaged in such domestic labors, Axochitl felt slightly insulted, as though he didn't trust her to perform such tasks correctly. As he continued doing so, however, she came to see that his real motivation was simply to share with her in every aspect of their life together.

Most astonishing to her was the first time he got up in the middle of the night to attend to their crying first-born child. On that occasion, she hurried him back to bed saying, "Mi amor, the child is hungry, and you have no means of feeding him. I do."

He paid heed to his wife's directive but cheerfully participated in all other aspects of caring for their son. On their present travels, they had left him in the care of Axochitl's mother and

Don Tomás, who had passed his transport company on to his son. Don Tomás had grown old and frail, but Arreola knew he could count on him and Papaplotl to care for the child as though he were their own. Besides, he had two doting aunts in Veronica and Patricia.

At any rate, they missed their little one terribly and were anxious to get back to him. Axochitl wondered if it was that that had made her husband so taciturn as he dried and put away the dinnerware. She put her arms around him from behind as she spoke. "What is it that troubles you, my love?"

He thought of brushing off the question, saying it was just a silence of satisfaction, but was aware that his wife knew him too well for the stratagem to succeed. He turned around and returned the embrace ten-fold. Axochitl melted into his strong, passionate caress but still sensed a vague tinge of desperation in it.

Consequently, she slightly separated herself and pulled him by his hands to sit down on a chair as she accommodated herself on one facing him, never letting go of those powerful yet delicate hands. "What is it, love?"

"Oh, it's probably nothing…"

She switched to Náhuatl as it seemed somehow more intimate. "Then why does it trouble you so?"

He followed her lead and continued in the same language. "I miss our son, and with this campaign so far away, I will not see him or you for months, possibly years."

"And…?" is all she answered, sensing that there was more to the story.

"And actually, with this campaign in Texas…" He hesitated to finish.

"…With this campaign in Texas, what?

His answer came with a broken voice. "I…I wonder if I'll ever see you and the boy again."

Now Axochitl pulled him up to standing and hugged him fiercely. "Have faith, my love. Texas is ours, is it not?"

He finally let his doubts express themselves in the violence with which he returned the embrace. "Is it? With the population so one-sided? They say that San Antonio is majority German. Can we—can *any* army—prevail over such a cultural onslaught?"

Axochitl was quiet for a time just clutching her husband with all the strength in those monstrously feminine arms. "Then if we can't defeat them, perhaps we should join them."

Arreola pulled away just enough to look into her eyes, astounded that she had given words to a thought that had rummaged about the underfloor of his own mind. He cupped her face in his hands. "Would you consider such a possibility…uprooting our family, raising our children in such a foreign culture?"

Looking straight back into his eyes, with a firmness of voice that matched her gaze, she said, "I would follow you and bring our children to the ends of the earth."

As he gazed into those eyes that radiated such love, such at once blind and all-seeing devotion, a chill of ecstasy flooded his whole corporeal being as he crushed her to himself. He kissed her passionately, longingly, then lifted her in his arms and carried her to the bedroom.

Chapter XV

This federal republic [the United States] *has been born a pigmy, so to speak. The time will come when she will be a giant, and even a colossus, much to be feared in those regions.*

--Count of Aranda

Poor Mexico, so far from Heaven, so close to the United States.

--Porfirio Díaz

The sun had just passed the meridian, and blazing light blanched the vague bits of color the surrounding vista provided: sandy earth, hay-colored clumps of grass here and there, a pale blue sky made paler by the glare of the sun, bedecked with a few thin wispy patches of white. Save for the haunting sough of the wind and the creak and groan of our wagon, a deathly quiet reigned over the desert. No bird sang, no critter scampered.

I was taken aback by how warm it had gotten compared to the night and especially the early morning. We'd dispensed with blankets by mid-morning and then peeled off whatever coats or sweaters we had on. Sitting there in just my shirt and jeans, I was still rather uncomfortably warm. This Texas weather, aside from that constant wind, sure is full of surprises, so different from Poland. I can see why it's so sere, though. We hadn't seen a drop of rain since we left Saint Hedwig.

I could see the initial traces of that glassy look brought on by sleep-deprivation in Miss Luz's eyes. I sorely wished there were some way I could take over for her—or relieve her in some way. I thought maybe keeping her engaged in conversation might help. I tried to think of something neutral so as not to push my curiosity beyond where it was welcome. "How much do you figure we got to make Fort Concho, Miss Luz?"

"We crossed the San Saba during the night. I'm hoping we can make it in another three or four hours."

"We crossed a river last night?"

"Not a very wide one."

"Boy, I must've been really tired. I'd have thought all the jostling of that would have sure woke me up."

Miss Luz just smiled and said, "It's not very deep either, and you obviously needed the shut-eye."

I was sure hoping that Miss Luz was wrong about the direness of Mister Macalister's condition. I'd seen advanced gangrene before, though, and those cases were not as serious as Mister Macalister's, and one of them turned out in the worst way. I could only hope against hope that that doctor at Fort Concho would have some medicine or technique that might clear up the infection. My brother Alex had told me that of late they were coming up with new medical treatments and discoveries all the time.

Maybe cutting off that leg might save him. Then I wondered how he'd adjust to being one-legged, as strong and vital a man as he is. Then he and I really would have something in common, excepting he'd be even worse off. I figured it was best to just leave that topic alone until we got there.

Miss Luz had left the story of the Alamo and how it affected Mister Macalister kind of hanging, and I was burning to know all about that. Again though, I could tell it was a tender subject and left it to her to take it up again if and when she felt like sharing. It turned out she kind of took an indirect route.

"Those years working the farm," she began, "and especially the fact of being married to Edeline, worked wonders for my brother. I could see that he was gradually beginning to relax that hard, crusty exterior a bit. He even began to joke every now and then—and it wasn't the graveyard humor that was the steady diet of the Rangers. It was a wonderful thing to see.

She broke into a huge smile accompanied by a chuckle. "It was an adjustment for him at first, of course, not having the entire weight of whatever enterprise he was engaged in on his shoulders alone. Taking rather than issuing orders I could tell, rankled a bit."

It amazed me how suddenly a kind of heaviness came back over Miss Luz as she paused. "It happened just in time, too. All the hunting and killing and watching young boys under his command die...well, I imagine enough of that can turn anyone mean. He was starting to excuse atrocities. Though he never participated, I could see him losing that sense that we were fighting human beings—people fighting for their culture the same way we were fighting for ours, however barbaric they were."

That heaviness in Miss Luz seemed to kind of float into the distance as a gentle smile replaced the frown on her face. "Well, thank God for Edeline. She was one incredible gal. I do so miss her. Of course, not as much as Gerardo does."

I wondered if she were going to tell me the story of what happened to Mister Macalister's first wife. I was darn sure curious about that, too. I wondered if it might have something to do with his son's kind of strange way of acting toward him.

She then let out an "ah" and shook her head in a way that seemed to be her chasing away those sad thoughts. A gentle laugh accompanied whatever came into her mind next. "Gerardo was so unprepared for falling in love. He came to me for advice, which was probably—no, definitely—a case of the blind leading the blind. Well, I am a woman…however damaged.

"He'd say to me, 'What have I done in my life that I can talk about with a lady, Luz? How am I supposed to act? All I know is fightin' Indians and training and leading men in battle.'

"Edeline and I had gotten to know each other some by then and she'd told me about her own experience with Indians. 'You'd be surprised,' I answered him. 'Edeline knows more about what it takes to settle this land than you might think.'"

"'Yeah, but… You think so?' he'd stammer." Miss Luz shook her head with a beaming smile. "He even had trouble talking to me about talking to her."

"So, how'd they finally come together?"

"Mostly because of her. She was one wise young lady for her age. She just seemed to have an innate understanding of Gerardo's discomfort. She took up the conversation single-handed, asking Gerardo about his life, his interests. I remember he had trouble with that topic: what interests could he have beyond the best way to fight Indians and military tactics?

"So she asked him about his hopes for the future, whether he'd thought about marriage and children. That was the first time I'd seen my brother blush." Miss Luz laughed out loud at the thought. It sure was good to hear laughter come out of her. I guess there's not a lot of time for laughter out here in Comanche country.

"Partly because of what she'd gotten from me...and I think, partly just her own wisdom about people, she told him of her own experiences with Indians—the atrocities she'd seen and come close to being a victim of when they were in San Antonio. It made him feel more able to share his own past with her.

"I could tell she was attracted to his strength and found his uncertainty with her rather charming. She never took advantage of it, though. Not once.

"So, we all settled onto our farm." She broke into a smile that had a tiny question in it. "I could see some ambivalence at first. Gerardo had gotten used to issuing orders and rarely having them even questioned. Really, he'd known little else in his adult life.

"Now, it was Jakob who knew about farming and Edeline about business, so he had to learn to negotiate, to persuade and weigh other people's opinions equally with his own. Even to take orders himself, sometimes." With a knowing grin, she finished with, "Believe me, that did not come easy."

Miss Luz let out a chuckle. "And I could tell when one rankled; he'd go completely quiet and just kind of simmer in silence. It was hard for him, being the one on the receiving end of orders and

direction since he knew as much about farming as I do about...
high finance. He gradually sort of sculpted himself and was sculpted into it, though.

"On the other hand, not having all the responsibility, not having to make decisions over and over that put lives at risk—even
sometimes knowingly sending men to their deaths—seemed to
make him blossom. A lot of old wounds healed. The many aches
and pains moderated. It actually looked to me like he grew younger
during those years."

The memory seemed to kind of make Miss Luz sad somehow,
and she went quiet for a time. I tried to respect it as long as I could,
but I was itching to know how it had all changed. There were so
many mysteries about this family I was to be a part of, things I
yearned to know. "So, was it what happened at the Alamo that
changed all that?"

Miss Luz let out a ponderous breath of air, and I worried I'd
overstepped my welcome in the conversation. So I just kept my
mouth shut and waited, and after a few minutes she finally began
that part of the story.

"The independence movement was the one fly in the ointment
that kept my brother from being completely at peace. Many of the
Rangers that had followed and fought with him came urging him
to follow them—lead them, really—to join Sam Houston's army.

"The urge to go, especially after what had happened in Liberty—and the same was happening all over Texas—fought with the
powerful sense of responsibility he felt for his new family. Gerardo
was approaching middle age by then, after all, and Jakob was beginning to slow down.

"When Edeline came to be with child, that decided things for him."

"Oh. Well then, how come…?"

"When she was about seven or eight months along, news came that cast him right back down into that burning pit of indecision. A lot of those boys who'd urged him to join the Texian army, who'd followed him into hell fighting the Comanche, had gone to fortify an old mission in San Antonio called the Alamo where some of the revolutionaries had gone to make a stand. I could feel his love and sense of responsibility for those boys tugging at him like the stubbornest mule."

As she paused before continuing, I could sense that the memory, whatever it was, was a deep wound. When she finally spoke, I felt like she wasn't only talking about Mister Macalister's feelings but her own as well. After all, she'd fought with them, too. "Every last one of those boys, all the survivors at the Alamo were executed without a second thought."

I knew that the battle at the Alamo had ended in the rebels' defeat, but I was bowled over to learn that there was such a massacre. "Wow Miss Luz, ain't that against the rules of war?"

Miss Luz let out a puff of disgust. "It's against all the rules of human decency. I found out from one of the Mexican officers when I got to Goliad that General López de Santa Anna had succeeded in convincing the legislature in Mexico to classify the rebels as pirates and so subject to summary execution. Humph, as though he wouldn't have done it even without their okay."

I remembered that Alex had told me something about that—at least that there were no survivors at the Alamo. Now I knew why it happened the way it did.

I was about to ask Miss Luz how the scoundrel could get away with something like that when she let out another "Ohhh" that hung like the darkest thunder cloud. "I watched as all the tiny bit of peace, of softness, my brother had allowed himself over the last few years just vanished in a flash. He aged right before my eyes.

"Gerardo had always had such a powerful sense of responsibility for others. Now that feeling was split, and that split was tearing him down the middle. I watched him retreat back to the Comanche warrior, the ruthless Indian fighter he'd been.

"There was no place, no space, in that person for sentimentality, for the gentility being a husband and father necessitates. I knew Edeline felt it as well. We agreed that Gerardo would stay out of a sense of duty to her, and that staying—abandoning his fellow Texians, as he'd see it—would eat away at him till little was left.

"We contacted a local midwife; she had a good record, even with difficult deliveries. We'd hired Camp Cookie by then to work the farm with us. He'd been an escaped slave that thought he was going north when in reality he was going northwest from New Orleans.

Jakob immediately hid him on the farm and insisted on paying him for his labor. Jakob had apparently been a virtual slave himself to his landlord back in Germany and hated that kind of servitude. While the family patriarch was getting on in years, he was still hearty enough to at least oversee all the farm labor.

"Now came the hard part, convincing Gerardo to go. I don't know how Edeline managed it, but she eventually wore him down. I know she told him he would be no help during the delivery or caring for the child, especially in his present state.

The midwife had assured her that the pregnancy was a normal, healthy one.

"At first, she wanted me to go with him. Of course, he wouldn't hear of that. But when I promised I would stay through the birth of the child, and with both of us urging him to go, he finally gave in. I could see in his eyes how much he hated going and hated the impulse that made him go, anyway.

"The next day he took off for a town called Goliad. There were Texian troops at a fort called La Bahía there that the leader had re-named Fort Defiance after they'd taken it over from the Mexicans. They had apparently been ordered by Sam Houston to retreat to Victoria in east Texas to consolidate with his army. Gerardo went to join them."

She broke off the story as her head nodded in exhaustion. "Miss Luz, I… I think you need a break. Is there any way I can…?"

She shook her head to ward off the sleepiness. "Guess I'm not as young as I used to be." Looking forward, she came to a decision. "You see that rise way off in the distance, *hijo*?"

"Yes, ma'am."

"From the top, you can see Fort Concho. It will take the better part of two hours to get there. I need just a brief rest, so drive the mules straight at it and wake me when we get there."

"Well Miss Luz, if I'll be able to see the fort, I could just drive us all the way there. Then you could get an even better rest."

She shook her head, no. "The way up and over is too tricky. Just push the mules as I've been pushing them, no harder. And if I'm still asleep when we get there, *wake me*. That's an order."

"Yes, ma'am. I sure will."

She handed me the reins and stepped back into the cart. I heard my mother ask her if everything was all right, and she answered that it was and explained what was happening. I turned when she addressed Mister Macalister, his head in my mother's lap. "*Hermano?*" I heard her say. I couldn't hear any response.

Little Amelia went right to her and hugged her, crawling right up into her lap. Then I noticed she wasn't sure who she wanted to be with more, Miss Luz or my mother. Then I heard my mother tell Miss Luz to lie down on the grain sacks. "Softer than floor," she said in her broken German. "Use one for head, eh...pillow."

When Miss Luz did lie down, that settled things for Amelia; she went right back to my mother.

I took advantage of the break just long enough to attend to necessities. I hoped that would give Miss Luz a little time to get to sleep before all the noise and jostling the wagon causes. It seemed to work as she was already lightly snoring when I got back to the rig and started up the mules. I looked back to Camp Cookie to make sure he knew what was going on, but I guess this family had been on these junkets so often that these things were part of the routine.

*A*s luck would have it, Miss Luz woke up just before we reached the rise. She quickly checked on Mister Macalister and then hopped into the buckboard, taking the reins from me.

She shook her head to clear it. "Getting up this rise is tricky, like I said. It gets steep about three-quarters of the way up. You can see, there," she said, pointing to the part she was talking about.

"Man, Miss Luz, will Camp Cookie be able to get the chuck wagon up that rise?"

"I told him last night to go around it. The cowhands and cattle will follow him."

It was actually a low mesa, and I hoped the way down wasn't as steep as the way up. I don't think I breathed the whole time we were on that incline.

Once we reached the top and got a little way toward the other side, I could sure enough see way off in the distance what looked like some buildings with a palisade of something, logs maybe, around it.

"How's Mister Macalister," I asked. "Was he able to answer you?"

"Vaguely. He's not delirious." She paused a moment as she clenched her jaw. "But he's on his way."

Then she had more directions that really put the fear of God into me. "Before we start down the other side of the mesa, I need you to get back in the wagon and warn your mother the descent will be rough. Tell her to put herself and Amelia against one of the front corners of the wagon and to grab hold of something as best she can to steady them. And put grain sacks between them and the hard edges of the wagon. You do the same and see if you can find a way to keep your stepfather from tumbling around too much. Stay there till we get to the bottom. We'll still have at least an hour to get to the fort."

I did like she said and boy, she wasn't kidding. It was all I could do to stay in the cart myself, much less trying to keep Mister Macalister, my mother and Amelia from being bounced out. I worried about Miss Luz herself, with nothing to hold onto being bounced around like...I don't know what.

When we finally got to level ground, I first made sure Mister Macalister was none the worse for wear. Boy, I guess my mother had gotten used to the smell coming from her patient. It liked to knock me over being that close. I asked her if she and the child were all right. She said they were. Then I did like Miss Luz had said and crawled back up into the buckboard.

"Is everyone all right? Are all of you still in the wagon? No broken bones?" she asked.

"Yes ma'am, I believe everybody's sound—well, except for your brother. But boy, you weren't kidding about that way down being rough. I was worried about you having nothing to hold onto but the reins—nothing to steady yourself."

"I've had a lot of experience; and being up here I can see which way we're going to lean or be knocked. I'd normally go around the mesa myself, but it would add up to half a day to the trip. I'm just glad everyone is all right and really thankful the wagon is still in one piece. I was concerned for it as well."

The sight of the fort was a really happy one for sore eyes. We'd made good time. I just hoped it would make a difference.

I really wanted to know what happened at that place Mister Macalister went to join the Texian army, but I guessed Miss Luz had too much on her mind. I was just glad we were back to the normal jostling of the cart. I noticed I had a few sore spots from the trip down. I decided I'd just let her continue if she was of a mind to.

"Go ahead and ask, *hijo*," she again anticipated me. Boy, how can this lady read my mind so easily? "The time will go faster telling you our history than my just worrying about Gerardo."

"Well Miss Luz, I-I don't wanna…"

Ignoring my hesitation, she just barreled ahead. "Jacob was born a week and a half later. Edeline and Gerardo had agreed that if it was a boy, he would be named after her father but with the English spelling and pronunciation."

I glanced around to see if I could see my stepbrother on his horse minding the cattle. When I saw nothing behind us, I remembered that Miss Luz had sent the others around the mesa. It must be one huge hill, going around it adding a half a day to the trip.

Miss Luz continued the story. "Edeline was back on her feet after a day and fully recovered the next. To live on this frontier, one has to be made of iron. She urged me to go after Gerardo right after the birth, thinking that I could somehow keep him safe. I had the same thought, of course, and set out the third day.

"When I got to Goliad, all the Texians were prisoners under the guard of Mexican troops. The troops were commanded by a General José de Arreola. Apparently, the Texian troops were surprised shortly after their retreat from Goliad. My brother said it was at a creek called the Coleto.

"He said that the colonel in charge, a Colonel James something…Fannin, I think. Anyway, he had stopped the train to let the oxen graze, just short of an *encinal*—a grove of oak trees—that would have provided cover. Gerardo overheard the colonel's staff urging him to not stop. The colonel didn't listen.

"That's one difference between him and my brother. Gerardo always listened to his men. He took my advice on many occasions. When he didn't, he was almost always right.

"Anyway, Fannin's troops were trapped in open country. They had to form a square three lines deep—or I think they call them 'ranks' in the army—to defend themselves on all sides. The first day they held their ground with only a relatively small number of dead and wounded. The second day, a large contingent of Mexican reinforcements arrived with a sizeable order of artillery. Colonel Fannin decided to surrender—with very little dissent.

"I was surprised and thanked the Lord that they weren't just immediately executed. The soldier that had told me about the order from the legislature designating the Texian troops as pirates was surprised by that as well.

"Because I was Mexican, I was allowed an audience with the commanding officer, General Arreola. He gave me free access to the prisoners as well as the Mexican troops. I found Gerardo uninjured but exhausted and weak with hunger like all the other soldiers. There was not a good supply of food even for the Mexican army, so the prisoners were on short to no rations at all.

"I had some food in my saddle bags and brought it to Gerardo, which of course he insisted on sharing with his fellow soldiers. He had to choose which of the prisoners he'd share with since there was no way to get even a tidbit to them all. He chose the ones who looked the weakest.

"The news that he had a new baby boy waiting for him at home lifted his spirits so much that a few bites of the food I brought seemed to satisfy him. 'And Edy?' he asked.

"'Strong as a horse, *hermano*,' I answered. 'Back to work after just two days.'

"With that he closed his eyes and just said, 'Thank God in heaven,' and sank back to rest."

I started to smile at the thought of the joy Mister Macalister must've felt at that moment, having a son. But then I wondered about the uneasiness, the distance, in his relationship with that son, now. What could have happened between them?

Then also, I sensed something in Miss Luz that kind of tempered the relief at finding her brother alive and well—and bringing him such wonderful news. There was something that stuck a pestering pebble under that happy turn of events.

I wondered what it could be. "Miss Luz, I…" I hesitated to ask, it felt so dark and painful for her.

She took a deep breath and exhaled with a powerful sigh. "I thought I had gotten over any feeling of kinship with the people of my birth. But what happened at Goliad made me so deeply ashamed that it finally turned whatever morsel of that kinship left in me into disgust and pure hate."

I could tell that Miss Luz needed a break from telling the story of Goliad, so I just sat and looked out at the countryside, hoping we'd be at Fort Concho in time to make a difference.

Chapter XVI

Greater love hath no man than this: that
he lay down his life for his brother.

--John 15:13

The ultimate measure of a man is not where
he stands in moments of comfort and convenience
but where he stands at times of challenge and
controversy.

--Rev. Martin Luther King

José de Arreola sat at his desk in Presidio La Bahía in Goliad staring down at the still sealed letter from his commander, General Antonio López de Santa Anna, with a profound sense of doom. He was sure it contained the General's response to his plea to spare the rebel troops who had surrendered to him at the battle of Coleto Creek, some relatively short distance away. He had no illusions about what the answer would be.

He remembered his commander's wrath when Arreola had pleaded with him to forgo an all-out assault at the Alamo. "My esteemed Commander, the rebels have had no relief for two weeks. They're bound to have no food left. We haven't let them have a good night's rest in all that time, either. They simply can't hold out any longer."

Arreola knew he was risking his commander's intense displeasure, but the thought of losing so many of their troops in such an assault horrified him—especially as it was so unnecessary. He also knew, however, that no quarter would be given the enemy unless he could further convince his commander to change his mind about their designation as pirates.

"We must show these rebellious traitors that there will be no mercy for them," Santa Anna replied with supreme confidence. "It is the only way to put down this insurrection of guttersnipes once and for all. We will show them the terrible fate awaiting those who defy the glorious and sacred state of Mexico."

"My general, I'm not so sure it will inspire fear so much as hate. People willing to endure isolation and uncertainty, the brutal savagery of hostile Indians, such want and misery as the men and women behind those walls now endure, don't strike me as a people easily daunted. They are a people who fought those Indians successfully, where we could not."

Arreola could tell that his last comment truly rankled his commander. The latter's answer came after he had smoldered a moment. Arreola knew he had to be more discreet. "People are the same everywhere, José. Rebellious sheep need to be reminded who is in charge and what the consequences for such treason are and always will be."

Arreola hesitated, feeling the swelling resentment his warnings were generating in General Santa Anna. But the prospect of such slaughter—such unnecessary slaughter—spurred him on. "I fear your metaphor of sheep might be misplaced, my worthy General. Might I suggest an alternative: a nest of angry hornets?"

Now the irritation began to show in Santa Anna's voice. "There are only rulers and ruled in life, General Arreola. We are the shepherds, and they are the rebellious sheep. They must be reminded of that undeniable truth!"

Arreola could tell that his commander was reaching his limit of entertaining voiced dissent. Consequently, he added very quietly and meekly, "May God ensure that it is that lesson that they learn." He still couldn't resist one final try, however: "We could spare our own rank and file, hundreds, perhaps even a thousand dead my General, by just allowing the rebels to surrender. They are bound to be starving."

Arreola could see the blood boiling behind his commander's eyes and knew he had overstepped. Had he not had the leverage of having saved Santa Anna's wife's and daughter's lives, it might have resulted in an unwelcome fate for him.

"*There is no glory in a bloodless victory, General Arreola!*"

By the vehemence of his commander's reply, Arreola knew that the debate was over. He was also convinced by that reply that any effort to spare survivors would be fruitless, as well as dangerous for him.

And so commenced the unspeakable carnage.

*N*ow Arreola sat at his desk in Presidio La Bahía overlooking the courtyard where over four hundred Texian prisoners of war—or pirates, depending on one's point of view—loitered on a temperate spring day. Before him on the desk lay that fateful letter, still sealed, still threatening.

He was all but certain of his commander's response to his pleas for mercy. How would he respond to what he was certain would be General Santa's denial and order of execution? The choice of how to proceed would indeed be stark.

He thought of his beloved wife, Axochitl, of his son, Tomás, named after Arreola's partner and surrogate father. Tomasito must have grown in the time he's been away fighting this almost certainly hopeless war. Would he remember his father? And if so, in what light would he remember him?

He thought as well of the daughter he'd only found out he had by letter from his wife. How he ached to hold them both in his arms! To gently cradle that tender female child that he may never know! To shield them both from the treachery and foulness of this life, the dearth of mercy, the endless war, the absence of hope.

He thought of a saying he'd read so very long ago, attributed to Plato: "Only the dead know the end of war".

With the thought of his son, the cruelly paradoxical nature of his predicament came clear to him: if he refused to execute the prisoners, he would be branded a traitor. Would his only son believe him to be so? The thought sent a grievous chill through him.

On the other hand, if he followed the order, he would be considered a hero in the eyes of the Mexican Republic. He would know, however, that it was in fact an act of cowardice—a course of action while consonant with his duty as a soldier, a higher power would most certainly consider a consummate evil. Though all the world might praise his name, he would know. *He* would know. What legacy would he really be leaving his son if he were to succumb to that so tantalizing alternative?

What a dilemma: to do what his conscience tells him is right and have his name showered in ignominy. Or to perpetrate such a dastardly crime and be considered a hero.

His fingers moved gingerly toward the letter, and he finally took it up as carefully as if it were a bomb ready to explode at the slightest jostle—or perhaps like some sacred relic. He lifted it above him, making of it an offering to God. His eyes continued beyond it as he looked up to Heaven and begged his Creator for guidance—for deliverance!

There he held it, as though some comforting angel might come and snatch it out of his hand. Finally, he brought it back down to earth, not in despair but rather in the knowledge that there was no one to relieve him of this so paradoxical fate. The choice was his and his alone.

This is a true test of leadership, he thought, *the* true test. It is the test not of the general, the statesman or the entrepreneur. No, it is the test for a child of God, a test that may determine the future of the Mexican Republic and the true worth of a man. It is as Christ and all those throughout history who have been martyred for principle were tested.

Hah! he snickered to himself, *it is the height of hubris, of pomposity, to compare myself to those paragons of righteousness.*

With that realization, he turned the missive over, exposing the fateful wax seal and, like ripping a scab off an infected wound, tore it open.

It bore no surprises. It read in script like the cold chiseled lettering on a tombstone: "Carry out my order of execution ON PAIN OF DEATH FOR TREASON!"

Now the only choice Arreola had to make was to select the words that would convey his answer to his Commander-in-Chief.

He had long ago considered the possibility of joining the rebels. He imagined that he would be welcomed with fanfare and celebration. Perhaps that thought was again the product of a false pride. For the plethora of rebels that have been returned to dust upon his order, his reception there might well be the hangman's rope.

He wondered what it was that made him hesitate, however. If he stayed and defied his commander's explicit order, there would be no question as to his fate. With the rebels he would at least have a chance. So what perverse sense of duty compelled him to stay, to face the same fate as those who would be, whether the order came from him or another, executed as surely as the night follows the day?

Of course, he thought there might be some among his troops who would remain loyal to him and follow his refusal to obey the order. That would put them in danger of a like fate as his would surely be. Could he live with that? He had gained such loyalty as much by his effort to prosecute this war with as little sacrifice of his own troops—and even those of the enemy—as humanly possible. Could he now expose them to such a fate?

Again, he laughed at his own arrogance. *You flatter yourself, José, to think that a common soldier or even an officer would share your fate out of loyalty.* At the thought, a quote from his readings concerning the independence movement in the United States came to mind: "Is life so dear or peace so sweet as to be purchased at the price of chains and slavery? Forbid it Almighty God!"

Humph, he thought, easy to say when you're safe in the statehouse or congress, much more difficult for a soldier facing a rifle ball, a murderous bayonet or the hangman's rope. Did the speaker of that statement participate in that country's war for independence?

Of course, there was no doubt in his mind that his bosom friend and subordinate, Colonel José de la Portilla, would without question follow the order of his commander-in-chief and President. It was rebellion, disloyalty, after all, that had come within a hair's-breadth of destroying Nicosito's entire family.

And he knew his companion had not the…what? Was it a matter of courage? Or was it simply a question of not having the imagination to see an allegiance to one's own concept of right and wrong above that of military protocol? There, there is that conformity to get along by going along. There are few, he thought, who can rise above that sentiment. Was he one of them?

Arreola's lips curled in a sad little smile as he thought of this man who now was like a brother—a younger brother. José Nicolás, after all, had not the breadth of consciousness to comprehend that this whole conflagration was a question of two opposing cultures and that the stronger would inevitably prevail in the end.

The question lingered, however, and ate at him: why did he not simply escape and join the rebels? Or why did he not simply escape, if he was so sure the rebels would prevail, and call for his family to join him in this independent state of Texas to be? Why was he participating in this ill-fated conflagration in the first place?

Could he not, as he had done in Mexico, start a business and enjoy the blessings of peace? watch and guide his children in their passage to maturity? grow old in the company of his beloved wife and die peacefully in the knowledge of her reciprocal devotion?

He searched deep within himself and could find no rational answer. Could it simply be a matter of hubris, a cheap affectation of vanity to have his life ended, like Socrates, for following the dictates of his conscience? How ironic that to gain the esteem of the few he must accept the opprobrium of the many.

Despite all the consideration of alternatives, however, he knew his mind was made up long before. And again, that famous Platonic dictum rambled restlessly through his mind. "Only the dead know the end of war."

So, he turned to the manner in which he would state his exception to his commander's ultimatum. He took a quill and sheet of paper and began: "My Esteemed Commander and President, it is with great regret that I find I..." Arreola stopped himself, thought for a moment and discarded the paper. *How inadequate,* he thought.

He tried again: "My Esteemed and Most Honorable..." This time he stopped himself even more quickly, crumpled up the paper and threw it aside. It occurred to him that there was not a limitless supply of paper in Goliad. In fact, he was forced to use the reverse side of missives that had been sent to him. Nevertheless, he tried again and again with no success. Nothing came that really conveyed the enormity of the event and of the pain it caused him to set it down in words.

He sat back and thought. When nothing came, he rose and walked to the frameless window overlooking the courtyard and looked down at the prisoners and the troops that guarded them. A memory from the distant past began to slowly take shape in his mind. As it finally coalesced, the déjà vu sent a rifling tingle through him that brought the memory into clarity.

It was from a similar vantage point that he witnessed the execution of peninsular Spanish prisoners held by Father Hidalgo in the very first Mexican rebellion so many lifetimes ago. It was the sight of that horrible event that made him determined from that moment on to save as many of the captives, surrendered or taken prisoner, as he could.

The feeling brought another related memory to the forefront of his mind: Father Hidalgo had told him that the Viceroy of New Spain, as Mexico was then called, whenever he received an order from Spain or from The Council of the Indies that was distasteful to him, he would send the same message back to his superiors: "I obey, but I do not carry out."

So succinct. So ambiguous and at the same time so clear. How it encapsulates his quandary so perfectly.

He rushed back to his desk and immediately penned the following message:

Obedezco, pero no cumplo.

With that, he immediately rolled it up and tied it off with the last bit of ribbon he had and marched to the door to his office to give the letter to his adjutant, Captain Ordáz, for delivery.

When he opened the door, however, he found the captain arguing with a Mexican woman with a considerably disfigured face. The argument immediately stopped at his appearance and the captain came to attention and saluted.

"Sir, this woman insists on having an audience with you. I have told her you are much too busy with official matters to attend to any civilian, but she continues to argue. Shall I have her removed, sir?"

Arreola paused a moment to take the measure of the woman before him and was surprised to find her doing the same with him. This intrigued him. "What is it you wish to see me about, madam?"

He also sensed a powerful integrity in her and a self-assuredness in her demeanor as she answered. "The prisoners, General Arreola," she answered in an ever-so-slightly stilted Castilian. So terse. So direct. So like the message contained in the letter for his superior. This was obviously a woman of considerable intelligence and discernment. She appeared to have the self-confidence of one who has experienced much in life.

"Please come in, madam," he responded to the great surprise of his adjutant. As he allowed her to pass into his office, he started to hand the letter to the captain but then for some reason held onto it as he followed the lady in.

As he escorted her to a chair before his desk, he addressed her. "First of all, you have me at a disadvantage, knowing who I am, when you are a complete stranger to me."

"I am Luz Macalister. Once upon a time, Doña Luz Cortez de Aranda."

Now Arreola was doubly intrigued, wondering how this *Mexicana*—or possibly *Española*—with such a distinguished name had come to marry an Anglo. And who might her husband be that he would marry such a disfigured woman. He would love to know this man.

"Doña Luz, it is a pleasure to know you, I'm sure. Please do sit down," he said, holding out the chair before his desk, seating her and then going to his own chair behind the desk and sitting facing her. "What is your interest in my prisoners?"

Luz had done her own due diligence in evaluating her present interlocuter to the degree she could. She perceived a fierce intelligence equal to her own. By his bearing and manner, she also thought she sensed a degree of integrity beyond the average soldier, or even army officer. Those conclusions led her to be quite direct. "You must not execute these prisoners of war, General Arreola."

Arreola noted that her petition was not presented as a plea or even a request but rather as something approaching a demand. Any of his peers faced with such boldness from a civilian, and especially a civilian woman, would have her immediately ejected if not imprisoned. For Arreola, however, such audacity only deepened his fascination. "Would that be because one of them is your husband, Madam?"

"Brother. I was adopted by the Macalister family when I was eleven after my family was killed by Indians."

"I see. I would be more than fascinated to know the details of your history, but I gather you wish to forgo that in favor of addressing the fate of the prisoners. Tell me please, Madam, what would you have me do with them?"

"Either keep them as prisoners of war or release them."

"Uhm. So that they can rejoin the rebellion and kill more of my men?"

Luz was silent with the knowledge that that is precisely what would happen.

Arreola considered the possibility of telling her directly that that decision had already been made. It would pose the risk of it being publicized, however. Plus, he found this woman so interesting that he wished to extend their interaction for at least a bit.

"As you can see, I have a hard enough time feeding my own regiment, much less over four hundred prisoners. As to the latter alternative, that would most certainly subject me to the fate you wish me to spare these men."

Luz carefully weighed the suggestion she was inclined to make. It was consummately risky. To save her brother, however, no risk was too fearsome to take. He had, after all, risked death for her as a matter of routine through much of their lives together. So, she played that ultimate card: "Not if you join us."

Arreola was quite taken aback by her suggestion, although he held his gaze as steady as he could in an effort to mask his surprise. By saying, *us*, she had clearly placed herself with the rebels, a group his commander-in-chief had labeled treasonous pirates, with no right to designation as an opposing army and therefore subject to summary execution.

Notwithstanding his self-control, the reaction didn't escape Luz's perception. She felt quite a sense of relief that her wager that he would not be incensed and immediately eject or imprison her was accurate.

"If you choose to perpetrate the crime of the Alamo, I warn you General, you will not in any way cower this people that even the Comanche could not intimidate. Rather, you will be bringing on yourself and the whole of the Mexican army such retaliation as would turn the stomach of the hardiest soldier."

Arreola sat back slightly in his chair, pondering the intense irony of the present situation: to be offered by this common and female member of the putative enemy a proposition he had been considering, and considering with a sense of urgency. The juxtaposition made his head spin.

He marveled as well at the irony of being warned by her of a result he had cautioned his commander against: that a people so independent, so self-reliant, who had actually challenged the fearsome Comanche and other ruthless tribes and fought them quite successfully, would not be scared into submission by barbaric behavior. Rather, they would be motivated to fight with the same measure of ruthlessness.

"Yes, Doña Luz, I am quite aware that it is a question of culture and not of right. Quite aware. I also know that fighting such an independent-minded and self-reliant people with lead and steel is at best a dicey proposition."

"There are Mexicans among your prisoners, sir," she pointed out. "*Tejanos*, they're called. The vast majority are those who came to the province on their own, separate from the efforts of the Mexican government to establish colonies here. They've built a life here, alongside the Anglos.

"And I think it is that same individual initiative that brought them here that also motivated them to start their own businesses or work on their own as carpenters, blacksmiths and the like. I believe it also induced them to trade with the Anglos and participate in their self-governing bodies, and finally to join the revolution. They are as dedicated to Texas independence as any Anglo."

Arreola wondered why he had the urge to share with this woman his reaction to what she'd just observed. Did he feel her to be a kindred soul? "Yes. I've noted that very phenomenon during my limited time in the province. I find it curious—huh, maddening, really—that all those entrepreneurs had to come here to realize their dreams because they couldn't in Mexico.

"But I know very well why. I had a business of my own, you see, a thriving one for a time. The powers that be, however, could not tolerate such success in an enterprise run by a common *mestizo*.

"So sad, and so profoundly at odds with all sensibility, since so many gained meaningful employment and bettered their lives as a result of our pottery mill. It created jobs in trade, supply, transportation, retail and other areas throughout the Mexican economy. It provided an infusion of resources for all those who prospered with funds to purchase goods and services that gave others quite remunerative jobs. It produced moneys that could have been, and were to an unfortunately small extent, invested in other concerns.

"How tragic that men seem to allow their prejudices to out-weigh their own self-interest—and that of their community. There is a saying in English that I came across in my studies: 'to cut off one's nose to hurt one's face?'"

"'To spite one's face,' yes."

"Hmm. I believe it is stated in the Bible that those who cannot create are compelled to destroy the creation of others. Sad. To stop Anglo immigration is to stop the tide from rising with the moon."

"Then why do you continue?" Luz perhaps ingenuously asked.

"A question I have repeatedly asked myself. And one for which I have no logical answer. Perhaps no answer at all."

Now Luz Macalister knew she could be even bolder in her proposal. "Then spare these men and join us."

Arreola thought for a moment, not taking his eyes off this extraordinary woman seated before him and sighed. "That would be...the rational thing to do."

He then stood, signifying that the audience had come to an end. "Doña Luz Macalister, you are an extraordinary woman. I sincerely thank you for the opportunity to get to know you, and I thank you for sharing your admonitions.

"I will take your offer, as well as your suggestions concerning the disposition of the prisoners, under serious consideration. Meantime, I suggest you refrain from sharing your attachment to the rebel force with anyone outside this office—for your sake and for mine."

Luz had stood with him and now offered her hand to shake. "You are a man of great honor and integrity, General Arreola."

Arreola's lips curled up in a rather ironic smile as he grasped her hand. She held his quite firmly. "Am I? Perhaps you could put that on my gravestone. I fear it will be an opinion held by few—at least of my own countrymen."

With that, he escorted her to the door. He addressed Captain Ordáz upon opening it. "Captain, see that this lady has access to her brother, a prisoner named Macalister. Then, dispatch one of our messengers to deliver this letter to Commander López de Santa Anna, post-haste."

Chapter XVII

If every action which is good or evil...were
under prescription or compulsion, what praise
should then be due to well-doing?

--John Milton

In social evolution, nothing is inevitable,
but thinking makes it so.

--F.A. Hayek

...there is nothing either bad or good but
thinking makes it so.

--Hamlet, IIii

José Nicolás Portilla struggled to identify the elusive sense of misgiving that rummaged about his brain and lodged so deeply in his viscera. Even before the surrender of the pirates at Coleto Creek there was a vague feeling of unease. Since that event, it had blossomed from a sensation of the world off-kilter into a potent sense of impending catastrophe.

At first, he'd tried to ignore it, unseemly in an officer of the Mexican army. But its growth insisted on being dealt with. He puzzled as to its origin. After all, under General Arreola's brilliant command their regiment had handily taken over Matamoros, gained a sizable number of volunteers there, acquitted themselves well at the Alamo, sacrificing many in the final assault. Then they had chased the rebel troops as they retreated east, caught and defeated a sizable contingent of them with only moderate losses at Coleto Creek.

Might that ill-feeling have something to do with the fact that he was now a father—and one of almost two years now? Though he hadn't married the *mestiza*, Carmen, who had joined the regiment before their departure for the northern territories, she had born him a child and he had come to deeply care for her and their child. Her devotion to him was unwavering, even fierce.

How being a family man had caused him to call into question so many things. How it had given rise to so many feelings and doubts he had never before entertained. As he was sworn to defend the rights and honor of his beloved country, so must he provide security for his loved ones. But the feeling was different somehow. How, he couldn't say, but different it was.

Now, the army had taken prisoner more than four hundred of the ungrateful traitors and retaken Presidio La Bahía and the surrounding town of Goliad. Together with their glorious victory at San Antonio and their own regiment's victories all along the Texas coast, the rebels were retreating in shameful defeat.

There should be celebration. These victories should provide him, his commander and friend and all their troops the sense of calm that confidence confers. There should be the impetus to pursue the rest of these faithless turncoats and teach them once and for all the fate that awaits such treasonous malefaction.

Still that feeling of pending catastrophe bedeviled him. Why had General Arreola, his commander and brother in arms, idled their army so long here? Why had the General done his best to see that the prisoners had at least some sustenance? It was costing them time and resources that were badly wanting. Aside from his troops, Nicolás had a special responsibility for mother and child, now.

According to his immediate subordinate, Captain de la Garza, the prisoners and even some of their own troops were eating anything that flew or crawled or slithered around the presidio. Of course, at least the troops could hunt. He'd heard of a few of them sharing their kills with the prisoners. He must put a stop to that.

A fight had broken out among the prisoners over a captured garter snake, by that time considered a rare delicacy. His commander, General Arreola, had ordered him to break up the melee. Again, he wondered why. What purpose could be served by keeping these rebels alive?

He could not consider questioning a direct order, however, and immediately selected a contingent of his troops to carry it out. When he and his squad made it to the brawl, however, he was surprised to find order already restored.

The same man that his commander's strange female visitor had asked to see, a man named Maquester, or something like that, had stopped the fight and was issuing orders as to how the snake would be divided and consumed. It was surprising to José Nicolás because this prisoner had no accouterments indicating he was anything more than a common soldier. Yet the others responded quite readily to his direction.

Could it be this inexplicable situation that so unnerved him? Did it have to do with the fact that his commander had tarried so long in disposing of these treasonous ingrates? They had lingered there in Goliad almost a week now, after all. What was General Arreola, his commander, savior and beloved brother-in-arms, waiting for? The Mexican Congress had officially designated these prisoners and all rebels as pirates and traitors. Their fate was unequivocal.

Coming directly from what he had witnessed with the prisoners and their response to this Maquester's leadership, Nicolás looked up at the frameless window—more of a rugged space where the stones that made up the wall of the fort had been left aside—to his commander's office.

He would never directly confront his commanding officer, or question his orders or strategy, not just because of the love he bore him or the reciprocal confraternity Nicolás felt from him. Nicolás had to admit that Arreola and he were in their proper places, the former's strategy and tactics that always impressed José Nicolás so much were ones he often would never have thought of on his own.

He did have the pretext, however, of reporting the successful quelling of the riot. He wondered how he might be able to parlay his report into eliciting from his commander his reason for the delay and his thinking in general concerning the prisoners and the war itself.

He approached the building serving the dual purpose of housing the army officers and operating as an office for the commander. As he did so, his inquietude seemed to increase with every step.

It was the strangest phenomenon. Never before had he felt the slightest unease in the presence of his commanding officer, save the times the general had had to reproach him for tactical errors. He had long ago made peace with the fact that he was a pure Spanish creole and General Arreola, his superior, a *mestizo*. Given the respect and great affection he felt for his commander, there was only the slightest quisling tincture of resentment at this state of affairs.

So, he reminded himself time and again how his whole family had been saved by this same *mestizo*, and how Nicolás himself had been given new purpose and status from his generous hand, the name Portilla blotted out from the record of "traitors". Still, a treasonous mole of anxiety burrowed ever deeper in the pit of his stomach.

Perhaps in order to defy those feelings, he marched quickly and determinedly up the stairs to the second floor and, despite Arreola's directive that the Colonel could come into his office without being announced, he followed strict military protocol.

Captain Ordáz, immediately sensing his superior's rigid formality, dutifully stood to attention at his approach, saluted and waited for the counter-salute. José Nicolás returned it punctiliously. "Colonel de la Portilla to report to the general the disposition of the recent disturbance among the prisoners," he stated with the same officiousness.

The captain was a bit surprised at just how formal his superior was being. Stress tending to be infectious, especially from superior to subordinate, he responded in kind, exaggerating the formality of his stance and salute. He immediately went to the General's office door, knocked once, opened it and announced Colonel de la Portilla's request for an audience with a formality that had previously slackened. "Colonel de la Portilla to see you, General sir."

Arreola noted the enhanced decorum and immediately sensed its origin. He had, after all, been fighting his own sense of doom since he sent the missive of refusal to his commander-in-chief.

"Please, send him in, Manuel," he answered, purposefully using his captain's first name in an effort to calm his own nerves by resisting his subordinate's studied formality.

He continued the stratagem with his immediate subordinate. "Do come in, Nicos. Your company is always much appreciated."

Notwithstanding the General's informal manner, José Nicolás was still compelled by his uneasiness to maintain strict decorum. He entered, stood smartly to attention and saluted grandly. Arreola, refusing to be sucked into the tension he felt from all quarters, returned the salute perfunctorily. "Please take your ease, Nicos, and sit down."

José Nicolás did so, somewhat disarmed by his superior's relaxed demeanor. There was an uncomfortable pause as Arreola waited for Nicolás' report on the commotion, perhaps taking a moment to try to get a sense of his friend's state of mind.

Finally, he felt forced to initiate the conversation but did so in a way as to try to melt some of the icy formality so at odds with the history of their relationship. "How have you been, Nicos? You've seemed preoccupied of late. Are Carmen and the child well?"

José Nicolás was quite disarmed by Arreola's manner. "Oh, uh...They're well, sir. Quite well."

"I'm glad to hear it. And yourself?"

"Oh, I'm...fine, sir. I, uh...came to report on the prisoner... upheaval, sir."

Another awkward pause further discomfited José Nicolás. Arreola decided to come to his rescue. "Well, by all means, Colonel, give me your account of how the matter was resolved. I'm most interested," he said as lightheartedly as he could.

"Oh, well…it seems it was resolved by the prisoners themselves. By the time I and my squad arrived there was one man—a common soldier it seemed—deciding how the prize would be divided. I can't imagine there was more than a single bite for even a handful of the soldiers.

"A funny thing, also: this soldier had no markings or dress indicating he had any authority, but to mine and my soldiers' astonishment, everyone seemed to listen to him and follow his… suggestions—which were delivered more like orders. I believe it was the same man who had the lady—the Mexicana—visitor: a… *Maquester?*"

"Macalister. Yes, his adopted sister was quite an imposing woman," Arreola commented with a touch of wistfulness.

"But sir, her face…"

"Oh, I assure you my interest was not in any way romantic. She just struck me as having a robust intelligence and the confidence of one who has experienced—and accomplished—a great deal in life. I take it from your account of the prisoner upheaval that her brother is equally formidable."

"Oh, I…suppose so, sir. How their army can manage itself with a plain volunteer taking control of such a situation is beyond my comprehension."

Such an utterance from his friend and protégé caused Arreola to take a moment to study him. That wasn't because it was in any sense, unexpected. Rather, it was sad confirmation for Arreola that his comrade and brother indeed had not the capacity to understand that true leadership derives not for one's station in life, but rather from his character and natural abilities.

The pause as Arreola considered this conclusion made José Nicolás uncomfortable, wondering what was going through the General's mind. "Sir...?"

"I must say it doesn't surprise me, Nicos, having fought them and watched their military prowess which, for a hastily assembled unit, is quite impressive. That was true especially at Coleto Creek. Completely surprised, they formed themselves into that square three ranks deep in record time, it struck me. I don't think their officers even had time to give the order before the square was well on its way to being formed."

"Well, they must have been drilled over and over by their leaders to do that very thing."

"Must they have? Their forces strike me as having had little time to be so organized. And the thing that surprises me most is that had their leader, Colonel Fannin, not dawdled, and they'd made it to the grove of oaks on the other side of the creek, we might have had—we *would* have had—a much rougher go of it, taking them on with so much cover."

Pointedly, General Arreola mused to his colonel and friend, "I consider that sense of initiative in the common soldier, however weakly led, to be a force that I'm afraid can only triumph in the end. Leadership will out eventually, as we witnessed during the recent prisoner turmoil."

Colonel Portilla was beyond being astonished as to be scandalized by his commander's seeming assessment that these ungrateful pirates would triumph. "Oh but, sir," he protested, "we defeated them handily, and took so many of them prisoner with only moderate losses."

"With considerably superior numbers and artillery, Nicos. Had they made it to that *encinal*, our losses would have increased dramatically. Mainly because they would have been fighting us more on a man-to-man basis.

"Consider Nicos: Once their left flank began to become porous with losses, you might, if you had taken the initiative, broken through and brought the battle to a quicker and more decisive end on the first day, resulting in even fewer losses on our side."

José Nicolás blushed with embarrassment. "But your orders, sir, they…"

"Yes, my orders were to weaken that left flank from a distance as much as possible. But you see, I didn't anticipate how quickly you would succeed.

"By contrast, I noted that apparently without an order from a superior, ordinary soldiers on their own went to fortify that vulnerable flank, and the opportunity was lost. I believe, other things being equal or not too far from equal, that battles, even wars and the consummate contest of cultures are won or lost ultimately on the basis of that kind of individual initiative. I wonder where that kind of self-motivation comes from."

Arreola took notice of his subordinate's discomfort. "Please, Nicos, don't be embarrassed. It's not just you. We all have to learn from our mistakes. I merely offer the criticism for your edification and growth as a leader." Arreola paused for a moment and then said with a certain emphasis. "You may have to take over command of this regiment one day, after all."

This suggestion truly exacerbated Nicolás' unease and turned it into a profound distress. Though he couldn't identify why, it seemed to the Colonel somehow consonant with his previous feelings of anxiety. "Oh but, sir, I could never replace you!"

Though Arreola knew he had Nicolás' brotherly affection, he could feel just a twinge of flattery—insincere flattery—in Nicolás' exception to the General's suggestion. There was quite a muscular bond between the two, but Arreola could always feel beneath it just a small scintilla of jealousy—a prick of resentment that Nicolás was a pure Spaniard under the command of a common *mestizo*.

He gently smiled at the reminder. "That day may come sooner than you think, José. I'm not invulnerable to a rifle ball or grape shot from a cannon—or other means of coming to one's always untimely end on this earth."

A wave of discomfort welled in José Nicolás at his leader's words. He felt a considerable misgiving in his commander and friend concerning the possibility of his homeland's success in quelling this rebellion. In fact, he had as much as said so!

Nicolás had had a suspicion of it from the very start of the campaign and it had only grown as the war progressed. How could his commander and friend doubt their ultimate victory with all their successes so far? He quickly dismissed, he thought, the notion that it might be something in his commander's common Indian blood.

Nicolás lacked, and knew he lacked, the temperament and character to command. He depended so mightily on the certainty of his commander, friend and brother that any chink he sensed in the armor of the latter's confidence was like stepping off solid ground into quicksand. Might he have felt a kernel of shame, of resentment, at that fact, considering the difference as to their origins? If so, it was buried so deeply beneath his fraternal feelings and admiration for his commander as to be unrecognized.

"My General, sir…" he hesitated to continue both because he felt he might be prying and because he was afraid of his commander's answer. "Are you all right, sir? It's just that I sense…well…"

"Doubt? A preoccupation?"

"Well…y-yes sir. I don't mean to pry, sir. It's just that the troops…I myself, sir…"

Arreola took up the question from his subordinate on his own. "…Depend on your commander's absolute confidence, his self-assurance, his supreme command?"

"Well…yes, sir."

"It is that very dependence that will lose us this war, Nicos, that will lose Texas, perhaps all our northern territories."

"But sir…! My General! My brother! How can you—?"

Nicolás was interrupted by a knock at the general's office door. He looked to his commander to order what must be Captain Ordáz to not interrupt their discussion, especially on such a horrible note. To his surprise and dismay, General Arreola told the captain to enter and state whatever the matter was. "What is it, Manuel?"

Irritated, Nicolás turned to Captain Ordáz to find out what was so important that he had to interrupt his conversation with his commanding officer. He noticed the letter in the captain's hand and was concerned that it was a reprimand for the general for having tarried so long there in Presidio La Bahía.

As he did so, he noticed a look of confusion or hesitation on the captain's face. In fact, his whole body looked uncertain, even fearful. He wondered why, considering that the letter in his hand was still sealed.

"S-sir," the captain stuttered, "I...I have a letter marked urgent from General López de Santa Anna."

There was a quiet moment before Arreola responded. "Then deliver it, Captain."

But Captain Ordáz hesitated, now with a potent look of fear on his face. Nicolás, puzzled and angry at the intrusion and now the apparent slight to his commanding officer, scolded him. "Captain Ordáz, if you have a message from our supreme commander for the general, then deliver it immediately! Why do you hesitate?"

"Sir, it...it is not addressed to General Arreola...but to you."

"*To me!*" Why on earth...? Nicolás looked to Arreola with utter astonishment, completely at a loss as to what to do.

With a measured fatalism, Arreola calmly said, "Colonel, you have a message, an urgent message from your commander-in-chief and president. It is your duty to immediately attend to it."

"B-but why would...?" Portilla rather stuttered.

"I imagine the contents of the letter will provide the explanation you seek." He turned to his adjutant. "Captain Ordáz, do your duty and deliver the letter to its intended recipient."

"Sir!" Ordáz answered and snapped to attention, then handed the letter to José Nicolás.

In a state of apprehensive confusion, Nicolás accepted the letter from Captain Ordáz, and the latter, sensing a coming blow of catastrophic proportions, quickly saluted and exited, his duty done.

For a good while, as Nicolás held the letter before him, his hands began to tremble. He looked up at his commanding officer, brother and friend. Arreola held his look with steady eyes. He said nothing and waited.

Finally, Nicolás could hold out no longer. He broke the wax seal and again hesitated before removing the letter from the envelope. As he unfolded the letter there contained, he cast a worried glance to Arreola, then looked down to glean the epistle's contents.

José Nicolás de la Portilla was shot to his feet by what he there read. All color drained from his face. His eyes became giant Os of trepidation. He could not believe he had read it correctly and, after a brief horrified look at his superior, repeated the action and then pored over it a third time. Now not able to escape its unequivocal directive, he looked up at his savior, his commander, bosom friend and protective brother. With a voice robbed of all substance he barely squeaked out, "My General…José! This…this can't be! It makes no sense!"

In a calm and certain voice as he rose to meet his brother's mystified gaze, Arreola corrected. "It will, Nicos. Let me tell you what I believe to be the contents of the message: that you are to relieve me of my command; that you are to assume command of the regiment yourself; and finally, that you are to effect my execution for dereliction of duty—the disobeying of a direct order."

Nicolás felt like a giant hand had entered and ripped all substance out of him. The room seemed to spin. He could not believe in the reality of the present situation. He was certain that he'd been catapulted into some alternate universe where everything was the opposite of the real, the true.

"My commander…my dear friend…my *brother*. How—how can this be? How in the name of God? What gross and preposterous error can have been committed here?"

"Unfortunately, there is no error, General Portilla. Our present situation has come about because I made a choice. Not an easy one and I'm not even certain that it was the right one. But, the decision made, I now have to live with the consequences."

"*What choice?*" What could you have done? What order could you have refused? And *why? Why?* How could you disobey an order from the supreme authority we have?"

"Because I'm counting on there being an even higher authority." Nicolás frowned in confusion, which his superior noted with paternal indulgence but would leave his subordinate to ponder the statement himself.

"And now, my *General*, my bosom friend…my brother, *you* have a choice to make."

Nicolás' eyes expanded into huge orbs of horror. "But…" he stammered, "w-what choice have I? It is a direct order from our commander, our sworn leader and president! That we both have taken an oath of allegiance to!"

Arreola was not at all surprised by his protégé's vehemence, his desperation. The more passionate were his pleas, the more calmly and rationally Arreola answered him. "Yes. Your duty is clear. And I can make it even clearer for you. Beyond sparing the prisoners and setting them free, it was actually my determination to join them in their fight for independence. So you see, General Portilla, that I am truly a traitor."

José Nicolás stared at him in bewilderment, his mouth agape, his brow furrowed in disbelief, nausea threatening to overwhelm him. "*Why would you tell me such a thing?*"

"I will let you ponder that, José Nicolás de Cos de la Portilla, General and Commander...friend and brother." With that he stood, went to the office door and opened it. "Captain Ordáz, your presence is required."

The captain came in, saluted and stood at attention, betraying his own alarm at the tension in the air. "Yes, my General, sir."

"I am no longer your commander, Captain. I have been stripped of my authority. Therefore, you will no longer address me as such. Your new general and commander stands before you here," he said, indicating José Nicolás. "You will now take me into custody to await my execution."

An astonished Captain Ordáz looked from one to the other, incredulous that he had heard his one-time general's words correctly.

Arreola, recognizing that he had to reinforce his declaration with a physical gesture, took hold of his general's insignia and tore them off with a formal but unmistakable violence. He then extended them to the astonished captain.

Ordáz, completely dumbfounded, looked from the tattered general's insignia in Arreola's hands up to his now former general's eyes and across the room to his erstwhile colonel, in despair as to what to do.

Intolerable silence reigned for seconds that seemed hours.

Finally, from the depths of his despair, Nicolás' military training, his time as second-in-command, his experience not only following orders but issuing them, took hold. (And could there have been mixed in, just a treacle of unconscious satisfaction for his pure Spanish pride?)

A voice not beneath but layered above his natural younger-brother self, Nicosito no longer but now General José Nicolás de la Portilla, came from him. "Captain Ordáz, do your duty and follow orders. Take this soldier, now stripped of rank and honor and imprison him…" and General Portilla hesitated before finishing, "…to await execution by firing squad with all due haste and formality," he finally was able to finish, fighting the urge to break down completely.

The captain was still stymied with uncertainty of how to proceed. So, Arreola took his hands and placed his general's insignia into them and exited the room. Ordáz hesitated a moment, glancing at his one-time colonel, and then followed Arreola out, leaving a General Portilla, eviscerated and crushed, blankly staring after them.

*O*n the third day after Arreola's arrest, General Portilla finally received an answer to his letter to General López de Santa Anna pleading for the life of his now defrocked brother. It was as stark and unforgiving as the one Arreola himself had received: execute the traitor or face execution himself.

Despite his Spanish pride, the burdensome weight of the position José Nicolás was so unpreparedly thrust into made him tremble with feelings of inadequacy. Several times a day during Arreola's imprisonment, Portilla had gone to him, begging him to renounce his confession of treason and follow the order from his supreme commander. He was certain that if his bosom friend and mentor did so, all would be forgiven, and his generalship reinstated.

But it was all to no avail. His former commander was adamant.

Now all avenues of escape from the hated order of execution had vaporized and been carried away on winds of military protocol. Portilla had not slept the night after his receipt of the directive from his commander-in-chief. Now, he knew he could delay no longer; the dawn would usher in the final denouement of this horrid, tragic tale.

In fact, he had slept only fitfully since the initial act of this drama. His general's insignia fit oddly on him. The responsibility for the actions of the whole regiment weighed upon him as an albatross of doom. He had to fight to keep it from pulling his shoulders earthward.

He looked out the window of what was now his own office to the courtyard below. The initial stirrings of troops and prisoners could be seen in the dimness of pre-dawn. He could just make out the members of the firing squad priming their rifles and a wave of panic forced him to turn away.

There on the general's—on *his!*—desk lay the letter containing the direct and inescapable order. He picked it up, started to re-read it but then quickly put it down. He tried to resist thoughts of his dear frie—of the prisoner—of the pris—of his *brother's* wife, his son…and the daughter he will never know. He fought the shameful tears that threatened to form and betray the required composure of command.

When one traitorous tear escaped and betrayed the self-possession he fought with all his strength to effect, he slammed his fist down upon the desk, square in the middle of the letter from his commander. He then immediately exited and passed Captain Ordáz who stood to attention and saluted.

When no counter salute was offered, he waited until the general descended the stairs and then sat, wondering at the abandonment of military protocol.

Portilla marched to the prison where Arreola was housed, passing by many soldiers who stood to attention and saluted, only to wait in vain for the appropriate response. The like happened as he passed the prison guard and entered the single-celled stockade.

The soldier-jailer did the same, but as the general waited before the heavy wooden door of the cell that housed the prisoner, the poor private, with the general still in his presence, stayed at attention, holding his salute, awaiting his general's countersign.

Portilla turned to him, scowling. Finally recognizing the reason for the private's neglect, the general saluted back as though he were swatting a fly. He said nothing, only nodding angrily at the door.

As the befuddled jailer opened the door, Arreola was already standing in the center of his cell facing who he knew would be his dear brother and executioner. The two stood staring at each other in silence, barely able to see in the tenuous light of predawn that crept, as though ashamed of the event that dawn would bring, through the cell's tiny window.

In that stare was Portilla's desperate plea for his friend and brother to repent and carry out their commander's order. Without words, Arreola apologetically but firmly communicated his dissent.

After a long and crushing silence, General de la Portilla lowered his eyes to the floor and stepped back, indicating to his prisoner to exit the cell and march to his place of execution. Arreola walked forward, stopped beside his brother, squeezed his shoulder in sympathy and complied.

They exited the stockade and made their way to the eastern wall of the fort. Nicolás could not look when Captain de la Garza placed the condemned man against the wall facing the firing squad. The captain offered a blindfold to him, which was refused. Brave though he was, Arreola trembled, as any man would in the like circumstance.

He had already made his final wishes known to Portilla: to be shot in the heart not in the face; to be given a Christian burial; and to have all his belongings and wealth sent to his family in Mexico.

Portilla had earlier arranged for Captain de la Garza to carry out the execution. However, when the captain started to give the orders to the firing squad, the general stopped him in mid-word. Somehow, he felt that his brother and friend deserved to have his time on this earth taken not by a relative stranger but rather by family. And to delegate that hated duty was cowardly.

So, he began. "¡*Listos*!" (Ready!) came out of him strongly, as he tried to live up to his newly bequeathed generalship. He tried to be as direct with the proximate order, but his voice broke in the middle of ¡*Apun-ten*!" (Aim!) the last syllable barely heard, so that the squad hesitated just a heart-rending second in carrying it out.

Portilla could not keep the tears from welling in his eyes as he stared at the ground before him and tried to give the final order. Those fraternal feelings now banished whatever pride he might have felt at now being in command. The delay was so long that the firing squad looked to their captain and glanced at each other wondering what to do.

Even when the general finally succeeded in mouthing the final order, his voice broke and the sound that came out of him was so tentative as to be inaudible. "Fue..." (Fi...). He tried again, but again the word would just not come above a hoarse whisper. It sorely grieved him that his brother was held in such agonizing suspense, but General Portilla was paralyzed.

José Necahuatl de Arreola, understood, however, and with a final gesture of love and compassion, issued the order himself, still unsure if the act was brave or cowardly: "¡*Fuego*!"

And the deed was consummated.

Chapter XVIII

Vengeance is mine saith the Lord. Therefore
if thine enemy hunger, feed him; if he thirst,
give him drink; for in so doing, thou shalt heap coals
of fire upon his head.

--Romans, 12:19-20

Between the radiant white of a clear conscience
and the coal black of a conscience sullied by
sin lie many shades of gray: not perfect but not beyond
redemption.

--Sherry L. Hoppe

"When the commanding officer, General Arreola, was executed, I knew, and your stepfather knew, what the fate of the prisoners would be, *hijo*."

We were less than an hour away from Fort Concho, I gauged by the distance. I was parched and hungry. I imagine we all were, but I knew Miss Luz wanted to get to the doctor as fast as possible. I did, too. I was still hoping there might be something he could do. Now there was no question that she was plainly showing the haunted eyes of the sleep deprived. I think maybe she was continuing the story in part just to keep herself awake.

"We tried to convince the others of the certainty of their fate," she continued, "but whether it was the predominant military protocol at the time or just plain wishful thinking, most just couldn't believe that four-hundred thirty-two men would be murdered out of hand.

"My brother told me that when they were marched out of the fort, despite being under heavy guard, the others were sure they would be let go. After all, they said, if they were going to execute them, why wouldn't they have done it while still enclosed in the fort?

"When they were stopped after a short march, Gerardo knew. 'Get ready to run for your lives,' he told those close to him. Most were still in denial. Though beginning to have their doubts, they waited, as that fateful human tendency to cling to the belief that faith will form reality, still possessed them.

My brother had already conceived of a plan: when the slaughter started, he would run a zig-zag course as fast as he could toward the nearest thicket or grove of trees. Most of the Mexican soldiers had muskets rather than rifles, which are very inaccurate, so he figured he had a pretty good chance.

"If he was hit, however, and the blow was not mortal, he would feign being dead. When they came to administer the coup de grâce, he hoped he would have gotten far enough that the soldiers would be widely dispersed, and he'd only have to deal with one of them. And if he prevailed, that might give him time to get to cover."

"Man, Miss Luz, why would they just execute people like that? Ain't there some law or maybe just a custom or something against it?"

"That soldier I told you about who had shared the news of the designation of the rebels as pirates actually came over to our side in disgust. Of course, he was the only one I knew of that did so. There is not that...sensibility in Spanish culture of thinking for yourself. An order from the authorities is taken almost like an order from God.

"A common soldier, even most officers, think, 'The masters decide what's right and wrong and my only obligation is to carry out their orders. I have no moral responsibility. The execution of pirates is justified—and justified because my commander says it's so.'"

"I always though pirates were thieves on ships."

"They are, usually. But any people who rise up in arms to—in the Mexicans' point of view—steal from the country, can be so designated.

"I wonder if ultimately, though, it was a matter of deep-seated fear...and jealousy."

"How's that?"

"The United States was growing, both in size and wealth, at an astonishing pace—you could say a threatening one to those that bordered them. Even before it became a republic in its own right, their people were pushing ever farther into the unoccupied frontier—all on their own initiative.

"By contrast, our little Mexican settlement I told you about was organized and ordered by the government to occupy a space in Texas. And as I told you, most of the people that made up our colony were aching to return.

"I think that tendency of the Spanish, the Mexicans, went beyond a preference or the craving of company. I think it's actually a fear of being alone—maybe originating in that rigid hierarchical social structure. I believe the Mexican army, or at least its commanding officer, understanding fear but not that kind of fearless initiative in their enemies, thought it could, by their ruthlessness, instill such a terror in the rebels that they would give up. They, and particularly Santa Anna, never imagined that it would just make them mad and vengeful."

I thought for a minute about what Miss Luz had just said about what I guess you could call cultural differences, but I was anxious to know how Mister Macalister survived the massacre. "So did it work out the way Mister Macalister thought it would?"

"More or less. He'd almost made it to a thicket of oaks when he stepped in a gopher hole and fell. He'd had balls whizzing by him so close that he could feel the heat of a couple of them, so he decided to just play dead there. He was lucky that the soldier who came to finish him off was going to use a knife to slit his throat and not the butt of his musket or a pistol. That murdering assassin had probably used his pistol on another poor prisoner—or prisoners; he might have just been out of powder or balls or both.

"When the soldier lifted my brother by his hair and put the knife to his throat, Gerardo used a trick he learned as a Comanche. He grabbed the soldier's hand and knocked him off-balance with his legs and feet so that the knife only grazed his lower jaw. Then he quickly rolled him over and got on top of him, twisted his hand the knife was in and plunged the weapon into the soldier's heart."

"Wow. So did he get away clean?"

"He made it to the grove of post oaks. Some of the officers were on horseback, however, and he knew he couldn't outrun them. He climbed one of the trees in the thicker part of the *encinal*, hoping they wouldn't look up there. Or if one of the mounted officers came close enough, he might be able to drop down on him and take his horse. He'd kept the Mexican soldier's knife.

"Boy, he's one awesome man."

I could sense the pride my comment had caused in Miss Luz. I could hear my mother in the wagon humming a Polish lullaby to little Amelia—or maybe to her and Mister Macalister. She'd already taught the child a little Polish.

"Yes, he is. He certainly is," Miss Luz answered with a heart-stabbing bleakness that seemed to snatch up all hope from the world and banish it to perdition.

I thought I'd better let the black cloud that had enveloped her dissipate just a touch before asking her to continue the story. It was taking quite a while, though, so finally I just decided that getting her mind off Mister Macalister's condition would be the only thing that could possibly help. "So how did he finally get away? Did it work out that he dropped down on a mounted soldier?"

"Sort of. First a soldier on foot stopped almost right under him. Gerardo moved a little to get directly on top of him, but the movement caused the tiniest rustle. I guess even the best trained Comanche is capable of making a careless mistake.

The soldier looked up and Gerardo had to jump him right away. The soldier had a little time to prepare, though, and went for his pistol. Fortunately, Gerardo made it to him in time to grab the gun so that it fired in the air. My brother made short work of him.

"But the gunshot was evidence of his presence and before he could climb another tree, a mounted officer came directly at him. In that moment he was lucky his Comanche ways came back to him in all their wiliness—and that the thickness of the trees constrained horsemanship. He side-stepped the horse, grabbed hold of the officer, mounted behind him and slit his throat all in one motion. Now he could get away."

"So did he hightail it east to get to Sam Houston's army?"

"Definitely not. I was still in the fort, you see. Besides, they would be looking for him going in that direction. The last thing they'd expect was for him to double back to the fort. The soldiers were still finishing off and mopping up the rest of their victims, whose bodies they piled up and burned. They'd still be occupied with that for a while and there were only a few soldiers left at the fort, so Gerardo figured he had a good chance for both of us to get away."

"Had they arrested you too?"

"No, but it was clear I couldn't leave until the soldiers made it back from the carnage. They didn't want any warnings or interference.

"When Gerardo got to the fort, he rode his horse straight into one sentry—knocked him unconscious. The other one fired his musket at him but missed. As soon as I saw him, I knew what to do. One soldier had just bridled his horse and was in the process of saddling her. I ran straight at him as he was lifting the saddle, knocked him down and jumped up on the horse. She reared, and since I was bareback, she almost threw me off.

"I managed to stay mounted, though, and headed for the gate. I felt the soldier's pistol ball whiz passed my ear as I rode for the gate. Gerardo drove his horse into the other sentry just as he was raising his pistol and knocked him clear outside the fort. He took off, knowing I'd be right behind him. A few of the soldiers managed to fire at us as we ran, but we rode the Comanche way and none of their balls came close."

"Man alive. So then did you head east to join Sam Houston's army?"

"We did. We stopped after about an hour to tend to Gerardo's cut along his jawline, which hadn't stopped bleeding. I tore off strips from my dress, trying to find pieces that weren't soaked with horse sweat, and put pressure on the cut. The bleeding stopped but when we continued on our way, it started again, started almost right away. I finally had to cauterize it with the knife Gerardo had taken from the Mexican soldier. We knew it was risky starting a fire and keeping it going long enough to make the blade sufficiently hot, but it was the only way."

"Boy howdy, that must've hurt like the dickens."

"Yes. That's why my brother has that prominent scar on his left cheek."

Suddenly, Mister Macalister weakly called out. My mother tried to attend to him, but he kept calling for Miss Luz. My mother said in her pigeon-German, "GP call you, Luz."

She immediately handed me the reins and said with a sense of urgency, "Head directly for the fort and keep the pace steady, *hijo*. I can tell the mules are exhausted."

She then made her way back to Mister Macalister. I couldn't hear what either of them were saying over the clopping of the mules' hoofs and the clack and grumble of the rickety wagon, but when Miss Luz got back in the buckboard, I asked her what he wanted.

She took the reins and went stone-cold silent. It felt like the earth swallowed her soul and all the mirth and laughter it contained. I respected the silence. Then finally resurrected enough to deal with affairs of the present, she quickened the pace of the mules up to a canter and said, kind of matter-of-factly, "He wants to die and be buried on the Lazy Eight." In the ensuing pause I felt the weight of the world press us earthward. "He knows."

The rest of the way to the fort we both hardly said a word. My mother asked me in Polish what her husband had said. When I told her, silence darkly reigned over all of us and seemed to extend to the limits of the earth.

*A*fter the doctor at the fort had had a chance to examine my stepfather, he took us aside. I could tell from his manner that there wouldn't be any good news. And I could see that Miss Luz knew it, too. I think she'd come to that conclusion as far back as when her brother first collapsed from his horse.

I was a little surprised that Jacob joined us. It struck me as kind of creepy that he was there but didn't seem much concerned. It didn't seem like much of anything got to him: the Indian attack, the bloody death of Mauricio the cowhand, his own father's injury and the mortal illness that came of it. It was like he was numb as an ear of cactus, indifferent as that constant west wind.

While the doctor spoke to us, I did my best to translate for my mother. "I'm afraid there's nothing I can do at this point. It's already turned into gas gangrene, which means the infection has traveled throughout his body. Cuttin' off his leg would just cause him a lot of pain without makin' a speck 'a' difference." He took a moment, addressing Jacob in particular. "I'm sorry, son."

I looked at Jacob. I couldn't tell if he had any reaction at all to the news. I was kind of surprised myself at feeling a potent sense of loss for a man I'd known barely more than a month.

"Let's get him back in the wagon," Miss Luz said. I felt like I'd kind of gotten to know her, so I wasn't surprised at her abruptness. I guess there's no place for sentimentality out here on the frontier.

"Now, hold on, Miss, uh…" the doctor cautioned.

"Luz," I said.

"Miss Luz. He'll be a lot more comfortable here. I've got some laudanum to ease the pain, and…you know, help him on his way… more comfortably." I noticed that Jacob seemed to take an interest in what the doctor said. I wondered why.

"He won't take it," Miss Luz dismissed the idea. "His last wish was to die and be buried on our ranch. That's the least we can do."

The doctor insisted. "Well, Miss Luz, you don't look like you've had a decent rest in days. Are you sure—?"

"The Lazy Eight is less than a day away. I'll rest only after I give my brother his final request." She turned to the rest of us. "Come on, let's get him up and over," she said, indicating Mister Macalister.

"Well, at least let me get some of our soldiers to carry him," the doctor offered.

"We'll take care of it," she answered in short order.

"Won't you let us hook you up with a fresh pair 'a' mules? Those you got look like they're at death's door."

"There's no time," she bit off. "They'll make it."

We lifted him up and carried him out to the wagon and this time, Jacob actually helped. That was the first time I'd seen him do anything for his father willingly. I was itching to know what made that ole boy tick, and what was going on between him and his father. I still felt kind of like an outsider, though, and knew it wasn't my place to scratch that itch.

Just as we were about to put him in the wagon, the doctor called out for us to hold off for a second. He had the straw mattress he'd had Mister Macalister laid down on in his office/quarters. "At least I can make the journey to your ranch a little less unpleasant for him." I could tell Miss Luz was touched by his gesture. I looked at my stepbrother and couldn't see any reaction from him one way or the other. Boy, I wished I could figure him out.

As we made our way out of the fort, some of the soldiers stood at attention in two lines on either side of our path. As we passed, they saluted in a gesture of respect. The name GP Macalister was apparently well known around Texas. That was the only time I could see Miss Luz holding back tears. Seeing her that way gave me the urge to do the same. I'd really come to care for her.

I couldn't believe she wasn't collapsing from exhaustion and lack of sleep. I figured getting her talking was the best way—the only way, really—I could help. I was dying to ask her about Jacob, but I still felt like it was up to her to talk about his relationship with his father if she decided to. It felt like a real sore subject. So, I asked her about what happened after she and Mister Macalister got away from the presidio in Goliad.

"We made our way east, met up with Sam Houston's army a little way from Victoria and followed him further east. A lot of the soldiers were complaining about Houston's orders of retreat. Some of them were actually talking about splitting off and taking a stand.

"At first, Gerardo just listened. I could see him trying to get a handle on Houston's thinking. Of course, my brother knew the size of Santa Anna's forces. And he knew what would happen if even the whole of Houston's small army tried to fight them in open battle. Gerardo's reputation as Indian fighter was known around the state, so some of the men asked if he would lead them if they broke off to engage Santa Anna's army.

"By that time, he had come to respect General Houston and had a feel for his thinking, his strategy. He told them that Houston was being smart. The part of east Texas he'd taken us to was swampy, which would make it harder for their soldiers to maneuver. Besides that, the Texians knew the terrain, the Mexicans didn't. He was tiring them out as well since finding food in that part of Texas for people who didn't know the area was an ordeal."

Miss Luz went quiet for a minute or two, and a weight of sorrow seemed to pull her earthward. I was worried about her still being basically sleepless for such a time. I wondered what on earth could have caused so drastic a change in her so suddenly. I soon found out as she took up the story of San Jacinto.

"I was worried about my brother. Through almost all his Indian-fighting days he'd maintained a sense of honor and kept his Rangers in line for the most part. I think the reason he quit is that he'd recognized in himself that that honor was being chipped away by the continual atrocities he witnessed—or the results of them, anyway.

"After Goliad, after the massacre of his fellow soldiers who'd already taken to his leadership, I felt that flint-hard callousness he'd only started to succumb to in his Indian-fighting years now take full possession of him. From that tree he climbed to hide from the Mexican troops, he'd watched as his fellow soldiers cried for mercy to the Mexican troops as they finished them off with rifle-buts to the head, throats slit or, more mercifully, a pistol ball to the back of their heads. He'd heard a couple—more than a couple—cry for their mamas as life slowly drained away.

"I wish that Edeline could have been with us; I couldn't think of any other influence that might have chased that demon from his spirit—or at least, softened its mastery of him."

I wanted to ask what Mister Macalister had done, but I knew better than to pry into something that had taken Miss Luz to such a dark place. After a moment, she took care of that for me.

"I tried to talk to Gerardo, but your stepfather is not one to share his feelings, especially ones that were as pitch-black as the ones he was experiencing in the aftermath of the massacre. I guess that simply isn't done out here in the frontier. There's just no time for them...feelings. I could near to smell the hate in him, the burning for revenge. Almost all of Houston's forces wanted to avenge the Alamo and Goliad. That poisonous bile in my brother seemed to infect his very soul.

"And they took their revenge. They certainly did."

She shook her head violently like she was trying to banish the ponderous haze her thoughts had taken her to and leap-frogged to another topic. "Why Santa Anna camped where he did, with no means of escape or retreat I'll never understand. Overconfidence, probably. His troops were blocked off by thick woods on one side and heavy marsh and a lake on the other.

"Houston knew the Mexican troops were exhausted. There'd been torrential rains. Roads turned into mud pits. He asked some of the *Tejanos*, including me, about the tradition of the siesta when Mexicans take a nap in the heat of the afternoon. It worked out perfectly for his Texian troops.

"When the order to attack was given, the rallying cry was "Remember the Alamo!" I heard my brother say under his breath, "Remember Goliad." He didn't yell it. It was more like a quiet oath of damnation for the Mexican troops.

"The slaughter was enormous. Houston and some of the other officers tried to stop it. Their orders were ignored until almost the end. You could hear Mexican soldiers pleading for mercy, yelling, 'Me no Alamo! Me no Alamo!'

"Their screams went unheeded." She paused a moment and then barely mumbled, "Even by my brother."

It was nighttime and I could see her head nodding and eyes closing every now and then. I sure wished I knew the way to the Lazy Eight. Of course, even then, I had no experience driving the mules in the dark. She actually started to lean forward a little and I just put out my arm to stop her. The gesture by itself woke her up.

"Miss Luz, don't you think we ought to take a couple of hours to sleep?"

"We don't have those hours before my brother d-dies, *hijo*." She was starting to stutter from lack of sleep. "Not to w-waste and still have Gerardo knowing he is on his own land when he goes. I so w-want to get him all the way to his home, to his Edeline. I can feel him fighting to stay alive and conscious till then. It's his final request. For all he's done for me and means to me, I have to honor it. I have to.

"Just sh-shake me if I start to fall asleep. There will be plenty of time to rest once Gerardo's final w-wish is fulfilled."

With that, she again shook her head, asked me to pour a little water in her cupped hand and splashed it on her face, rubbing it vigorously. Then she continued the story. Now, however, her words were coming out kind of forced and stuttering.

"I n-noticed that during the heat of the battle that Gerardo kept his pistol...l-loaded. I knew what he was saving it for. He'd used his rifle, his knife, the butt of his rifle, a saber he took from one of the Mexican soldiers he'd killed, but not once had he f-fired his pistol. I knew he was searching for one soldier to use it on: General José Nicolás Portilla, the ma..." she seemed a bit befuddled for a moment..."the man who'd given the order for the ma-massacre at Goliad.

"I knew it was useless to try to reason with my brother. The executions had finally warped his sense of honor beyond repair. I was h-hoping against hope that General Portilla had been killed by someone else. I was afraid such an act of revenge, of-of hate, would taint my brother's s-spirit, change him in some irreversible way.

"My hopes to avoid such an act went un-unfulfilled. Somehow, amid all the chaos, we saw a man with a general's uniform pushing a woman holding something in-in her arms into a tent. As we neared, I could see it was General Portilla.

"He turned around to face us just as we st-stopped, standing before the entrance to the tent. I could see that he was unarmed.

I also feared that the woman he was hiding was his w-w-wife. I looked at my brother and then at him. I could tell that he recognized Gerardo. He had personally escorted me to visit my b-brother at La Bahía—Fort Defiance.

"There seemed to be a kind of…kind of silent communication between them. General Portilla had not raised his hands, but rather stood as though before a firing squad, unable to escape, perhaps even kn-knowing that his fate was inevitable—even deserved.

"It was the only time I'd seen such a look of barbaric hate coming out of my b-brother. I knew there was nothing I could do to stop him. I th-think he took his time raising his pistol just to impress upon Portilla the virulent contempt he felt for him. Portilla looked back with what looked to me like acknowledgement.

"Finally, Gerardo pointed his pistol and put a ball right between the eyes of his victim, which kn-knocked him back into the side of the tent.

"From inside it came a s-scream of horror. Gerardo and I looked at each other, and I could see a cr-cracking of the ice of his hate at the sound. After a moment, Portilla's aggrieved widow came out of the tent, trying to cock a p-pistol Portilla had apparently left her with. I quickly glanced at my brother and knew he would not defend himself against a woman he had just made a w-widow.

"This woman had obviously never fired a gun in her life. Cocking one of those old blunderbusses requires quite a bit of strength, and so she continued without su-success to cock it. My brother simply dismounted and moved to face her. But he made no attempt to disarm her.

"Finally, she ma-managed to pull the hammer back into p-p-position. Gerardo just stood facing her, again making no effort to disarm her or to avoid the shot. I wonder if he r-recognized what his thirst for revenge had done to him, so that he felt that the taking of his own life might bring the scales of justice back into balance.

"The lady also had trouble pulling the trigger of that old relic. She held it with both hands. But as I saw that trigger slowly start to move, I lifted my own pistol, aimed and fired a shot directly at her heart. She fell insta-instantaneously.

"Gerardo didn't even turn to look at me. He continued to stare at the two bodies wrapped in the tent before him. What he was thinking and feeling flowed out of him like a malignant w-wave of rot. Its stench seeped into me and set all my f-flesh tingling with the death of compassion and joy.

"Then something truly extraordinary happened. A ch-child, a sweet innocent female child appeared at the entrance to the tent. Gerardo immediately turned to her and then to me. On his face I could see the r-realization that he'd made this little girl an orphan. I'll never forget that look of horror—like I'd never s-seen from him before. And not again until...another loss."

I wondered if she were talking about Mister Macalister's first wife. I of course wasn't going to ask. It seemed like she went right back to the story to avoid the topic, anyway.

"I started to dismount, but Gerardo stopped me. He watched the child for a m-moment and then approached her. I could see her looking innocently up at him. Sh-she didn't look afraid, only curious. He knelt down before her...and she smiled.

"He spoke to her in Spanish. '*Hola, preciosa. ¿Cómo te llamas?*'"

"'Amelia,' she answered. '*Tengo tantos*,' she s-said as she held up two fingers. I couldn't believe she was so calm. She hadn't seen her mother and f-father lying lifeless on the tent which had folded around them. Amid all the noise and slaughter, though, it was eerie, her p-p-poise. Had she grown accustomed to it, traveling with the army? Was she in the s-state of shock? Why on earth had Portilla brought his wife and daughter with him? Had she just-had she just come to join him without asking p-permission and Portilla simply had no choice?

"It's not unheard of in the Mexican army to travel with one's w-wife—or…other women." She'd added that last bit in an undertone with a kind of distaste, so I figured she was talking about mistresses or prostitutes. "The answers to all those qu-questions, however, lay dead, enfolded in canvas."

"Wow, Miss Luz," just kind of heaved out of me after a moment. This child they "rescued" had the same name as the child in back with my mother. "Was this little girl you found little Amelia's mother?"

"She was."

"So you must've like adopted her, huh?"

"I kn-knew before my brother even picked her up that he would consider it his duty to take her as his own and raise her. *Este…*" I could see that Miss Luz was having trouble concentrating from sheer exhaustion. "Uhm…he-he p-picked her up and for a good while just hugged her against him. I'd never seen him before or since be so tender with anyone else—even with Edeline.

"Finally, he turned and…and l-looked up at me. I just nodded; there was no need to say anything.

"Well, what happened to her?"

"We raised her as our own. There's a k-kind of understanding on the frontier, with so many children losing their parents to Indian raids or war or disease…or just plain ba-bad luck: You take care of them; if there are no known relatives to be found, you r-raise them yourself. Edeline didn't hesitate for a…a moment. She treated Amelia as her own from the very first t-time Gerardo handed the child to her—didn't even ask for an explanation till later on."

Miss Luz broke into another little rueful smile. "That little girl would have had quite a talent had she l-lived beyond her teenage years. My brother spoke English to her, I addressed her in Sp-Spanish and Edeline spoke to her mostly in German. So she was p-pretty much tri-trilingual. I wonder what she could've done with that."

"Oh, she's not with us anymore?"

"She died in ch-childbirth. That was a little under two years ago. We named her daughter after her. She's now an orphan just like her mo—her mother—even though we have a suspicion who the father is."

"Who's that?" I blurted out without thinking.

Miss Luz went quiet at my question, and I could've kicked myself for prying into something so intimate. "Gosh Miss Luz, that's sure none of my business. I'm sorry."

Her lips curled up in a smile of understanding. "It's natural enough to be cu-curious. We don't know for sure, though; she went to her death re…refusing to say who it was."

Miss Luz went quiet again for a time, and I surely wasn't going to stick my nose into what was none of my business like I'd just done. She was fighting to stay awake though, and I struggled to find something to talk about in order to help.

I'd noticed that when she'd mentioned having a suspicion of who Amelia's father was that it looked like she started to turn back behind us but stopped herself. There were plenty of ranch hands it could've been, I suppose. But again, that was none of my business.

"How far from the Lazy Eight are we, Miss Luz?"

"Not much more than four…four or five hours, *hijo*. We'll be there s-soon." She was slurring her words more and more from sheer exhaustion.

"Why don't we get one of the cowhands to drive the mules so you can get some rest?"

"Look back behind us, *hijo*." I looked and could barely tell in the soft moonlight that it seemed we were all alone. "I told them and Cookie to stay at the fort and get some sleep. Rest them, their horses and the cattle. We took more cows from the Kotulas than we'd set out to, and losing Mauricio made us dangerously sh-short-handed. They didn't…they didn't need to be involved in this mission to get my brother back home before he dies."

"Even Jacob?" I asked her with a kind of an emphasis, curious as I was about my new stepbrother. I hadn't heard two words cast in my direction since meeting him at the Kotulas. There, he just silently nodded—and more like nodded at me rather than to me. I was dying to know what was going on between him and his father. I didn't dare ask, but again, somehow Miss Luz knew exactly what I was thinking.

"I don't think you asked about J-Jacob to know whether he was traveling with us, *hijo*."

I tried to think of some answer to mask my curiosity about something that was no concern of mine. Nothing came to mind, though, and I just started with one thought after another, starting to speak and realizing before any words came out that each was a dead end.

Miss Luz came to my rescue. "It's all right. You're a m-member of this family now and have every right to know what you've gotten yourself in-into. I could feel your cur...curiosity, even your anxiety, about your stepbrother's relationship with his father."

"Oh Miss Luz, I-I still feel like an outsider. I don't want to pry into something that's—"

"No, *hijo*. You have every rrr-right. And the character of your stepbrother is something you need to understand. With his father's death, the Lazy Eight will pa-pass to him. You need to be prepared for that. The story of my b-brother and his first born and only son—that is, before you—is one of bitter, bitter heartache and tragedy that too often occurs out here on the frontier.

"Well Miss Luz, I really don't consider myself—"

"*He* does. So listen now to a history full of s-sorrow and regret."

Chapter XIX

*A man never stands as tall as when he
kneels to help a child.*

--Knights of Pythagoras

*The hardest decisions in life are not
between good and bad or right and wrong,
but between two goods or two rights.*

--Joe Andrew

*Sometimes the most heartbreaking choice
is that between two unavoidable evils.*

--Anonymous

I woke up in the back of the cart where Miss Luz had ordered me when I'd again almost fallen asleep and gone over the side of the buckboard. I had a hard time shaking off the sleepiness as I crawled back up in the buckboard beside her. It was pitch black except for a soft, haunting glow cast by the moon as it made its way toward secreting itself beyond the horizon.

"Good morning, *hi-hijo*," she greeted me, trying her best not to betray the haunted look and slurring speech of one beginning to fail from lack of sleep.

"Good morning. Is it morning or night?" I asked.

"I suppose it's in-nbetween," she answered shakily.

"How long was I out?"

"Oh, I'd say less than two hours. How do you f-feel?"

"I'm all right, thanks."

The temperature had dropped considerably from the daytime and that constant west-Texas wind cut like a saber and chilled to the bone. I noticed Miss Luz was trembling to beat the band. I supposed that was a combination of the chill, the lack of sleep and the sparse rations we'd allowed ourselves in order to get to the Lazy Eight as fast as possible.

I reached back into the cart and pulled the blanket I'd found on top of me when I woke and wrapped it around Miss Luz. "Miss Luz, I sure wish I could spell you so you could get some sleep."

"Actually, you ca...can. The mules know the way home from-m here. All you'd have to do is get them going if they come to a s-stop. I nodded off a few times even up here and woke w-with the mules just stopped and grazing."

I tried to get her to take the blanket with her, but she wouldn't hear of it. "I'll be protected from the wind, especially if I surround myself with grain sacks. You'll be exposed up here. D-don't worry. I won't have any trouble s-sleeping." With that she handed me the reins and climbed back into the cart and was lightly snoring almost instantly.

In the ensuing silence, that blanket wrapped tightly around me against the icy wind, I had a chance to really enjoy the nighttime Texas sky. Its sable blackness spread out in awesome glory, festooned with glittering sparks and occasional steady points of light spread in delicate celebration of nature's majesty. The moon had gradually secreted herself beneath the earth's distant edge and no cloud besmirched the haunting display. So a sky awash in sequined majesty spread its glory from horizon to welcoming horizon.

Yet something weighed on its consolations.

I was surprised to find myself yearning for my brother Alexander to be here with my mother and me to share witness to such awe-inspiring grandeur. I longed for him to know my Aunt Luz, for so I now considered her, the most luminous point of light in all the firmament's finery.

Sensing the coming pitch of the darkness before dawn, I marveled that it was Alexander I wished to share this dazzling display of God's creative mastery with. Like that anonymous thief in the night, the thought crept into my mind that it was really the interrupted story Miss Luz was preparing to tell that made me yearn for my brother's company. I wondered why my desire to share it with him was so strong.

Of course, from the somberness of her mood before she'd lain down in the wagon, I couldn't imagine it was a tale I would want to hear alone. But I marveled that it was Alexander whose company I yearned for.

Now all alone with the stars and only the wheedle of crickets, the creak and grumble of the wagon and an occasional howl from a lone coyote to serenade me, I was free to reflect on all that had brought me and my family to this pass. It struck me that I had quite a tale of my own to tell.

I think Alex would have some insights into what it all means. He told me he'd realized that he'd been looking for meaning and— what did he say...*purpose*—in all the philosophy he'd read, in all his studies of economics and science and mathematics, political science and history.

And all of it failed him, he said—left him alone and empty. It was as a result of losing our father and baby sister that he came to the realization that the only thing that could really sustain a body—or spirit—was actually family, friends and a belief in a higher power. He'd said that those were the only things that kept him from despair.

I'd always felt a...a kind of sadness in him. Well, I guess I'm giving myself too much credit there. It was after our father and sister died and we'd pulled together as a family just as we got to our destination that I'd started to think of him not as a spoiled brat but as a really unhappy...*person*.

It made me wonder how much Mariana and I, with the way we treated him, robbed him of that feeling of family. Were we just jealous of his abilities? I wonder if it was his feeling of being so alone that had turned him away from God in the first place.

Curious thing about that belief in a higher power, though: he said he *chose* to believe, that none of us can really know for sure one way or the other. I sure am glad he didn't share that thought with Mama.

Then he went into things that were just beyond me, things about faith and reason or something like that.

I had questions of my own on that account. For instance, why would God now give me and my mother a new family only to take it away just like that? What kind of purpose can it serve? Well, maybe I can have a new family even without Mister Macalister. I sure hope so. I've always known I needed family.

There's that old saying that Alex, before the change in him, called a cheap excuse for believing in "such fairytales," as he called them then: that 'God works in mysterious ways'. "Just a way of avoiding the truth that there's no such being," he'd said he believed then, "and that everything that happens, happens randomly; that the only meaning in our lives is what we make of it."

I don't know. I just feel better believing than not believing. Like Alex says, how can anyone know for certain one way or the other?

I had been driving the mules for about two hours, I figured, when Miss Luz woke up (although when you're by yourself with nothing much to do, time seems to play a lot of tricks on a person). Anyway, she climbed back up to the buckboard wrapped in a coat I didn't even know was back there and shook her head mightily to chase away the sleep-induced cobwebs. I was amazed that she looked pretty well refreshed after such a short break.

I started to hand her the reins. "No, you continue driving the mules while I wake myself up completely. It's almost daybreak. Once the sun is up, we should be able to see the old homestead. It won't be long—maybe another hour—and we'll be there."

She poured some water, the little bit left in the last canteen, into her hand and rubbed it over her face and shook her head again. As curious as I was, I wondered now if I really wanted to know the history behind the strange feeling between Mister Macalister and his son.

Of course, she again read my mind and said, "You definitely need to know how the tension between Gerardo and Jacob came to be."

She didn't say it like it was a story I'd find interesting or amusing. She said "*needed* to know" not *wanted* to know. And so she began. Innocently enough at the start, but with a palpable sense that it was leading into the abyss.

"By the time my brother and I made it back to the farm," she started, "little Jacob was closing in on two years of age. Sam Houston had tapped Gerardo to participate in negotiations with Santa Anna and the Mexican government. Well, there was no real difference between the two. Antonio López de Santa Anna was in every way what the Aztecs called a *tlatoani,* a chief with supreme power, considered for all practical purposes a god.

"I stayed to help care for the child, Amelia. It was funny about that little girl. Because Gerardo was so busy with all the tasks General Houston put him to, she spent most of her time with me. But there was no question whom she preferred. As soon as she saw my brother coming, her eyes would light up like the brightest stars in heaven and she'd run to him and would not let go for all the gold of Croesus.

"Whenever he was there for a meal, she insisted that he feed her. If I tried, she'd just shut her mouth closed like a bear trap. She'd only go to bed if Gerardo was there to tuck her in and kiss her goodnight. She came to absolutely worship my brother.

"I assume because of Gerardo's natural leadership, Houston also put him to work decommissioning the troops, the few who didn't immediately hightail it back to their farms and ranches but waited to be paid. Unfortunately, that had to be done mostly with a pittance plus IOUs.

"Almost to a man those who stayed thirsted for Santa Anna's execution. They started fashioning nooses as soon as they heard he was captured. It fell to Gerardo and a few others to convince the majority of them the wisdom of Houston's plan to trade the Mexican president's life for Mexico's renunciation of all claims to the province of Texas.

"Santa Anna agreed—of course never intending to honor the treaty. It took an all-out invasion by the United States to finally settle the matter."

Miss Luz adjusted herself on the buckboard, shook her head to chase the sleepiness away and let out a profound but quiet sigh. I suppose it was to prepare herself to get to the rest of the story, which I could tell would be a heartbreaking one.

"We finally made it back to the farm near what had been the town of Liberty," she continued the story. "That Captain Bradburn whose abuse of Edeline had brought her together with my brother had had it burned to the ground. It looked like some former townspeople had started trying to build it back up but then eventually had given up. There were a few buildings started, walls built, then abandoned.

"When we made it back to the farm, we were both surprised at how little it had deteriorated, considering that Edeline only had Camp Cookie for help. All the able-bodied men had gone to join the Texian troops. Those two must've worked day and night to keep it going. Edeline had that look, that look of fatigue of one caring for a child and running a business and a farm singlehandedly."

"It must've been one happy reunion," I said.

Miss Luz paused kind of thoughtfully. "It was...mostly." She seemed to notice my reaction to her qualification. "Gerardo went straight to Edeline and paused before embracing her. Just for that brief moment he held her at arm's length. It seemed he just had to make sure he wasn't dreaming, that he was really home to the woman he loved more than the morning air and the stars at night.

"I could see Edeline understood, too, as she waited while he just swallowed her whole with his eyes. I can still feel the embrace myself when they finally melded into each other. It was as close as I've ever seen to two people becoming one. It gave me gooseflesh then. As I think about it now, it still does."

I waited a moment before speaking, but my curiosity finally got the better of me. "Uh, Miss Luz, you said…mostly."

"Yes, *hijo*." She took a deep breath like she was trying to figure out the best way to tell me the rest of the story. It encompassed many years and I guess a lot of issues, so I kind of understood.

"When Edeline put little Jacob down to embrace her husband, I noticed how the boy reacted. He'd had his mother all to himself for all those almost two years of life. Now here was a man coming between them, on whom she showered some of her love, maybe even more than she did on him.

"He grabbed his mother's skirt and started whimpering. My brother knelt down and tried to pick him up, but he hid behind his mama. 'Jacob, that's your daddy,' she said in German, 'there's no reason to be afraid.' She'd apparently spoken to him almost exclusively in her first language from the time he was born.

"In those two years, my brother had forgotten the little German he'd learned speaking—or trying to speak—with his father-in-law. It was too bad that Jakob had died just days after Gerardo left to join the war for independence. Besides Gerardo being an absolute stranger to Jacob, there was a language barrier for a time. And…it seemed to me that it lasted longer than it should have.

"Gerardo made an effort to relearn some German but, like I said, though he has many abilities, languages were not one of them."

I wondered how and which kind of questions I could ask and not be a busybody, but I was real curious about how it had turned out the way it did. Miss Luz was quiet for a time, and I was afraid she was falling asleep, so I just blurted out, "So is that why they don't really seem like…" I was gonna' say like father and son but I didn't want to be…what's that word Alexander used…*presump-shus*(?). As usual, Miss Luz came to my rescue.

"I think that kind of started it. It at least got things off on the wrong foot. I think Edeline inadvertently had a hand in it—of course, without meaning to at all. When Gerardo and I went away, and then her father died so soon after, little Jacob was all she had. She only saw Cookie when there was a question about the plowing or planting or harvesting or the care of the livestock. I think, naturally enough, she kind of spoiled Jacob. He was the only companionship she had. And she was his everything.

"When the boy's father came, she obviously had other obligations. Jacob now had a rival for his mother's love and attention. The first night Edeline went to bed with her husband and put the boy on a separate mat, he cried and cried until he was allowed to be by his mother's side. It took months before Gerardo and Edeline could consistently sleep as husband and wife. I guess to him, this new man in their lives was an intruder."

"Well…uh…" I hesitated to ask her to go on.

"Ask, *hijo*. You need to know."

"Weren't they ever able to work it out?"

"Oh, it...got better. But I don't think it ever got to be a really normal relationship between a father and his son—if there is such a thing."

"What do you mean, 'such a thing'?"

"As a normal relationship. From what I've seen in my life, there's no such thing as normal. There's good and bad, better and worse, closer and more distant, but where relationships are concerned, maybe where life itself is concerned, I don't think there's any such thing as 'normal'.

"Gerardo tried. He took the boy riding with him when he was still too little to ride by himself—almost always with Amelia between them. I often wondered if Jacob resented that as well, having to share his father with another 'intruder'.

"At first, Jacob seemed very stiff riding with his father and adopted sister. And I don't think he ever completely relaxed or felt totally secure. As the boy grew, my brother taught him how to ride and care for livestock, how to shoot a rifle, how to form and use a lasso, all the things that fathers do for their sons out here on the frontier.

"But with all the experiences Gerardo had had in his life, seeing his own family despoiled and murdered, his time as a Comanche going on bloodthirsty raids. Then, once we escaped, turning around and hunting and fighting them and seeing the results of their barbaric attacks on other settlers—seeing his fellow rangers starting to commit their own atrocities.

"Then finally, there was the massacre at Goliad. I even think his act of vengeance at San Jacinto hardened him to a point that it was difficult for him to show any tenderness. With the life he'd led, tenderness, sentimentality, was an invitation to catastrophe, to death."

Miss Luz paused, and I could tell there was something really significant or odd she was coming to. I turned to her as she just looked out into the blackness.

"But it's funny," she continued. "Amelia was always the exception. He was always gentle and loving with her, at least in his own rough-hewn kind of way. I still to this day wonder why. How had he kept that tenderer part of himself alive for her? Was it because he felt guilt for killing her father and being the cause of her mother's death? Can guilt have such a positive effect?

"It was fortunate for him, and for Jacob as well, that Edeline had enough love for both of them—the three of them, actually. She just kept a steady devotion that finally eased my brother back from his distance. It seemed to me that her love and her patience were boundless. I wonder if that comes from an essential strength, or if that capacity to love is what gives a person such strength of character.

"Gerardo's soul was scarred by all the war and killing and vengeance he'd experienced. Somehow, Edeline seemed to understand. He would sometimes go into dark places where he put up walls between himself and the rest of the world. During those times he'd hardly eat and not have two words to say to anyone beyond orders. I'm sure that didn't help his relationship with his son.

"Edeline was never resentful. She just waited patiently for the darkness to pass. Interestingly enough, it was usually Amelia that broke through the ice. She was another one full of love, just like her adopted mother. She wouldn't nag or even say anything or get fussy. She'd just, at the end of the day, after we'd all had our supper, crawl up into my brother's lap, curl up into him and often fall asleep right there. It never failed to thaw Gerardo out of his iciness. Her devotion to him never waned.

"And I wonder if there was something else going on. Something I felt from little Jacob when that would happen. Could he have been jealous of Amelia's closeness to his father—even though he himself never warmed all the way to him? It must have been confusing for the boy."

Miss Luz paused again to shake away the sheer exhaustion I knew she was suffering. It gave me a chance to reflect on what the deal was between Jacob and my new stepfather. It still felt kind of funny calling him that.

Anyway, I got the sense from Miss Luz that there was more to the story. There wasn't a feeling of finality in what she'd told me so far. "Well, I guess I can see how all of that might've poisoned the bond between them," I said, kind of hoping it would spur Miss Luz on to tell whatever the rest of the story was.

I hesitated to push, however, because of the feeling I got from my adopted aunt. Those times she went quiet like she was now I could sense she was building up to something. I waited a long time just listening to the constant wheedle of crickets, the creak and groan of the wagon, the occasional yap and howl of a coyote in the distance, the whistling wind and the steady breathing of my mother and little Amelia I could barely hear as they slept in the wagon behind.

Finally, I couldn't help myself. "Uh…Miss Luz was it just that? I mean…could they never, like…I don't know, get past all that?"

Miss Luz looked up at the starlit sky like she was trying to parse all the mysteries of life. She took a deep breath and exhaled with a quiet, determined sigh. "They did, *hijo*. It was never the kind of bond like there was with Amelia, nor with the two daughters that followed: your two sisters you'll soon meet. But there was a bond." After another breath, she quietly continued, "for a time."

My mother suddenly woke up and asked me a question. I conveyed it to Miss Luz. "My mother wants to know how far we are from the ranch. She says Mister Macalister's breathing is getting very shallow and…how would you say it in English…hard? forced?"

Miss Luz shook her head hard to chase away the final webs of drowsiness. "Tell her we'll be there in less than an hour." She took the reins from me as she continued. "And see if you can get that information to your stepfather as well."

I climbed over the back of the buckboard and gave the message to my mother, trying not to gag from the smell coming from Mister Macalister. I guess since we were riding into the wind the odor wasn't so bad up in front. I wondered how on earth my mother and little Amelia could stand it. I suppose you eventually get used to anything.

I went to Mister Macalister covering my nose as best I could. "Mister Macalister? Sir, can you hear me?"

"…Yes, boy," he sort of exhaled out, "What…is it?"

"Miss Luz wants you to know we'll be at the ranch in less than an hour."

"Tha's good. Tha's…goo…" kind of crept out of him like a sigh.

The message delivered, I climbed as fast as I could back to the buckboard. I wonder if there's anything that smells worse than rotting flesh. I felt kind of guilty complaining about it though, considering what Mister Macalister was going through.

"Mister Macalister's still conscious. I was able to get the message to him." Miss Luz just nodded.

We rode in complete silence for a good while. I caught myself nodding off and reached over to grab the canteen and splash my face with water. There wasn't any left. Miss Luz handed me a piece of jerky. "Chew on this, *hijo*. The chewing will help keep you awake." I noticed that that was exactly what she was doing.

"But you know you can always go in the back and sleep." She looked over at me with like a half-smile I could now see in the pre-dawn light. "But I know you want to hear the rest of the story. It is one you need to know.

"When Texas was finally admitted into the union there was a push to settle the lands farther west—where we are now, although there is now land even farther west still to be settled. With statehood, the federal government set up forts here and there to help with the effort. When Fort Concho, which we just left, was established, free land was offered in the area to encourage development."

Miss Luz must've thought of something a little happier than the story she was now telling as her lips curled up in a knowing, if restrained, smile. "There was always something restless in my brother's Scottish blood. It thirsted for a challenge—some new feat to accomplish, a new frontier to tame. I have to admit that I too was never content with just being. I was always excited when life threw a complication or adventure my way.

"It was in that forced Mexican settlement when I was a child that I really felt alive. There were so many new things to discover and understand. Even after the massacre when I was all alone, yes, I was lonely and scared, but together with those feelings there was a kind of excitement, a thrill of discovery…the challenge of survival."

She thought for a moment, looking up at the lightening sky. "I suppose that was why I eventually felt more at home with the Macalisters than with my own—my former—family."

Miss Luz paused for a moment, I supposed to reflect on what she'd said about the difference between her two families and the difference between her and the members of her Mexican family. Then she continued the story of Mister Macalister and Jacob.

"Anyway, the opportunities and my brother's restless spirit added up to Gerardo immediately looking for a buyer for the farm and applying for a land grant out west—this land we're on right now. I think that if it weren't for the fact that we've built the Lazy Eight into the size and success it is, and my brother always working himself to the bone to make it bigger and more successful, that we would have continued moving west.

"Now, with Edeline buried here, Gerardo would never leave."

"Miss Luz, how…" I again had to stop myself from poking my nose where it didn't belong.

"That's part of the story, *hijo*; the main part."

Somehow it seemed that Miss Luz no longer had that haunted, sleep-deprived look as she prepared to unravel the mystery of Mister Macalister and his son. She sat up straight in the buckboard and let out a thoughtful breath of air in seeming preparation.

"The time we spent developing the Lazy Eight, at least after the initial few years of scarcity, were the best for the family. We'd gotten a good price for the farm, thanks to Edeline's bargaining know-how. We brought the few cattle we had on the farm to the Lazy Eight and built from there. My brother had a knack for crossbreeding, I knew horses like the back of my hand and Edeline put her business savvy to work just as successfully with cattle and sheep as she had with grains and cotton.

"We sort of threw together a temporary house, but we built it on a solid foundation that we could use to make it into a real home later, which we did bit by bit. I suggested we build a second one, a safe house, out of clay, of adobe. Adobe can't be penetrated by arrows or bullets and is fireproof. We made it with narrow slits just wide enough for a rifle to poke through.

"During that time, the government finally got most Indians onto a reservation in the Oklahoma Territory. The only problem was that they—at least the Comanche and their Kiowa brothers—would still go on raids, then retreat to the reservation where they'd blend in with the so-called 'pacified' Indians. Indian agents from the government never seemed to understand: it's in the Comanche's nature to pillage and raid; you can't pacify a tornado.

"But as time went on, the raids began to diminish. Not only were we safer, but we were losing fewer and fewer cattle and horses. Those were the bountiful years. We added onto the house, Edeline had two girls a good three years apart. The first was named after Gerardo's mother, Fiona. The baby of the family was named after Edeline's mother, Lorelei, but they gave her the middle name of Luz, after me. I was so grateful for that."

Miss Luz smiled and seemed to swell a bit as she continued. "Lorelei Luz. I think it's a very beautiful name. Edeline and Gerardo called her Lorelei or sometimes Lori. I always called her Lucita, for obvious reasons. And everyone seemed fine with that. It was a little bit of intimacy between the two of us. I could never have children; Lucita was as close as I could come."

Miss Luz paused a moment in what looked like a kind of rapture. This time I would keep absolutely silent and do nothing to interrupt it, these moments of happiness seeming so rare on this journey. Finally, she just put a kind of cap on the subject by saying, "I do love that little girl. Although she's not so little anymore. No, she's a beautiful young lady, now."

"I can't wait to meet her—and her sister."

"I'm looking forward to introducing you, *hijo.*"

After that comment, Miss Luz went quiet, I suppose thinking about her namesake and, I guess you could say, foster child. We were bound to be coming on to the ranch, so I wasn't going to do anything to motion her back to the story of Jacob and his father. As usual, it turned out I didn't need to.

"Years had gone by and there had not been a single Indian raid on our property, nor on any of the surrounding settlers' places. We figured the fort being so close made the Comanche keep their distance. The ranch had grown and prospered, and the blessings of peace had a salutary effect on the whole family. And that's exactly what we were, one big family.

"Oh, there was still some tension between Jacob and his father, and strangely, Fiona seemed to have picked up some of it from her brother. I noticed the difference between the two girls right from the time they were born. Fiona was stiff in the arms of Edeline, and in anyone's who held her. She was fussy and cross from the start and had a hard time keeping her milk down.

"Lucita was just the opposite. She was at home with everyone and just molded herself to whoever chanced to pick her up. She only cried—and at that it was barely a whimper—when she was hungry or needed her diaper changed."

Miss Luz paused, and I could feel her mood darken. I didn't want to spoil the good feeling she was having at the memory. "Miss Luz, I...I imagine we're almost there. You don't have to—"

"Yes, I do. I definitely do, *hijo*. Especially since my brother will no longer be with us and your stepbrother will take over the ranch. For that, I do.

"I suppose we got careless, all those years of relative peace and prosperity. We had almost forgotten about the adobe fortress. The children sometimes made it into a make-believe fort, but that was about all it was used for. We were even talking about tearing it down, mold it into bricks for other purposes."

This time Miss Luz paused it felt like the storm of the century was about to break. Just the feeling made me stiffen in my seat. "When they came," she darkly began, "we were spread out in all directions across the ranch. Gerardo and Jacob were out searching for strays. Lucita was in the barn, bottle-feeding a lamb whose mother had died in childbirth. Fiona and I were in the corral pacing one of the mustangs the boys had brought in from the wild.

It was August, hot as an oven with a sweaty horse blanket wrapped around you. There wasn't a whole lot for the hands to do, so we were down to just two of them. Cookie had gone into the little settlement of San Angelo for supplies.

"I don't know who saw them first. Adolfo, one of the two hands who were with us in the corral, threw Fiona over his shoulder and headed straight for the adobe fortress. Seeing that, I hightailed it to the barn for Lucita. She was too young to have had any experience with Indians, so I had to just grab her by the collar and drag her to safety, ignoring her pleas for me to explain what was going on.

"Once inside, I looked through one of the slits and could see my brother and Jacob ahead of the Indians making for the fortress at a blistering run. Adolfo and Chris, the other hand, were at two different slots trying to pick off Indians with their rifles. I took the one between them and did the same.

Gerardo and Jacob barely made it to the fortress in time. I opened the door and let them in just as the Indians were surrounding us. A bullet and two arrows sank themselves deep into the door as I was closing it.

"Gerardo had taken his rifle from his saddle and went to another slit on the opposite side to fire. The smoke and smell of gunpowder was choking. Suddenly my brother stopped shooting and looked around. 'Edy!' he cried. 'Where's Edeline?'"

"He started for the door, but I stopped him. 'There she is, *hermano*.' I pointed to her in the arms of an Indian mounted in front of him. He took careful aim and dropped the Indian riding behind her. She was a good rider, but nothing compared to an experienced Comanche. Immediately as she gathered the reins, another Indian grabbed her off the horse and onto his own and started away from us.

"Gerardo was able to get that one as well, but the horse went down with him and her. She managed to get up but after a few strides another one scooped her up and threw her across his horse in front of him. My brother aimed and pulled the trigger; nothing happened but a dismal click. 'Who's got ammunition?' Gerardo demanded looking at the rest of us.

"Only Chris answered. 'I figure I got two left, GP.' He grabbed Chris' rifle out of his hands and aimed. They were getting farther away and close to being out of range. But Gerardo was able to drop that Indian as well. Edeline got up from where the horse had fallen on both her and the Indian. It looked like she was hobbled by the fall.

"They were too far away at that point for anyone to go after them, and we were down to one rifle with one bullet. Another Indian took up Edy as she stumbled toward us. Gerardo looked at me and I just nodded. 'Do it, brother. You know what her fate will be if you don't.'

"Jacob ran to his father screaming, 'No, Papa! No! We'll go after her! Please, no!' I grabbed Jacob and held him as he continued to scream. Gerardo raised the rifle but hesitated. 'Gerardo!' I yelled, 'You must!'

"Then finally, he fired. Only Jacob made a sound, screaming, 'Noooo!'

"The rest was a deathly silence."

Chapter XX

There is special providence in the fall
of a sparrow. If it be now, 'tis not to come;
if it be not to come, it will be now; if it be
not now, yet it will come. The readiness is all.
Since no man of aught he leaves knows,
what is it to leave betimes? Let be.

Hamlet, Vii

As the sun broke above the horizon, the softest, gentlest light brought the ranch house into distant view. It seemed to glisten in the early morning light. Almost dreamlike, house, barn and corral emerged shyly through a mist so thin as to be next to non-existent. Our journey was finally at an end, but the adventure, I felt, was just beginning. For my mother and me, would it bring peace or heartache? I guess there's always a bit of both in this life no matter the place or time.

There's a tenderness about the dawn, before the blazing Texas sun reaches its height and furiously burns off all grace and gentility. Birds unknown to me greet its arrival with cheerful, lilting song. There were some new ones here I hadn't heard before. If Alexander were here, I know he'd be about identifying each and every one. Maybe someday he can be.

It's strange about the desert. It's so different from Poland. At first, it seemed so completely and mournfully empty. It was sort of like the way I felt about this new family when I first met them.

They are people of few words, sparse, reminiscent of the scarcity of plant life and the endless, vacant sky covering the desert with blue wonder. It kind of makes you feel small, surrounded by such vast, empty space.

But in the days and nights we spent on it, I came to see a raw but rapturous beauty in it. Its openness invites you to breathe deep and free. The lack of greenery draws from you such a profound appreciation of every isolated lump of grass, the scraggly scrawny beckoning green of a mesquite tree, or the dusty grayish green of a huisache. And when you come upon a creek or a river lined with tall cottonwoods sporting delicate but lively green leaves, bullrush, cattails and river grass, it's like arriving at an oasis, such a sight for sore and vacant eyes.

I'd never seen such spectacular sunsets! A golden-reddish glow exploding across the western sky like God had reached out his hand and sloshed a bucket of finely blended paints across the horizon's edge as a blessing upon the earth. And those rare times there were a few clouds to reflect the light, they did so in dazzling pinks and carnival oranges and somber maroons to purples to blood-reds.

But at night...oh, the night sky was a dizzying banquet of glittering brilliance, so thick with stars it was like a sheet of twinkling fury.

It was all in keeping with the odd feeling I was having about finally reaching our destination. I mean, I was glad our journey had finally come to an end. I was glad we'd managed to grant Mister Macalister's final wish—that is, I hope he hadn't died in the short time since I last checked on him. We were at least on Lazy Eight land.

I felt a barely perceptible grain of discomforting doubt beneath the soothing unction of journey's end.

The feeling suddenly hit me that I would miss this man among men—that I would *really* miss him. Such a surprise, happening in the short time I'd come to know him. Could that be an effect of the empty desert as well, that bonding to the few people you come to know seems to happen so quickly and so strongly? Funny that at the same time those bonds are expressed in such a strict formality.

Does the sparseness of people as well as greenery lead you to appreciate those contacts more, just like you love the sight of a florid creek or river in the midst of scarcity? Did that help in some way for the settlers to unite like they did and cooperate as an army to hold their own against the powerful Mexican military?

The colonel at Fort Concho had been kind enough to send a messenger on horseback ahead of us to the family to inform them of the present situation—namely, Mister Macalister's condition—so it wouldn't be so much of a shock. I wonder that we didn't see the soldier crossing our path as he returned. I guess maybe he took a different route back.

Miss Luz hadn't said a word since recounting the story of Mister Macalister's first wife's death. That story pretty much silenced me as well. Boy, I just couldn't imagine: watching your father kill your mother? However necessary it was, I could see how that would send a boy into a tailspin and poison his feelings for the man who gave him life—for everyone and everything.

To my great surprise, Miss Luz started up again just where she'd left off. "Jacob was eleven at the time of his mother's death. For such a long time, maybe a year, he didn't speak at all. For some of that time, he didn't do much of anything, either. Anytime my brother or I would ask him to perform some chore, he'd just look at us like he didn't understand. He'd have nothing to do with his sisters or with me and he avoided his father like the plague. Anytime he saw my brother approaching he'd walk away and ignore his father calling after him.

"He'd show up for meals some of the time, but when he did, he'd just pick at his food like a bird. It was some time before he ate anything at all. Where he spent his time beyond that no one knew.

"Sometimes I'd see him coming from the creek, but without a fishing pole, and dry as a bone, so what he did there was anybody's guess. He'd saddle a horse and be gone for most of the day. Sometimes he'd just stand at the corral or sit atop it and watch the horses for hours. What was the fascination? What he did with the rest of his time was a complete mystery.

"At first, all of us tried and tried to speak to him and get him to answer. All he'd do, though, is nod or shake his head 'no'—and sometimes he wouldn't even do that. If you asked him a question that required words to answer, he'd just point or simply walk away. Eventually, we kind of gave up. I guess we just got used to him being mute.

"I tried to talk to Gerardo about it, but out here on the frontier things like that, mental things, are mostly ignored. Stiff upper lip and all that. 'He's had a terrible shock, Luz. Just give him time, he'll come out of it,' was all my brother would answer. That's how things like that are handled out here.

"To a degree, my brother was right. Jacob eventually started answering in one or two words at first. It was interesting that he did so with Camp Cookie before anyone else. The hands were next, then his sisters and finally, myself. But it took years before he said anything to his father. And when he did, he always addressed him from that moment on as 'GP', never Dad or even Father.

"I knew that was a deep wound on Gerardo's heart. But to people like my brother, you would never talk about something like that. You just swallow it hard and deal with the bellyache it gives you. I wonder how many years that took off his life. I wonder if the heartbreak of it hastened the infection in his leg.

"Jacob was always such a sensitive boy. He didn't even like to hunt or slaughter a cow. I suppose my brother was right to some degree, though. He did eventually start answering us at least. But since the death of his mother, he's never been the same."

Miss Luz again went quiet for a bit, but I felt like she had more to say. So, I just waited. Finally, she quietly but clearly said, "I don't think my brother was the same for a long time, either. I'd say he never got to be except that… something in your mother touched him, touched him deeply. God bless her for that."

Boy, I hadn't thought about that. It's a strange feeling, thinking your mother could inspire something like that. I guess I'd never thought of her as a…a person, a woman; she was always just Mama to me. I guess that's a whole new thing for me to think about.

There was one thing I was still curious about concerning Jacob, too. I didn't think I had any right to ask about it, so I said something as neutral as I could think of. "Boy, that's…tough. Really tough. I guess I can understand—at least to some degree. I…well."

"Go on and ask, *hijo*. You know most of the secrets of your new family now. You might as well—you *need* to know them all."

"Well Miss Luz, I...I wonder how Jacob seems to be so...like nothing seems to get to him. He doesn't seem to even care—about much of anything. And why wasn't he able to help his father with the arrow? I mean, I understand, or think I understand about the feelings he has for his father, but..."

I was embarrassed to be curious about something like that, so I couldn't continue. Turned out, as usual, I didn't need to.

"You've seen the flask he drinks from all the time?"

"Yes, ma'am. That was something I was curious about, too, I gotta' admit."

Her face kind of twisted into a wince like the memory was painful. "After that Indian attack there were other isolated raids, not just by Indians but cattle rustlers as well. Sometimes they were mostly white or Mexican with a few Indians in the mix. One time, Gerardo and Jacob and I with the ranch hands had just gotten back from getting a rough count of the cattle on the range preparing for a drive to the markets up north.

"Just as we dismounted, we heard gunshots and the cattle start to stampede. We immediately mounted again and went after the rustlers and the herd. We had the deuce of a time scaring them off by dropping a few of them. One of the hands got caught in the stampede and was trampled. He survived, but he was never much help after that. Since he'd been so faithful when he was whole, Gerardo kept him on doing the few chores around the house he could manage.

"During the chase, my brother and Jacob were after two Indians running ahead with the heard. Gerardo dropped one with the last bullet he had in his rifle. For some reason, the other one turned around and was riding hard back toward them. The one Gerardo shot must have been his brother or something.

"They both stopped. 'Jacob, shoot that Indian,' my brother ordered. Jacob raised his rifle but hesitated. 'Damn it, boy, *shoot!* He's comin' after us!' Jacob finally shot, but the Indian used his thong to drop to his horse's side, the Comanche way. Gerardo pulled his pistol and started shooting, trying to drop the horse. 'Shoot the damned horse!' he yelled at Jacob. The boy raised his rifle but again, hesitated.

"The renegade was getting close enough to be in pistol range and Gerardo managed to hit the horse just as the Indian let loose an arrow that hit Jacob's horse. The horse reared. Jacob was unprepared and was thrown. But his foot caught in the stirrup, and he was dragged until Gerardo managed to get to him and stop the horse. The Indian fell under his own horse and couldn't get his leg out from under him. Gerardo took care of him on the run after Jacob.

"Jacob's ankle was badly broken, and he was bruised and cut and scraped all over his body. He's lucky he even survived.

"My brother brought him back, unconscious. We immediately hitched up a wagon and took him to Fort Concho. At that time there was someone there with at least some knowledge of medicine and set Jacob's ankle. He was treating his other wounds when Jacob came to. When he did, he just howled, screamed in pain.

"The doctor and my brother and I tried to calm him down, but he was just in too much pain. 'I've got something to ease the pain,' the doctor said."

Miss Luz took a moment before she finally said, "That flask Jacob carries with him is whisky with a touch of laudanum mixed in. He's slowly killing himself."

With Miss Luz clearing up the final mystery of these Macalisters—or what I hoped was the final mystery—the reality of being an outsider in a whole new family, *this* whole new family, was sinking into me. What would be my place? Would I have one, or would I somehow be able to carve out one for myself?

What about my mother? What would her position be? How would she be treated without Mister Macalister there as her husband? Would we even be able to stay? And if not, how would we get back to the Kotula ranch? Would they take us back?

"There it is *hijo*, the homestead of the Lazy Eight," Miss Luz said as she nodded to the structures with an air of comfort tinctured with a shade of concern. "And there are your sisters waiting for us on the front porch. I know our arrival with such sad news will be a deathblow to my Lucita." I wondered at the fact that Miss Luz only mentioned the one sister.

I guess the messenger sent from the fort had accomplished his mission. The two sisters ran to meet us as we approached. They immediately went to the back of the wagon and climbed in. "Papa!" the younger said as she fairly pounced on him, hugging him with a desperate fury. I could tell that the elder, Fiona, was struck by the horrible smell coming from her father, and just knelt down at his feet with a hand on his ankle.

I felt real bad for them, knowing all too well what it was like to lose a father betimes. Although I don't suppose there's any time that makes it easier. My mother, with her consummate discretion, pulled away to let the two girls have all of their father.

As we pulled up, an elderly Mexican man came out of the house, doffed his hat and held it in his hands against his legs as he crossed himself. Miss Luz pulled to a stop right in front of the house, put on the break and handed the reins to the Mexican man. "*Hola*, Adolfo," she greeted him. "*Espera aquí.*"

The younger of the two sisters rose up on her knees to let her father breathe, and now both held each of his hands in theirs, weeping torrents of tears. Miss Luz climbed back around them and hugged them hard from behind. "Hello, girls. I am so sorry. There is nothing to ease this horrible loss, but at least you have the chance to say goodbye."

My mother got out of the side of the wagon and kept a respectful distance. I did the same. I saw Mister Macalister try to raise his head.

Miss Luz took charge. "John Michael, Adolfo, let's slide my brother out on his mattress and take him inside where we can all take our leave of him."

"No," came like a breathless squawk out of Mister Macalister. "Put me...by...Edy...and gather...round."

Without a moment's hesitation, Miss Luz arranged us to carry out Mister Macalister's final wish. With my mother and I on one side and Adolfo and Miss Luz on the other, we slid Mister Macalister out of the cart and struggled to carry him over to where his former wife was buried. His daughters followed.

"Lay me...by her...side, he wheezily croaked out. "Rozi... come," he said, holding out his left hand. With little Amelia in one arm, my mother took hold of Mister Macalister's hand with her other hand. Fiona and Lorelei Luz came immediately to the side opposite my mother, on top of their mother's grave. They both grabbed their father's other hand. "Oh, Papa…" Lorelia sobbed out.

"Don't…fret…Lori…Fi, I'm…leaving you…with…two fine…mothers and…a new…brother. You'll be…fine. I…love you…both so mu…"

"Oh, Papa…we love *you*," Miss Lorelei cried out in a broken voice. "We love you so much," Miss Fiona echoed.

"John Mich…," Mister Macalister tried to lift his head, seeming to call out for me. Come…."

I looked over at Miss Luz, not sure of what to do. Why would he want to say any final words to me? Miss Luz just indicated with a nod for me to go to where his head lay, while she stayed at his feet.

He let go of my mother's hand just long enough to pull me down right by his mouth, then reached for her hand again. I could just make out what he said. "Lazy Eight…must…survive. XIT business…won't. King…family. Lazy Eight…family. Must last! See to it…boy. *Swear*."

Again, I looked up at Miss Luz, completely at a loss as to what to do or say. How could I do anything to keep the ranch going? He should be saying this to Jacob. I wondered why he wasn't there. He could have made it by now if he'd left the others behind and come on his horse. Miss Luz just looked down at me with eyes that urged me to answer.

"Promise…me…boy!" Mister Macalister said with what sounded like desperation. I took a quick look at Miss Luz who nodded at me with an urging, almost a demand.

"Well, yessir," I answered. "Yessir, I...I promise."

And with that, I noticed his hands holding his daughters' and my mother's hands went limp. With his last breath he exhaled a barely audible, "good. Tha's..."

Fiona and Lorelei collapsed on him sobbing. My mother put her hand on his forehead and lovingly closed his eyes. Then Miss Luz, Adolfo and my mother crossed themselves in reverence. Out of respect—and heartfelt sorrow—I did the same. Little Amelia, I guess sensing the grief of others, buried her head in the crook of my mother's neck as copious tears rolled down her cheeks.

I stood and looked at Miss Luz, completely perplexed. How was I to...? What did the survival of the Lazy Eight have to do with me?

Miss Luz just returned my look with a constant, confident air. It seemed a look that spoke volumes, thoughts I struggled to decipher. It had an urging that bore into me like a carpenter's drill and had the air of a commandment.

No word was spoken. No horse whinnied or mule brayed. No bird sang or critter scurried. A deathly, reverential silence reigned over and beneath Mister Macalister's daughter's heartrending sobs.

I finally could not contain my own tears.

I did not try. They were my signature on the oath I'd sworn to my stepfather.

*A*nd the west wind moaned a soft, mournful dirge.

My heartfelt thanks to the following:

T. R. Fehrenbach, for his book,
Lone Star, A History of Texas and the Texans

Enrique Krause, for his book, *MEXICO, Biography of Power*

Timothy J. Henderson, for his book,
The Mexican Wars for Independence

S. C. Gwynne, for his book, *Empire of the Summer Moon*

Wikipedia, for copious information

Roderic L. Notzon, for consultation on military matters